MAD ABOUT EWE

COMMON THREADS BOOK #1

SUSANNAH NIX

WWW.SMARTYPANTSROMANCE.COM

COPYRIGHT

Made in the United States of America

Print Edition: 978-1-949202-73-1

CHAPTER ONE
DAWN

S low walkers were a scourge upon the city streets.

It was all very well to live a leisurely, low-stress life, taking plenty of time to stop and smell the roses—so long as you did it off to one side so those of us with somewhere to be could get past you.

"Pardon me!" I chirped politely as I zipped around a young man strolling down the dead center of the sidewalk with his phone pressed to his ear.

He was too engrossed in his conversation to hear me, and as I drew abreast, his arm shot out to gesticulate at the person on the other end of the phone.

Fortunately, I had ninja-like reflexes when it came to navigating Chicago sidewalks, and I managed to avoid taking a forearm to the face by ducking under the offending appendage. I threw a glance over my shoulder as I hurried past, but the man hadn't even noticed me—or how close he'd come to breaking my nose.

Unsurprising, really. I'd found as I progressed through my forties that men didn't seem to see me anymore. It was as if age had rendered me invisible to them, no matter how faithfully I dyed my gray roots copper brown, or how many steps I added to my skincare regimen. (Nine, if you're wondering. I was up to nine steps, and seriously considering adding two more.)

Never mind Mr. Forearm Tattoo, I had more important things to worry about. The store was supposed to open—I glanced down at my watch—five minutes ago. *Fudgsicles!*

I picked up the pace, dodging around obstacles and pedestrians like a high-speed Ms. Pac-Man, breaking into a sweat despite the chilly spring weather. Chloe had been scheduled to open this morning, but she'd called in sick an hour ago. I'd still been in my pajamas, unwashed and unshampooed, enjoying a rare late morning in, when she'd phoned to tell me she'd woken with a sore throat and fever.

Sidestepping a yawning young woman in scrubs headed for the hospital a few blocks away, I skipped over the leash of an old man's wayward dog while giving a wide berth to a deliveryman balancing a stack of boxes. I was moving at a solid clip and making good time until I came up behind a pair of spandex-clad women walking two abreast down the sidewalk ahead of me.

"Excuse me," I said to the back of their matching Lululemon outfits and bouncy ponytails.

No response. They continued chattering at one another, as oblivious to me as the young man on the phone had been. Apparently, my invisibility wasn't limited to men.

I'd simply have to go around. If I made myself smaller, I could just squeeze by on one side—

"Excuse you," one of the women said when my handbag bumped her elbow as I squeezed between her and a parked SUV.

"Sorry," I answered reflexively, feeling my face flush with a mix of anger and embarrassment.

It wasn't my fault Ms. Lululemon had been rudely blocking the sidewalk, yet I couldn't help the sense of shame that clawed its way out of the pit of my stomach over a small correction from a stranger. My dearly departed mother's voice rang in my head, admonishing me from beyond the grave: *Be polite, Dawn. Say you're sorry, Dawn. Don't get in the way, Dawn.*

I grimaced and picked up the pace, knowing the sour feeling left by that one insignificant encounter would likely hang over my mood for hours. On the bright side, the sidewalk was mostly clear ahead, and I was able to make the final stretch of my journey down East Randolph without further mishap. I felt a small surge of happiness as I caught sight of the yarn store I'd opened last year.

Mad About Ewe was my pride and joy. Of course I was also proud of my two children, and of course they also gave me joy, but they were both grown, independent humans who made their own decisions these days. There was only so much credit I could take for them anymore. Mad About Ewe, on the other hand, was all mine. The first thing I'd done entirely on my own in my whole adult life.

I'd written up the business plan, picked out the property, furnished the interior (with some guidance from my artist best friend, Angie), and selected the inventory with painstaking care. Although some of the start-up capital had come from my divorce settlement, I considered it fairly earned compensation after twenty-four years of marriage to a world-renowned pulmonologist who'd spent more time at the hospital than at home helping me raise our children and keep our household running.

To be honest, I'd felt more like a personal assistant than a wife for a lot of my marriage. Two years after signing my divorce papers, I was still relishing my freedom. My younger son was off at college and the older one, a recent graduate, was living on his own. Which meant I had the house all to myself, and my time was my own to devote to my new career as an independent businesswoman.

As I drew nearer to the shop, I spied Linda, my most faithful customer, waiting on the sidewalk outside and looking rightfully impatient. *Fudgsicles.*

"Good morning, Dawn," she said with a judgmental eyebrow arch. "You're four minutes late."

"Yes, I know, Linda. I'm sorry. Chloe called in sick this morning." I unlocked the door and held it for her to follow me inside.

As I moved around the store turning on the lights and readying things for a new day's business, Linda made a beeline for her favorite chair. There was a grouping of cozy couches and chairs by the front window where people were welcome to sit and knit for a spell, when the space wasn't in use by one of the knitting or crochet groups that held their regular meetups at the store.

Linda came in almost every morning to sit and visit for a few hours over her knitting. She was retired and lived alone, and I had the sense she didn't talk to many people outside the time she spent in the store.

"What do you think, crème brûlée or southern pecan this morning?" I asked as I moved to the coffee maker. I always kept a carafe of coffee on hand, as well as a selection of teas and powdered hot chocolate, so customers could enjoy a warm

3

beverage while they knit or shopped for yarn. It encouraged them to stay longer, and the longer they stayed, the more likely they were to buy something. It also made the store feel more homey, which was part of my business mission statement: *Create a comfortable home for fiber arts lovers to gather and shop.*

"Feels like a crème brûlée day to me," Linda answered as she unfolded the Joji Locatelli Odyssey shawl she'd been working on for the last several weeks. It was knitting up so beautifully I'd been considering starting one of my own with some of the new Malabrigo Dos Tierras I'd gotten in last week.

The bell on the shop door rang, and I glanced over my shoulder as I counted out scoops of flavored coffee grounds. It was a man who'd just entered, which was unusual but not unheard of. He stood with his back to me, gazing at the window display Angie had created for the store. It was an eye-catching installation, with sagging clotheslines full of colorful hand-knit hats, scarves, and socks suspended over a pair of giant knitting needles supporting a swatch of rainbow-striped garter stitch. It had enticed quite a few curious onlookers into the store.

"Let me know if you need any help," I called to the newcomer. He didn't respond, so I finished setting the coffee to brew before I went to properly greet my first customer of the day.

He'd drifted over to the section of shelves stuffed with a spectrum of Cascade 220 colors. As I approached, I noted that he was roughly my age—or a bit younger perhaps—with an attractive salt-and-pepper beard and silver-threaded hair.

"Is there anything in particular I can help you find?" I offered, affecting my cheerful customer service smile.

He turned to look at me, our eyes met, and my stomach dropped onto the floor next to my sensible dressy flats.

It wasn't. It *couldn't* be.

But it was.

I'd know those piercing brown eyes anywhere, even thirty years later when they were surrounded by deep crinkles and a silvery beard. They belonged to Mike Pilota, my former high school crush. Varsity football player, student council president, and homecoming king Mike Pilota. The best-looking guy in my graduating class.

In other words, someone who'd been totally out of my league, and whom I'd none-theless pined over for four long and miserable years.

He'd changed over the last three decades, but not that much. Miraculously, he still had all his hair and his athletic physique. In fact, he was extraordinarily muscular for a man in his late forties. One might even go so far as to call him jacked.

His face sported quite a few more wrinkles these days—in that way that looked so unfairly handsome on older men—and he was more hirsute than I was used to seeing him. In high school, he'd been clean-shaven and had worn his hair in one of those unfortunate brush cuts that had been so popular in the eighties. Now, in addition to the beard, which lent him a pleasantly lumberjacky appearance, his hair was thick and wavy on top, brushed back from his forehead and trimmed shorter on the sides.

But those eyes. They were exactly the same: deep-set, dark, and intense. The giddy feeling they inspired in my loins plunged me right back into high school.

Mike and I hadn't moved in the same circles back then. I doubt he ever would have known I existed if it hadn't been for Pizza My Heart, the pizza parlor where we both worked in the evenings and on the weekends. From the time I turned sixteen to the day he left for college, Mike and I spent ten to twenty hours a week slinging pizza, garlic bread, and soda pop together.

Yes, as a matter of fact, I had applied for the job at Pizza My Heart because Mike worked there. What can I say? I was a teenager ruled by my hormones.

The job had allowed me to spend time with Mike, even talk to him a little. I wouldn't exactly say we were friends, but we were friendly. We were acquaintances, which was more than we'd been the two years prior.

Therein lay the problem: I was not what you'd call a smooth operator in my teenage years. Oh, I'd tried to play it cool, but cool wasn't exactly in my wheelhouse back then. These days I liked to think I'd adopted a classic style that complemented my natural features and personality. But in 1988? I looked like the inside of a Contempo Casuals had vomited all over me—and my fashion sense was by far my best feature.

In addition to braces, acne-prone skin, and a haircut better suited to a Golden Girl than a teenager, I was not socially adept. My best conversational overtures consisted of awkward attempts to repeat jokes I'd heard on *Who's the Boss?* the night before. I was, in summary, a massive dork.

Nevertheless, I remained ever hopeful that one day Mike would look past the metal mouth and bad skin to realize his undying attraction to me. I was so optimistic, in fact, that in the summer after graduation—our last summer together at Pizza My Heart before Mike went off to college in Ohio—I screwed up my courage to ask him out on a date.

It did not go well.

His expression in response to my proposal that we catch a showing of *Turner & Hooch* was not unlike that of Janet Leigh when Norman Bates pulled back the shower curtain. The sight of Mike's face frozen in shocked surprise still haunted me occasionally in my anxiety dreams.

"Oh. Um. Uhhhh…" Mike had dragged that last syllable out for what felt like an eternity, his mouth hanging open like a hooked walleye as he struggled to verbalize a response. *"I can't. I've got…stuff. To do. Stuff to do. So I can't. But, um, thanks?"* Then he'd turned on his heel and speed-walked out of my presence as fast as his muscular legs would take him.

Like I said, it did not go well.

That was what I got for shooting my shot. But I didn't bear Mike any ill will. If anything, I was grateful for the lesson. It had taught me not to aim for the stars. I was more of a middle-distance girl, and that was fine. Somewhere between the ground at my feet and the visible horizon was where I belonged. It was useful information, and it had saved me a lot of unnecessary embarrassment over the intervening years.

And now Mike was standing in front of me, thirty years after crushing my hopes, looking just as dreamy as he'd been at eighteen. Dreamier, even. It was easy to be attractive at the age of eighteen, but attractive men in their late forties were rare unicorns indeed.

My eyes drank him in. All six-plus feet of him. A solid hunk of a man at any age.

He didn't remember me. That much was clear from his blank expression. I'd spent the last three decades reliving the humiliation of his rejection, and he didn't remember it at all. He didn't remember *me* at all. Typical.

But then something changed in his expression. I could actually see the moment his memory kicked in. "Dawn…Dawn Czworniak, right?"

Dreamy.

I couldn't help grinning. At least I'd made an impression, even if it wasn't a good one. I hadn't been completely forgettable.

"That's right," I said, before correcting myself. "Well, Dawn Botstein these days. I haven't been Czworniak for twenty-six years."

"You're married, then?" He betrayed no reaction to this information. It was simply a fact, utterly unrelated to him.

"I was until two years ago. I'm divorced now." I felt it important to put that out there. Not that I really thought there was a chance…but if there was, I wanted Mike to know I was currently unattached.

He looked faintly embarrassed, as one does when they realize they've stepped into uncomfortable conversational territory. "Sorry."

I shrugged to show it wasn't a sore spot for me. "I used the divorce settlement to open this place, so you could say I made my lemons into lemonade. What about you?" I asked, unable to restrain my curiosity. If Mike was a married man, I needed to get my lustful feelings in check, pronto.

His forehead creases deepened fetchingly—*damn men and the attractiveness of their wrinkles*. "What about me?"

"Are you married?"

He affected a faint grimace. "Twice—and divorced twice too."

I nodded in sympathetic commiseration while trying not to look happy to hear that. "So what have you been up to all these years? Last I heard you were in Ohio."

"I was, yeah. I just moved back to Chicago in February after my dad died, to be around more for my mom."

"I'm so sorry." This time my sympathy was genuine and profound. I'd lost both my parents in the last ten years and knew how difficult it could be. "My condolences for your loss."

"Thanks," he mumbled, dropping his eyes to his feet.

I took pity on him and changed the subject. "What brings you into the shop today?" I asked, reverting back to my customer service persona. "Are you a knitter?" It wasn't common for men to knit, but it wasn't unheard of either. I counted several men among my regular customers—including a famous television star who was an avid crocheter—so I never made presumptions based on gender.

Mike shook his head. "No, it's for my mom, actually. She used to knit, and I was thinking it might be good for her if I could get her to take it up again. Give her something to focus on other than…" He trailed off with a grimace.

"Sitting around the house missing your dad?" I offered gently.

"Yeah. Exactly that." Mike's eyes met mine with a grateful look that was so unexpectedly soft and tinged with sadness, I felt guilty for the way it made my toes curl and my stomach flutter.

The man was mourning one parent while caring for the other, and here I was internally squealing over a little eye contact like I was sixteen again. *Shame on you, Dawn.*

I pulled myself together and refocused on the matter at hand. "What kinds of things did your mother used to knit when she was knitting regularly? Can you remember?"

Mike rubbed a hand over his face while he thought about it, and I looked away, lest the sight of his thick fingers stroking that luscious beard send my hormones into carnal overdrive.

"She knit me and my dad a few sweaters," he answered as I moved to straighten a perfectly straight display of hand-painted yarns.

"Anything else?" A sweater project could be tricky to pick out for someone if you didn't know their tastes or skill level.

"Blankets," he said. "There's a few around the house she made."

I dared a glance at him. "Knit or crocheted?"

"What's the difference?" he asked with another of those damnably attractive frowns.

"Get her one of those nice afghan kits!" Linda called out from her seat by the front window. In my preoccupation, I'd completely forgotten she was in the store and near enough to hear every word of my conversation with Mike.

"Good suggestion," I called back to Linda. "Follow me," I said to Mike and set off for the display of afghan kits by the register. "These can either be knit or crocheted," I explained as I showed him some of the different patterns and colorways available.

"They're a bit pricey though," I warned, not wanting to make assumptions about his budget. Good quality yarn was a luxury item, and a blanket required a lot of it.

"That's no problem," he said as he flipped through the selection.

While Mike was busy studying the afghan kits, I surreptitiously leaned toward him and—god help me—I sniffed. That's right, I was sniffing the man right there in the middle of my store. And he smelled...*scrumptious* was the first word that came to mind. Like he'd just finished rolling in a pile of autumn leaves and then walked past an oven full of baking bread. For real. He smelled like warm yeast rolls and fresh air. I could have eaten him up on the spot.

"What about this one?" he asked, turning toward me. "Are these good colors?"

I felt my face heat and quickly looked down at the kit in his hand to hide my flush. I didn't know what had come over me. I hadn't felt this way around a man in—I couldn't even remember the last time, to be honest. Probably sometime in the Pliocene Epoch.

Since my divorce, I'd made only two cursory attempts at dating, but the results had been so awkward and unsatisfying in both cases that I'd given up the endeavor entirely. I'd begun to suspect that part of my life might be over. I was nearing fifty, and menopause was just around the corner. Perhaps my libido was waning, or maybe I was just tired of men. The prospect of dating one certainly seemed like more trouble than it was worth when I had a satisfying substitute in my nightstand drawer that boasted a rechargeable battery and a lifetime guarantee—which was more than any man I was likely to meet could offer.

Until now.

Until Mike Pilota walked back into my life, and I found myself blushing like a schoolgirl as my insides quivered with an excitement I hadn't felt in years.

I cleared my throat as I pretended to examine the afghan he'd selected. "I think it's lovely."

"Really?"

I looked into his deep brown eyes, which seemed to glimmer at me as his face crinkled into a smile. It was the first time he'd smiled since he'd entered the shop, and it turned my knees to jelly and my stomach to a roiling kaleidoscope of butterflies.

There were dimples under that beard somewhere, I remembered. Two of them, one on either side of his beautiful, perfect mouth.

He was gazing at me expectantly, waiting for me to respond, but my tongue suddenly felt too large for my mouth. All I could manage was a weak nod.

"Good." His smile got a little wider as his eyes remained on mine for what felt like a long time.

Too long.

My chest prickled as I felt the flush creep down my whole body, making me unbearably hot all over. I was dying. Trapped in that too-long moment like a fly caught in a spider's web. I couldn't look away, not when Mike Pilota was gazing into my eyes, but I wasn't sure I could stand to stay that way for another second without literally combusting in front of him.

"I'll take it," he said, finally breaking the spell as he held his purchase out to me.

I grabbed it and practically sprinted behind the register, grateful to put some space between us. Slipping on my reading glasses, I rang up his purchase as quickly as my shaking hands could manage and endeavored to ignore the way my blood pressure spiked when his fingers grazed mine as he passed me his credit card.

Down, girl. Don't make a fool of yourself—again.

"I hope she enjoys it," I said as I bagged up the afghan kit and handed it across the counter. So what if I'd dropped one of my business cards into the bag? I did that with most new customers—when I remembered.

"Me too," Mike said, and his eyes latched on to mine again. "Thanks for your help. I really appreciate it."

The butterflies in my stomach ramped up to a flapping vortex. "That's what we're here for," I replied with an awkward chuckle. *Very smooth, Dawn. Well played.*

"It was really good to see you again."

"Same," I answered weakly. Then added, ever pathetic and hopeful, "Maybe I'll see you around."

The corner of Mike's mouth tugged upward. "I hope so."

My brain shorted out. All I could do was stand frozen in place as his words bounced around in my head like a game of Pong.

Mike Pilota hoped he'd see me again. Holy crap!

He'd already turned to go. He was moving toward the door. Soon he'd be gone, possibly forever.

"Mike!" I called out.

He stopped and turned back.

I hurried over to him, stopping just in front of his broad chest. I had to crane my neck to look up into his face, which was open and curious as he watched me.

"Would you like to have dinner with me tonight?" I blurted before I could chicken out.

With a mortifying sense of déjà vu, I watched his expression cloud. His mouth fell open briefly before his lips pressed together in a grimace. He looked deeply uncomfortable. I knew what he was going to say before he said it.

"I can't." He eyes skated away, looking everywhere but at me. "I'm busy."

Of course he was. Why had I thought he'd want to go out with me? What madness had possessed me to repeat my mistake of thirty years ago?

Fortunately, in times of crisis my brain went into autopilot mode. I felt a mechanical smile tweak my lips. "No worries," I heard myself say as I waved my hand to show how little I cared. "Forget I asked."

Mike opened his mouth as if to speak, but at that moment the bell on the shop door rang as a pair of customers came in. My false smile got even wider as I turned to greet them, then froze on my face. It was my nemesis in Lululemon and her companion from the sidewalk earlier.

The two women smiled at me warmly and asked if I had any Miss Babs yarns. It was clear from their expressions they didn't remember me. Why would they?

As I pointed them toward the stock of Miss Babs, I heard the bell on the door ring again. Glancing that way, I saw Mike walk past the window outside and disappear down the sidewalk.

That was that. He was gone. Out of my store and out of my life.

I'd humiliated myself in front of him twice, but there would not be a third time.

You've had two chances to date me, Mike Pilota, and that's all you get.

I mentally shook my fist at him to drive home just how done I was with him.

That would teach me to fantasize. I'd forgotten for a moment, but now I remembered. I was a middle-distance sort of person, and I always would be. There was no use in shooting for the stars.

"Men," Linda harrumphed from her chair by the window. "Can't live with them, can't tip the lot of them into a volcano and start society over without 'em."

"Amen," I murmured as I went to pour us each a cup of coffee.

CHAPTER TWO

MIKE

She wore a yellow dress. It reminded me of a Cheerios box.

Her name was Jessica, and I'd met her at work. She was a reference librarian at the Humboldt Park branch. She'd smiled at me when I was there updating the Wi-Fi network, so I'd asked her out.

I hadn't really expected her to say yes, but I figured what the hell, worth a shot. My sister kept telling me I needed to get a life, and I guess she might have had a point. I'd been back in Chicago since February, and my social life was basically nonexistent.

In my defense, things had been tough the last few months. My dad had passed just before Christmas. Heart attack. He went suddenly, which I suppose could be considered a blessing in a way, but it didn't feel like that. It felt more like a catastrophe.

Mom was living alone for the first time in her life at the age of seventy-nine, and my sister, Kelly, already had her hands full with her own family. I'd been living in Columbus, Ohio since college, but there wasn't much of anything keeping me there, so I moved back to Chicago to help keep an eye on Mom.

In any case, I guess my sister's nagging did the trick, because I'd asked Jessica to dinner on the spur of the moment, and she'd accepted.

Because my invitation had slipped out spontaneously, I hadn't put any real thought into it. If I had, I would have asked her out for lunch or coffee or after-work drinks first, to gauge whether we had anything in common before bringing out the big dinner date guns. But I hadn't done that. Nope, I'd jumped straight to asking her out to dinner. On a Saturday night, no less.

No pressure or anything.

Jessica smiled at me across the table, and I tried not to squirm in my seat.

"Do you want to get a bottle of wine?" I asked, hefting the massive wine list. It was heavy enough to use as a blunt weapon, and I realized too late I'd made another critical error.

"Sure," she told me, fluttering her thick eyelashes. "You choose something."

I didn't know fuck all about wine, except white was supposed to be for chicken or fish and red was for...everything else? But we hadn't ordered yet, so that was no help.

"Do you like red or white?" I asked, flipping through a list as long as a phone book.

"White, if that's okay." She smiled again, showing off perfect teeth. "Red wine stains my teeth."

Six more page flips finally brought me to the start of the white wines. I was still reading through the first page—although why, I didn't know, since it was all gobbledygook to me—when the waiter appeared to take our drink order. In desperation, I randomly chose the second-cheapest bottle of chardonnay, which was at least a kind of wine I'd heard of.

After the waiter retreated, Jessica and I both turned our attention to perusing our menus. I was sweating in my blazer. I hadn't been on a first date with a woman in six months, and I'd fallen out of practice. As my eyes swept over the list of entrées, a sudden fear that I'd forgotten to apply fresh deodorant seized me.

Breathe. It's just dinner. She's just an ordinary woman.

She was beautiful though. And young. Younger than I'd realized when I asked her out last week. I eyed her surreptitiously over the top of my menu. She'd worn her blonde hair up at work, and her clothes had been considerably more conservative, all of which had given the impression she was older.

Now that I was looking at her with her hair down and a pretty date dress on, I put Jessica's age closer to thirty-five. Maybe even thirty. *Christ.*

What the hell was she doing on a date with a twice-divorced IT guy pushing fifty?

At least I still had my hair. That was something, even if it got a little grayer every week. And I'd managed to stave off the middle-age spread by going to the gym regularly, which was more than I could say for a lot of guys my age.

The waiter returned with our bottle of wine. I always hated this part. You couldn't really have a conversation with the server standing right there—not that Jessica and I were doing much talking—so there was nothing to do but sit there awkwardly and watch him open the wine. I'd never gotten used to being waited on by other people, so watching someone else perform a menial task for sub-minimum wage compensation made me uncomfortable. Even more uncomfortable than I'd already been.

Once he'd finished wrestling the bottle open, the server poured a small amount into my glass and waited patiently for me to approve it. I sampled it and tried not to make a face. I didn't like it, but I wouldn't know good wine if it bit me in the ass. Anyway, I wasn't about to send it back, even if it tasted like Windex.

I gave the waiter the okay, and he filled up our glasses before asking if we were ready to order our entrées. Jessica chose the saag paneer and I went with butter chicken.

"Cheers," Jessica said, lifting her wineglass after the waiter left.

I clinked my glass against hers. "Cheers."

She sipped her wine, and I saw her nose wrinkle in distaste as she set it back down.

"You don't like it?" I asked.

"No, it's good." She gave me an over-bright smile. "It's just a little oaky for my taste."

Oaky? Wasn't all wine made in wood barrels? I thought oakiness was a given. "Sorry," I muttered, embarrassed. "We can get something else if you like."

"No, it's fine." She reached across the table and laid her hand on mine. "Really."

I tried to relax. It wasn't like I was particularly invested in this date. I barely knew Jessica, but she was definitely too young for me. Maybe to some guys that'd be a bonus, but it wasn't my style. Not anymore. My second wife had been eight years younger than me, and I was convinced the age difference had contributed to some of our problems. Now that I was single again, I preferred to date women my own age.

Like Dawn Czworniak.

Before today, I hadn't thought about her in years. Running into her in that knitting store this morning had really knocked me back.

I almost hadn't recognized her, she'd changed so much since high school. Dawn had always been cute, but now she was beautiful. The mop of unruly hair I remembered had transformed into short, elegant waves, her spindly teenage figure had filled out into attractive curves, and there was a confidence to her utterly unlike the Dawn I used to know.

Her eyes were the same though. That was how I'd recognized her. Those big green eyes with hints of gold in their depths. They'd always been so expressive, those eyes. You could always tell exactly what she was thinking.

Dawn and I hadn't known each other well, but we'd spent plenty of hours working overlapping shifts at Pizza My Heart. Talking to her had helped pass the tedium.

I'd known back then that she had a crush on me. Her eyes revealed all, poor kid. But I hadn't reciprocated her feelings. In high school, I'd had very particular—some might even say shallow—ideas about what I wanted in a girlfriend, and Dawn Czworniak hadn't fit the bill. But I'd liked her. I'd enjoyed spending time with her.

These days I valued different qualities in a woman than I had in the arrogance of youth. It was one of the lessons of my first failed marriage. Finding someone you could actually talk to and enjoyed being around was worth a hell of a lot more than the things I'd thought were so important back then. You couldn't have a conversation with a pair of long legs, or enjoy a laugh with a woman's bust size. Personality was what mattered most. Compatibility. Empathy.

As I sat in Taj's Indian Restaurant, unable to think of anything to say to Jessica, I wondered if I'd still enjoy hanging out with Dawn.

It had taken me by surprise when she'd asked me to dinner. If only I hadn't had plans with Jessica tonight already, I would have said yes in a heartbeat. I'd wanted to ask Dawn out for another night, but it didn't seem right. I felt like I should at least give this date with Jessica a fair shake before I started making plans with another woman. Didn't I owe her at least that much?

Jessica removed her hand from mine and took another sip of her wine. This time she didn't make a face. "So, Mike. What do you do for fun?"

I didn't have a good response to that question. I really needed to get myself an interesting hobby, if only for conversational purposes. This whole dating thing would be easier if I could talk about my passion for hiking or brewing craft beer.

The only answer I could come up with made me sound like a dud. "I like to play video games."

Jessica's strained smile told me exactly how unimpressed she was by my answer. "My last boyfriend was addicted to Fortnite. I could barely drag him away from the screen long enough to eat." She let out a humorless laugh, from which I gathered it had been a point of contention in the relationship. Maybe even the reason they broke up.

At least my video game playing hadn't caused my divorce. More like the other way around. As my marriage failed, I'd retreated further into games as an escape.

"I never really liked Fortnite," I said, and saw her relax a bit. Score one point for me.

"I watch way too much Netflix," she volunteered, as if this was somehow comparable. "Right now I'm obsessed with _Glow_."

"Never heard of it. My mom watches a lot of Netflix though."

Wrong thing to say, I realized as I watched Jessica's expression go glassy again. I was back to zero.

I reached for my wine and took a drink, even though I didn't really like wine. Jessica was right, it was too oaky. Drinking it was like licking the underside of a coffee table.

I squirmed in my seat again, wishing I hadn't worn a blazer. "Are you from Chicago originally?" I asked, trying to get the conversation back on the rails.

She nodded. "Born and raised. You?"

"I grew up here, but I've been living in Columbus since college. I just moved back."

Her expression brightened. "Did you go to Ohio State?"

"Yeah, I did." I didn't mention that I hadn't actually graduated. It wasn't a fact I liked to volunteer if I could help it. Most people I worked with assumed I had a bachelor's. The only ones who knew better were the ones who'd read my résumé.

"Me too! What year were you?"

"Ninety-three." I watched her face as she did the math to calculate my age. She didn't flinch or anything, so she must not be too shocked. "What about you?" Since she'd asked me, I figured the question was fair game.

Please tell me she's not in her twenties. Please let her be older than that.

"Two thousand five."

I let out the breath I'd been holding. That made her twelve years younger than me, so thirty-six. Not as bad as I'd feared, but still not great. Twelve years was still a pretty big age difference. Bigger than I was comfortable with.

At least we'd identified something we had in common. We were able to talk about our alma mater and favorite hangouts in Columbus until the waiter arrived with our food.

The butter chicken was the best I'd ever had. If nothing else, I felt confident I'd picked a good restaurant. Until about halfway through my plate, when I noticed Jessica watching me. She'd barely touched her own food.

"Do you not like it?" I asked, gesturing at her plate.

"No, it's great." She gave me another of those strained smiles.

I'd fucked up again somehow, but this time I didn't know what I'd done. Was I chewing too loudly? Eating too fast? Was there something caught in my teeth?

"I don't really like Indian food," she said.

So much for picking a good restaurant. I guess I should have asked her preferences before making the reservation. Another lesson learned. "Shit, I'm sorry." I winced. "And I'm sorry I said shit."

This time her smile was more genuine. "It's okay. You couldn't have known."

"Do you want to go someplace else?" I wasn't sure where we'd be able to get a table this time of night on a Saturday, but I was willing to try.

She shook her head and reached for a piece of naan. "No, really. It's fine."

"Do you want to try my butter chicken?"

I saw her hesitate before shaking her head. "That's okay."

"It's delicious. Come on, give it a try." I pushed the plate toward her.

She reached across the table and stabbed a piece of chicken with her fork. She chewed it slowly and offered me a smile. "It's good."

"Really?" I tried to discern if she was lying. I couldn't imagine anyone not liking this butter chicken, but there was no accounting for taste.

"Really. That's delicious, actually."

"Do you like it better than yours? Do you want to trade?" I'd already eaten half of mine, so it wasn't exactly a fair trade.

"No, you don't have to do that."

"I don't mind. Here." I relieved her of her saag paneer and put what was left of my butter chicken in front of her.

She smiled at me. "Thank you."

"No problem." I dug into the saag paneer, which was also excellent.

Jessica finished off the rest of my butter chicken and another piece of naan. I made it two-thirds of the way through her saag paneer before throwing in the towel.

"Still think you don't like Indian food?" I asked as the waiter cleared away her empty plate.

Her mouth curved as she reached for her wine. "I may be changing my tune. You've opened my eyes to new possibilities."

I returned her smile. "Glad I could be of service."

"Do you do this a lot?" she asked.

"What?"

"Dating."

"Not so much lately." I started to reach for my wine, then changed my mind and took a drink of water instead.

"I thought so."

I grimaced as I set my water glass down. "Is it that obvious?"

19

One of her shoulders lifted. "I do a lot of online dating. Most of the guys I meet do this all the time. They've practically got it down to a science. You...not so much." She gazed at me through her lashes. "You seemed nervous when we first sat down."

"I was."

"I think it's sweet. And refreshing." She had a nice smile. And a nice face. And a nice personality.

Unfortunately, none of it did anything for me. There was no spark. No connection. No urge to get to know her better.

After I paid the check, I walked her to her car. She thanked me for dinner, and I bid her goodnight.

I didn't try to kiss her, even though she looked like she wanted me to.

On Sundays, I went to see my mom. She still lived in the house I grew up in, in Edison Park. The place looked like a time capsule from 1980—wall-to-wall carpet, dark wood paneling, laminate countertops, and all.

"Hey, Mom!" I called out as I let myself in the front door.

"Is that you, Mike?" she answered from the living room. Every Sunday I came at this same time, and every Sunday she asked if it was me.

"Yeah, who else would it be?" Setting down the afghan kit I'd bought, I took off my shoes and left them on the mat inside the front door.

"I don't know. It could be burglars." She was sitting on the old floral couch in front of the TV. She was always sitting on the couch in front of the TV. She didn't seem to do much of anything else. Then again, all I did was play video games when I wasn't at work, so I had no real room to talk.

Today she was watching some British mystery show that looked like it was made in the nineties. I bent down to kiss her cheek. "Did you want me to ring the doorbell from now on instead of letting myself in?"

Her nose wrinkled. "I don't want to have to get up from the couch. Just call me or something next time and give me a little warning."

I wished she would get up from the couch. It'd be a hell of a lot better for her than sitting all day. "I did call earlier, and it went straight to voice mail. I tried texting too. Where's your phone?"

"Oh, it's in the kitchen." She waved her hand vaguely in that direction. "I turned it off to charge it."

I tried to keep the irritation out of my voice. "What'd I tell you about that? You don't ever have to turn it off. Just leave it on all the time." She needed to keep her phone on her in case of emergencies. If she fell or something, it wouldn't do her any good all the way in the kitchen.

"But I don't want to waste power." She was obsessed with the idea of wasting power. Always shutting down her computer and compulsively turning off lights she wasn't using. I was pretty sure she sat around at night in a dark house with nothing but the light from the TV to see by.

"It's not a waste of power, and when you turn it off I can't get a hold of you. I want you to keep it on and with you all the time. In case of emergency." We'd had this conversation approximately a hundred times already, but she never listened. Or maybe she listened and then chose to ignore me. My mom was as stubborn as I was.

I headed into the kitchen to find her phone. The counter around the sink was stacked with dirty dishes again. At least it looked like she'd been eating this week.

When I was a kid, my mom had been a neat freak. Never a dirty dish left in the sink or a crumb left on the counter, and woe unto anyone who tracked in mud or left their dirty clothes on the floor. We'd all had to pull our weight keeping the house tidy, but Mom had been the grand marshal of cleanliness, issuing orders and checking our work to make sure no mote of dust was left unturned.

Since I hadn't been around much the last thirty years, I didn't know when that had changed. But it had definitely gotten much worse since Dad died. Mom had been letting things stack up around the house, and it worried me how she didn't seem to care anymore.

Finding her phone plugged in next to where the old landline used to be, I turned it back on and carried it into the living room. I'd set up a charger for her next to the couch, so I didn't know why she'd been charging it in the kitchen instead of close by.

"Here you go," I said as I plugged it in and set it on the end table next to her. The table was covered with empty coffee cups, unopened mail, and more dirty plates. "Leave it on from now on, please. Can you do that for me?"

She gave me a distracted nod, her eyes fixed on the TV. "Sure." Someone had just gotten murdered by a falling gargoyle statue on her show.

"How are you feeling today?" I asked.

"I'm fine."

She always said that, but she obviously wasn't fine. She hadn't been fine since she lost Dad.

My parents were married for fifty-four years. Could you even imagine? The longest I'd ever lasted in a relationship was seven years. That was my second marriage. The first one we barely made it a year.

My mom was twenty-three when she met my dad. I didn't think she knew how to live without him. It was like he'd taken a piece of her with him when she lost him.

"I got you something, Mom." I went into the entryway where I'd left her present, belatedly realizing I probably should have wrapped it or something.

She pulled her eyes away from her show when I came back carrying the big white paper bag I'd gotten from Dawn's shop. "You didn't have to do that."

"I know." I sat down on the couch and placed the bag between us. "I wanted to."

She looked inside and frowned. "What is it?"

I reached into the bag and took out the big bundle of different colored yarns wrapped up in plastic. "It's an afghan kit. It's got everything you need to knit a blanket. All the yarn, the needles, and the instructions."

"Oh, that's nice." She said the word *nice* the same way she said she was fine.

"I thought you could knit while you watched your shows. You used to love to knit."

"I can't believe you remember that." Her eyes had gotten a faraway look. She reached out a hand and caressed the yarn through the plastic. "Thank you, dear. That's very sweet."

Then she turned her attention back to the TV.

I stood up with a sigh and folded up the paper bag to put in the recycling bin. When I turned it upside down, something fluttered out and landed on the floor.

"What's that?" my mom asked as I stooped to retrieve it.

"It's a business card for the yarn store where I got the afghan kit from. Do you want to keep it?" I traced my thumb over the Mad About Ewe logo. It was colorful and hand drawn, with tiny knit patterns inside the fat part of the letters. "Maybe you want go there yourself sometime?"

"I don't know why I'd want to do that. Throw it away for me, will you?"

As I walked it over to the wastebasket, my eyes lingered on Dawn's name below the logo. *Dawn Botstein*. That was the name she used these days—her married name. But she was divorced now, like me.

Instead of tossing the card, I slipped it into my pocket.

"How are you doing for food?" I asked my mom. "Do you want me to take you to the grocery store?"

She was back to watching her show. "There's no need. I have a delivery scheduled for tomorrow."

Although I understood the necessity, I kind of wished my sister hadn't showed my Mom how to order groceries online. It was one less thing to get her out of the house.

I went into the kitchen and washed all my mom's dishes. Then I scrubbed the sink, wiped down the counters, and swept and mopped the floor. I knew Mom would complain if I tried to vacuum the living room while she was watching her show, so I went to change the sheets on her bed next.

After I'd carried the dirty sheets and towels down to the basement laundry and started them to wash, I went back upstairs and cleaned mom's bathroom. All Dad's stuff was still in there, like he might come back any day now and need it again. His aftershave, his razor, even his toothbrush sitting in the holder next to Mom's.

I felt a band tighten around my chest as I cleaned around Dad's things. I knew better than to try to get rid of them, but I hated the thought of my mom staring at them every day. I didn't think it was helping her get used to him being gone.

When I was done cleaning the bathroom, I walked down the hall to my old bedroom. It was still pretty much the same as it had been when I'd lived here. My parents hadn't had any reason to use it for anything else, so it existed in a sort of stasis, as a shrine to my high school days.

I didn't come in here much. There wasn't a lot from high school I wanted to revisit. The sports trophies and pep posters that decorated my old room didn't hold any meaning for me anymore. I wasn't proud of my achievements back then, or particularly fond of the person I used to be.

I'd bought too much into my own hype in my youth. I'd thought because I was on the varsity football team and popular at my high school that it meant I was hot shit. Looking back on my teenage self and some of the things I'd done, I didn't like that guy very much. He'd been kind of a dick.

It was a rude awakening when I got to college and realized I wasn't special after all. I wasn't good enough to get a football scholarship or a spot on the team at Ohio State —or any of the other schools I'd applied to, for that matter—which meant I wasn't one of the anointed ones anymore. Without my status as an athlete giving me an artificial boost, I was nobody. Just an ordinary Joe at a school of sixty thousand other ordinary Joes.

College-level classes turned out to be more of a challenge than I was prepared for, and I spent way too much time fucking off and partying. By my junior year, I was on the verge of flunking out. But more than that, I'd grown tired of the struggle and couldn't see the point. I had a decent part-time sales job, and my boss had made it clear I could transition to full time if I wanted. So I dropped out.

Maybe it was a mistake, but it was a mistake twenty-eight years over and done with, so it didn't much matter. Mostly, I tried to avoid thinking about the past.

As I stood in my old bedroom, my eyes skimmed over the relics of a life that didn't feel like mine anymore, until I found the high school yearbooks lined up on the bottom shelf of my bookcase. I went over and dropped into a squat as I pulled out my senior yearbook. Carrying it over to the bed, I flipped it open. My old twin mattress creaked under my weight as I sat down to thumb through the pages.

A flood of memories assaulted me. People I hadn't thought about in ages, faces I'd forgotten, moments from my so-called glory days freeze-framed in black and white. There'd been a lot of good times, and a lot of friends. More than I remembered.

I flipped to the senior pictures, and landed square in the Ps. My own face stared back at me, thirty years younger. Wearing the ugly blue tuxedo and ruffled dickey they'd forced on all the senior boys for yearbook portraits. I'd been too cool to smile in my photo. Stupid kid.

A few page flips back brought me to Dawn's senior picture in the Cs. I stared at her bright smile, just as open and charming as Dawn had always been. Even wearing that ugly feather boa they made all the senior girls wear, she looked lovely. Why hadn't I appreciated it at the time?

Her short, fluffy haircut reminded me of Molly Ringwald's in *The Breakfast Club*, but I didn't have any room to talk, considering the mullet I'd sported my junior year. The things we used to think were cool in the eighties.

That was the heart of the problem right there. I hadn't thought Dawn was cool enough. She wasn't part of the popular crowd. She wasn't an athlete or a cheerleader or on the dance team. She was in Model UN and the Latin club. She took honors classes and was two full grades ahead of me in math. I remembered she went to prom with some dweeby kid who'd started up our high school's first computer club. That dweeby kid went on to found a multimillion-dollar tech company ten years later.

Instead of looking down on people, Dawn was friendly. She smiled all the time, at everyone. She didn't care who you were.

And I was such a dumbass I thought that friendliness made her uncool. I'd barely given her the time of day at school, even though I'd liked talking to her when it was just the two of us at work. What an asshole I was.

I still remembered the day Dawn had asked me out. It stuck with me, one of many pinpoints of shame in the bulletin of my life.

She'd been nervous. Stammering a little. Although I knew she liked me, I hadn't expected her to pull the trigger. We'd been working together for two years at that point, and I was only a few weeks away from leaving for college. When she'd asked me to a movie, it caught me flat-footed. I couldn't think of anything to say. Part of me had wanted to say yes, knowing it'd be fun to go to a movie with Dawn. But another part of me, the dumbass part, had been behind the wheel that day, and he'd been afraid of how it would look if any of his friends saw us together. So I'd turned her down, awkwardly, inelegantly, and regretfully.

Just like I'd turned her down yesterday. That was twice now Dawn had put herself out there, and twice I'd shot her down. I doubted I'd get a third chance.

The tragedy of it all was, both times I'd wanted to say yes.

CHAPTER THREE

DAWN

I was surrounded by pregnant women. There must have been a dozen of them in the waiting room at my ob-gyn's practice. Young, beautiful, glowing, in the prime of their lives.

And then there was me. Past my prime childbearing years, with menopause breathing down my neck.

Hopefully.

That was why I was here. To see if the recent changes in my menstrual cycle were the result of my fertility's last gasp, signaling my entrance into the shriveled old crone phase of my life.

I couldn't wait. I certainly wouldn't miss my period or the cramps, sore breasts, and mood swings that came with it every twenty-four to twenty-eight days. While I didn't relish the side effects that were likely to accompany menopause, I felt fairly confident I could muddle through them with dignity. I had no use for my fertility anymore, and as the years piled up behind me, I found myself increasingly ready to move on to the next stage.

A nurse leaned out of the door to the back part of the office and all eyes in the waiting room swung her way, waiting to see who would be the next lucky contestant called to the stage. "Dawn Botstein," she read off the file in her hand, and I lifted my purse strap onto my shoulder as I got to my feet.

As I followed the nurse into the back, my eyes traveled over all the pregnant women in the waiting room. Shifting uncomfortably in their seats, rubbing aching backs and painful joints. While the nurse checked my weight and left me in an exam room with instructions to change into a paper gown, I searched my heart for regret, but all I found was relief. Seeing those pregnant women and remembering the discomfort, inconvenience, and uncertainty I'd experienced with both my pregnancies, I felt even more grateful to be past that part of my life.

I'd loved being a mother, but two children had been plenty for me. I was enjoying my retirement from my previous career as a stay-at-home mom to two rambunctious boys.

Make that three boys, I thought with a sigh as my ex-husband's name lit up the screen of my phone.

"Hello, Jerry," I said as I answered the call, trying to keep the annoyance out of my voice.

"What's the name of our dentist?"

It had been two years since our divorce. Had the man really not managed to get himself to a dentist in all that time? Probably. I'd always scheduled all his appointments for him, just like I'd done for the boys.

I made a mental note to start making both my sons schedule their own dentist appointments from now on.

I gave Jerry our dentist's name, and he proceeded to describe to me, in great detail, the loose filling that had inspired his need for a dentist appointment. As if the state of his teeth was something I still cared about.

While he monologued about his loose filling like it was some sort of unique and interesting condition rather than a mundane occurrence that had happened to nearly everyone multiple times in their lives, I set my phone down on the exam table, only half-listening as I changed into my glamorous paper gown.

"Yes, well, good luck," I said, picking up the phone again once I was paper-clad, and interrupting when Jerry finally took a breath.

"Do we have insurance I have to show them?"

This time I didn't try to hide my irritation. "*You* have dental insurance through your hospital retirement plan. *We* no longer have the same insurance, remember?" I'd had to acquire my own health insurance after the divorce was finalized, which meant saying goodbye to the hospital's cushy employee plan.

If Jerry noticed my tone, he didn't acknowledge it. This was how much of our marriage had played out. Me feeling quietly resentful and him not noticing.

What a way to live for twenty-four years. I wouldn't go so far as to say I was grateful he'd taken up with another woman, but perhaps on some level I was. If he hadn't initiated the separation, I'm not sure I ever would have found the motivation to leave what I had never acknowledged to myself was an unhappy marriage. I'd always been very good at pretending, and I had a lot of years invested in pretending my marriage was perfect.

I'd been devastated at first, of course. I'd grieved for the loss of my marriage and the life that was all I'd ever known. How was I supposed to know who I was if I wasn't Dr. Botstein's wife?

But I'd worked through all seven stages of grief and had come out the other side with a surprising sense of relief. Relief that I didn't have to manage Jerry's life anymore, or listen to his self-important stories, or subsume my own desires for his. It had been a difficult adjustment at first, going from being part of a family of four to being a woman who lived alone. But now I relished my freedom. I could lounge around the house braless, dance in my underwear to whatever music I wanted at whatever volume I liked, and make what *I* wanted to eat for dinner without having to cater to anyone else's tastes.

Plus, I had my business now. It gave me a reason to get up in the morning and left me pleasantly tired at the end of every day. It gave me a purpose, and a reason to feel pride in myself and my accomplishments that I'd never had before.

As divorces went, I'd been extremely lucky. It hadn't been pleasant to learn Jerry had cheated on me—with a much younger woman, naturally—but truth be told, we hadn't exactly been in the throes of passion for quite a while. Roommates might be a more accurate description of the last decade of our marriage. I almost couldn't blame Jerry for seeking out greener pastures, an at least I no longer had to feel guilty about my failing marriage.

And I could say this much for Jerry: he'd had the decency to own up to the infidelity and take his lumps. His personal sense of honor and integrity was too strong to try and stick it to me after he'd broken his marriage vows, and so the divorce had been both amicable and equitable. I got the house we'd raised the kids in, a comfortable alimony, and a decent cash settlement for my share of the vacation and rental properties we'd owned.

I'd let go of most of my anger. When I spoke to Jerry now, all I felt was mild irritation. But there was comfort in knowing the irritation was only temporary. These days, our conversations were brief and intermittent. Once they were concluded, I could go back to enjoying my Jerry-free life.

I smiled faintly to myself as Jerry narrated the contents of his wallet while searching for the proper insurance card. I couldn't even feel resentful. These little interactions with him kept my perspective in check by reminding me exactly what it was I'd lost —and what I'd gained.

"That's it," I told him when he finally unearthed the correct card. "Just give that to the dentist if they ask. Now I've got to go. I'm at the doctor's office, and you know how funny they are about cell phones."

"They're not funny about it," Jerry said. "There are very good reasons for the rules against cell phones." He paused, and I braced myself for a lecture about cell phones and patient care, but instead he surprised me by saying, "Are you all right? Why are you at the doctor?"

"I'm fine. It's just my annual," I lied. Touched as I was that he'd actually expressed concern, my health was no longer his business. I wasn't about to start describing my irregular menstrual cycles to him. Anyway, I was certain it was nothing out of the ordinary. No reason to cause unnecessary worry.

I got off the phone with him with plenty of time to spare before my doctor finally bustled in, looking faintly harried as usual.

Dr. Norman was an attractive Black woman, approximately my age, with a very faint Jamaican accent. She'd been my gynecologist for the last ten years, but I'd been a very boring patient with no extraordinary conditions, so we'd only seen each other once a year on average. I wasn't entirely sure she remembered me from visit to visit.

She greeted me cheerfully, sinking down onto the rolling stool while she read over my chart. "It says here you've been having some irregular bleeding, is that right?"

I described how my periods had seemed to come and go with increasing frequency the last two months, and she asked a series of questions about other symptoms, none of which I'd experienced.

"Are you sexually active?" she asked, and I snort-laughed. Dating was the one aspect of my new life as an independent single woman I hadn't embraced yet.

Part of it was laziness. Dating was an awful lot of effort, and I couldn't seem to muster the motivation to expend my energy on an activity with such a low chance of paying dividends. There was also the fact that I simply hadn't found myself attracted to anyone—aside from my brief and regrettable encounter with Mike Pilota the other day.

But the biggest reason I hadn't made more of an effort on the dating front? Fear. I was a tremendous chicken.

I hadn't slept with anyone but Jerry in twenty-eight years. And it wasn't like our sex life had been particularly adventurous. *Dull, rote,* and *no great shakes* were the phrases that leapt to mind—not to mention all but nonexistent the last few years we were together.

The truth was, I was afraid to sleep with anyone else, because I was fairly certain I would be bad at it. Even if I wasn't, the idea of getting naked in front of a man I'd just met terrified me. At my age? In my current body? Madness.

And then there was the intimacy of the act itself. The vulnerability. How did people expose themselves like that in front of someone they barely knew? It seemed inconceivable to me.

"I'll just take that as a no, then?" Dr. Norman asked, looking up at me with a smile. She had friendly crinkles around her eyes that always set me at ease.

"Definitely a no," I agreed.

"Well, then, let's do a pelvic exam and see if we can figure out what's going on."

I lay back on the table with my feet in the stirrups and a paper blanket tented over my knees and tried to relax as I was subjected to the uncomfortable ordeal. Tragically, it was the most action my nether regions had seen in ages.

When she was done, Dr. Norman snapped off her gloves and told me I could sit up. Ignoring the slimy discomfort between my legs, I clutched the sad paper blanket around my knees as I prepared to receive the news that menopause was upon me.

Whoever had invented these ridiculous paper garments was definitely a man, and probably a sadist, to boot. There was absolutely no dignity to be found when you were clothed from neck to knees in a stiff, sandpapery gown that left your ass hanging in the breeze.

After she'd washed her hands, Dr. Norman began busily making notes in my chart. "I'm going to order some additional blood work," she said without looking up.

That sounded…ominous. And not what I'd expected to hear.

"Is everything all right?" I asked. "I thought it was just early menopause." I tried to smooth my gown over my chest, and the sound of the rustling paper was like a portentous rumble of thunder in the quiet of the exam room.

Dr. Norman gave me another of her crinkly smiles. "Let's not get ahead of ourselves."

I didn't find her smile quite as reassuring this time.

CHAPTER FOUR

MIKE

My sister and I had been meeting for lunch every couple weeks since I moved back. Kelly worked in human resources for a real estate company in Uptown, so whenever I knew I was going to be at one of the branch libraries up that way, we tried to get together.

Our favorite spot was Ernie's, a family-owned diner near her office. It wasn't usually too noisy or crowded, and they made a mean patty melt.

"She's not doing well," I told my sister. We were talking about Mom, like we usually did at our lunches.

"I know that," Kelly said irritably. "You think I don't know that?"

I bit into my sandwich instead of replying. Kelly often got irritable when we were talking about Mom. I couldn't blame her, under the circumstances.

"Sorry." She rubbed her head with a sigh, her brief flare of temper waning as quickly as it had waxed. "I shouldn't have snapped at you."

"It's okay," I said as I wiped Russian dressing off my lips. I'd gotten the Reuben today for a change. It wasn't as good as the patty melt, but it was pretty decent. "We're both worried about her."

Kelly shook her head as she took a sip of her iced tea. "I'm not used to having help with Mom."

"I know." My voice grew soft. "But I'm here now. I'm trying to help."

While I'd been off living the carefree life of a single man, Kelly had been doing a lot more for Mom and Dad than I'd ever appreciated. I was trying to make up for it now, but I still carried a lot of guilt. My little sister had a family that needed her, on top of a full-time job, and I'd left her to deal with our aging parents on her own while I'd whiled away my leisure time playing video games.

Some big brother, eh?

Kelly reached over and plucked a french fry off my plate. She'd ordered her usual Greek salad with chicken breast slices, but always ended up eating half my fries. They served great fries at this place. Crinkle fries like the ones you got in school cafeterias, but made fresh instead of frozen, and deep-fried to crispy perfection.

I spun my plate around to give my sister easier access. "I tried to get her to go to the grocery store on Sunday, but she wasn't interested. She'd already scheduled a delivery."

Kelly nodded and helped herself to another fry. "I brought the kids over last weekend and we tried to get her to go out for ice cream with us, but she said she didn't feel like leaving the house. I got the sense she couldn't wait for us to leave."

That concerned me. Mom loved those kids, and she loved ice cream. Her not even wanting to go out for ice cream with her grandkids was a bad sign.

"She's depressed, isn't she? I mean, clinically." I was no expert, but from what I'd gathered, my mother was displaying all the signs.

"Maybe. But I don't know what to do about it." My sister looked tired. She was three years younger than me, but despite the fact that she dyed the gray in her own dark hair, I couldn't help thinking she looked older than me.

"We need to get her to a therapist or psychiatrist or something."

Kelly made a scoffing noise. "Good luck with that. I tried already. I couldn't even get her to talk to her GP."

"There's got to be something we can do."

"You can try talking to her." My sister shrugged as she pushed her salad around on her plate. "Maybe she'll listen to you."

SUSANNAH NIX

I doubted it, and I could tell from my sister's tone that she did too. The only person my mother had ever listened to was our dad. With everyone else, she'd always been as intractable as the fabled immovable object. Now that Dad was gone and she'd retreated into herself, I didn't know how to reach her.

I picked up my sandwich again and took a bite, mulling over the problem as I chewed. "Do you think I should move in with her?"

Kelly looked up from her salad, frowning. "I think you two would drive each other up the wall in exactly five minutes."

"Yeah, but would it be good for her?"

"I don't know." She seemed to consider it as she stabbed a piece of chicken. "I think she'd probably hate it. And I think it'd make you miserable." Her eyes met mine. "Even more than you already are, I mean."

I felt myself scowl. "How many times do I have to tell you? I'm fine."

Kelly made another scoffing noise, this time accompanied by an eye roll.

My sister was convinced my life was a pathetic shambles. I'm not saying she was wrong, but the fix wasn't as simple as she wanted it to be.

She thought I was just lonely. That all I needed was a girlfriend, and all I had to do to get one was go out on more dates until I found a woman I liked.

But what was missing from my life was more than just a girlfriend. It was meaning. A sense of purpose. The feeling I had a place in the world. Value.

Maybe I was in the throes of a midlife crisis. Only instead of buying a red sports car I couldn't afford and dressing like a twenty-five-year-old who'd time-traveled from the 1990s, I'd quit my job and packed up my whole life to be closer to my family. Which was either touching or incredibly sad, depending how you looked at it.

My sister thought it was a little of both. Touching that I'd done it to take some of the burden off of her, but sad that I'd had so little tying me to the city where I'd lived for the last thirty years that I could move back home at the drop of a hat.

I hadn't thought of it that way when I'd decided to do it. It was supposed to be a fresh start. New job, new apartment, new life. That was the idea anyway.

I'd thought maybe things would be better here, although I didn't know why. My new job with the Chicago Public Library wasn't much different than my old one with

34

Columbus City Schools. My new apartment was smaller and shabbier than my old place in Columbus, but it was all I could afford here on my salary. Other than that, and the fact that I saw my mom and my sister more often now, my life was pretty much the same. Different song, same melody. I went to work, I went to the gym, I went home and ate a frozen dinner while vegging out in front of a video game. The end. Lather, rinse, repeat.

I knew I needed more than that, but I didn't know what. And inviting a woman into my empty life wasn't the cure-all Kelly thought it was. I'd tried that. Twice. If I'd learned anything from my failed marriages, it was that you couldn't expect to find personal fulfillment in another person. If you weren't happy with yourself, you weren't going be any happier with someone else. You were only dragging them into your unhappiness with you.

"But would it be *good* for her?" I persisted, changing the subject back to Mom. "Even if she hates it, maybe it's what she needs."

"I'm not sure I see the point of making her miserable in a different way." Kelly reached for one of my french fries. "You know how much she values her privacy and alone time."

"She has too much alone time now. That's the problem."

"Yeah, but if you move in, that's like going from one extreme to the other. I'm afraid having you up in her space all the time might make things worse for her instead of better."

Secretly, I was relieved to hear Kelly say this. As much as I wanted to help my mom, I dreaded the thought of moving back into my old bedroom and coming home to that house every night. It would be an even bigger step backward than the one I'd just taken, and I wasn't exactly eager to immerse myself in the memories of my unfulfilled youth.

Not to mention, although I loved my mom, she had a tendency to criticize and see the negative in every situation, which was a trait I'd detected in myself and tried to overcome. We were a little too much alike, my mom and me. I worried we might bring out the worst in each other if we were forced into close quarters.

"Besides," Kelly said, pointing an accusatory fry at me, "I refuse to let you turn into a sad middle-aged dude who lives with his mother. It would absolutely kill your chances of ever having a social life."

On that point, we agreed. If I thought dating was awkward now, it'd be straight-up mortifying to have to tell a woman that I lived with my elderly mom, so there was no chance of me taking her back to my place.

"Speaking of which," Kelly continued. "How was your date on Saturday with—what was her name? Jessica?"

"It was Jessica, yeah, and it wasn't too bad. But I won't be seeing her again."

"Why not?"

"She's too young for me."

"How young?" Kelly's face lit up in amusement. "Too young to rent a car? Too young to drink? Is my big brother robbing the cradle?"

This time I was the one who rolled my eyes. "She's in her thirties."

My sister looked disappointed. "That's not so bad. Only a ten-year difference. At our age, ten years is nothing."

"It's a twelve-year difference, and it's not nothing to me."

"Have you considered maybe your standards are too high?"

"It's got nothing to do with standards. She's a perfectly nice woman. We just didn't have anything in common."

"Hmm." Kelly chewed on her lip, and I guessed what was coming next. "You know, I've got a couple single friends I could fix you up with."

"No way." I shook my head decisively. The last thing I wanted was to date one of my sister's friends. Talk about a recipe for disaster. If and when it didn't work out, I'd never hear the damn end of it.

"Well if you won't try online dating—"

"I'm not that desperate," I growled.

"It's not just for desperate people anymore. Get with the times, big brother. It's for anyone looking to meet someone new. And it makes it easier to weed out the ones you don't have anything in common with. I'm telling you, you should give it a try."

"No, thank you." My aversion to online dating was probably irrational, but I wasn't ready to go there yet.

"Maybe you should get a dog," Kelly suggested.

It was an option I'd actually considered and ruled out already. "My building doesn't allow pets. Also, I work eight to five and can't afford to pay for doggy daycare."

Kelly's face settled into a frown as she regarded me. "Seriously, Mike. I'm worried that you don't have any hobbies or friends. You're no better than Mom. You need to get a life."

My sister was right about that. I just hadn't figured out how.

CHAPTER FIVE
DAWN

On Tuesday, a celebrity came into the store.

I didn't bat an eye when Nico "The Face" Moretti walked in the door. My customers, on the other hand, batted several eyes and all of their eyelashes as the famous comedian entered their midst. I couldn't blame them. Nico was heart-stoppingly gorgeous in that superhumanly symmetrical way actors and models tended to be. The first time I'd met him, it had left me breathless. His comedy show wasn't really to my taste, but Nico very much was.

Nico was to everyone's taste, because on top of being profoundly handsome, he was also down-to-earth, charming, and incredibly sweet. It was impossible not to like him, regardless of how you felt about his television show, which included naked Jell-O wrestling as one of its regular features.

I watched Nico pause inside the door and gaze around the shop, his green eyes twinkling with amusement as they took in the three female customers who were trying very hard not to look like they were gawping at him. When his gaze finally found me, he broke into a warm smile as he sauntered my way.

"Mia bella!" he hailed cheerfully.

Did I mention he was Italian? And spoke the language fluently? It didn't get much dreamier than Nico. (Except possibly for Mike Pilota, but I'd vowed not to think about Mike anymore.)

"Nico!" I matched his smile with one of my own. "How's the baby?" Nico and his wife had been regular customers since I'd opened the store last year, but I hadn't seen as much of them since their first little one's arrival. Understandably.

Now that I was looking at Nico up close, I could detect subtle hints of the sleeplessness most new parents experienced. A slight shadow darkened the skin around his eyes, and his smile shone with somewhat lower wattage than usual.

"Beautiful." His tired eyes grew extra twinkly at the mention of his daughter, and he whipped out his phone to show off the latest picture. "I don't want to brag, but I'm pretty sure she's the most perfect baby in the whole history of the world."

I smiled admiringly at her chubby little cheeks. "Not sleeping through the night yet though, is she?"

He let out a wistful sigh. "No, not yet. But we're getting closer. I can feel it in my bones."

I gave him a sympathetic smile. I could remember those days all too well. "She'll get there. They always do." Anticipating the reason he'd stopped in, I moved toward the register. "I've got the Baby Soft Bamboo Cotton you wanted behind the counter." Nico had called last week to place a special order for five hundred grams of the lilac colorway. He was an avid crocheter and his wife was a knitter, so I didn't know which one of them the yarn was intended for.

"Excellent! Elizabeth's been itching to start a new baby blanket."

"How's she enjoying her maternity leave?" Nico's wife was an emergency room physician. I'd known her for years, much longer than I'd known Nico, because my ex-husband had been her mentor when she was in medical school and during her residency at Chicago General Hospital.

"She's only going up the walls a little," Nico said with a grin. "Less so once she figured out how to knit and breastfeed at the same time."

"You know, I could have made the arduous journey next door to leave your order with the doorman," I said as I counted out the skeins to make sure they were all there. Nico and Elizabeth lived in one of the condos in the building above the shop. In fact, it was Elizabeth who'd suggested this location to me when the retail space became available.

Nico's grin grew flirtatious. "I know, but then I wouldn't have gotten to fondle your yarn—and you know how I love to fondle your yarn."

I flicked my hand at him, shaking my head in amusement. "Fondle away."

Nico wandered off to browse the in-stock yarns, and I smiled as I watched him reach out to squish a particularly cuddly alpaca blend.

"Is that Nico Moretti?" one of the other customers whispered, bringing her purchase to the register.

"It is," I confirmed as I rang her up.

She cast a longing look at Nico as he gave one of the silk yarns a squeeze. "He's even better looking in person."

As I watched her throw several furtive glances in Nico's direction on her way out the door, I felt a pang of sympathy for him. Imagine knowing people were watching you like that everywhere you went. It must be exhausting. But Nico always seemed to take it in stride.

There was another jingle as the door of the shop opened again, and I smiled as my best friend Angie walked in.

"Good morning!" she called cheerfully as she joined me behind the register and stowed her large boho bag under the counter. A pair of the handmade earrings she sold on Etsy jingled as she moved. Today she wore interlocking circles of gold wire that hung down long enough to peek out from beneath her smart black bob.

Angie had never needed to dye her jet-black hair during her high school goth phase, and she still didn't dye it now, wearing her silver streaks with pride. I envied the way they'd grown in stripy, giving her a dramatic, witchy look. I envied a lot about Angie: her creativity, her colorful personality, her fearless fashion sense. Her absolute confidence in who she was and where she belonged in the world.

Ever since I could remember, Angie had been who I wanted to be when I grew up. Bright, colorful, loud. Irrepressibly herself. Only I hadn't grown up to be Angie, of course. I'd grown up to be me. Dull, predictable, humdrum Dawn, who tried a little too hard to be exactly who everyone expected her to be.

"Well!" She straightened, resting her hands on her hips as she turned to face me. "You'll never guess who's been put in charge of our thirty-year high school reunion."

"Oh god," I groaned. "Is it time for that already?" Thirty years seemed like an impossibly long time ago, when it still felt like only yesterday that the two of us were learning to drive in Angie's mom's old Volkswagen Beetle. How had we gotten so old?

"I went to my ten-year high school reunion a few years ago," Nico said, joining us as he set a skein of a pastel pink superwash wool on the counter with the rest of his order. "It was harrowing."

"Nico!" Angie turned a beaming smile on him. "I didn't see you lurking over there. How's the bambino?"

He answered her beaming smile with one of his own as he brought out the baby photo again. "Perfect."

"Of course she is. She takes after her daddy."

His expression turned thoughtful. "I think she takes after her mother, actually. I'm pretty sure she's got Elizabeth's nose, although it's hard to tell, since babies' noses are all sort of smushed and potato-like."

"Crocheting something for the baby?" I asked him as I added the pink yarn to his order.

"I was going to try making some bibs. I never realized how much babies spit up. She's constantly leaking from one end or the other."

As he spoke, I noticed a telltale white stain on the front of his shirt. "Speaking of, you seem to have a little on your shirt."

He looked down at his chest, licked his thumb, and tried to wipe away the stain. "Ah well." He shrugged, giving up and flashing me a cockeyed grin. "Spit-up happens."

I finished ringing him up and made him promise to give hugs to Elizabeth and the baby for me before I handed over his purchase.

"Bye, Nico!" Angie called cheerfully, and every eye in the store watched him saunter out the door.

"So the reunion…" I reminded Angie when Nico had gone. It was easy to get distracted when Nico was around. People tended to forget not only their train of thought in the presence of his handsome famousosity, but even their own name at times.

"Right!" Angie said, turning back to me. "They've roped some new sucker into chairing the reunion committee, and you'll never guess who."

I lifted my eyebrows and waited for her to astound me with the news, although I had a feeling I could guess. Angie had served on the committee that had planned our last two class reunions. It wasn't a great leap to suss it out.

Her eyes lit up with excitement. "Me! That sucker was me!"

"Why would you agree to that?" I recalled Angie being extremely frustrated by her previous experiences on the reunion committee. There had been a lot of disagreement about how things should be done, and a lot of infighting as everyone tried to get their own way.

Angie shrugged. "Because they asked. Finally."

"What happened to Tess?"

Angie's smile took on a self-satisfied twist. "Bossy Tess quit the committee."

Teresa McGregor had been our student council vice president, class valedictorian, and president of half the after-school clubs, which meant you couldn't really do anything at our school without bumping up against Tess and her controlling tendencies.

Angie shrugged. "I can only assume there were so many complaints about the last reunion that she got her feelings hurt and quit in a snit."

"Aww, that's kind of sad. She worked really hard on it." I'd never minded Tess as much as Angie had. In fact, we were still pretty friendly. But then I'd never felt the need to compete with her the way Angie had. The two of them had butted heads repeatedly over the years as they vied for control of their favorite extracurricular clubs. Angie had some controlling tendencies of her own.

"Don't you dare feel bad for her," Angie shot back, glaring at me. "We *all* worked hard on it, but she was the one who forced through all her bad decisions so the result of our hard work was a reunion with the vibe of a proctologists' convention."

I snorted in amusement. "I've been to a couple of medical conventions, and I can promise you proctologists throw much better parties." I moved to straighten up the bookshelves, and Angie followed me.

"See! That's my point! Anyway, with Tess out, they needed a new chairperson, and Donal Larkin asked me to do it. This is my chance to finally bring my vision to fruition. This thirtieth reunion is going to be our best reunion yet."

"Why doesn't Donal Larkin do it himself? He was the class president, after all."

Angie lowered her voice so it wouldn't carry to the customers browsing on the other side of the store. "Because he's a corporate attorney who knows fuck all about event planning. The guy probably can't even take a shit without his assistant reminding him to do it. He just wants it off his plate."

"Well, congratulations." I smiled at her. "I know you'll do a great job."

"Thank you. I do need one teensy-weensy favor from you."

"What?" I asked, already guessing what it was.

"Volunteer for the committee. I need to stack it with my own people, so my good ideas don't get railroaded like last time."

I sighed dramatically. "Fine."

Helping to plan a reunion I wasn't entirely sure I even wanted to attend wasn't my idea of a good time, but I'd do it to support Angie. Besides, what else did I have to do with my free time? At least Angie would be there, which would make it more fun. And, if I knew her, the meetings would be over drinks at her favorite pub. It wasn't the worst thing to commit to.

"Yay! Thank you! I knew I could count on you!" She threw her arms around me and gave me a quick squeeze to show her gratitude.

"It's funny you should bring up the reunion," I said, remembering my own recent blast from the past. "Because someone from high school came into the store on Saturday."

"Who?"

I felt myself blush as I said his name. "Mike Pilota."

Angie's eyes widened. "Pizza My Heart Mike?"

I nodded. Angie was well acquainted with my old crush on Mike, having been forced to listen to me pine over him for pretty much all of high school.

"Oh my god! Did you die? What was he doing *here*, of all places?"

"Buying yarn for his mother."

Angie clutched her chest dramatically. "Damn, that's so sweet. What does he look like? Please tell me he's fat now. Is he bald? Does he look like an old, fat banker?"

"None of the above, as a matter of fact. He's extremely fit and has a very sexy salt-and-pepper beard to go with his full head of hair."

"Double damn! It's so unfair that he's still hot."

"It is pretty unfair," I agreed.

Men had it so easy. They didn't have to deal with childbirth or hormonal changes making their bodies swell and sag. They really only had to expend the bare minimum of effort to stay fit and fashionable, and yet it was still somehow more than most of them were willing to do. I'd noticed most men seemed to give up completely around thirty or thirty-five, letting their fashion sense and hairstyles become as stuck in time as their taste in music.

Granted, many of them did have to deal with hair loss, which was one of the few afflictions of aging that disproportionately affected their sex. But Rogaine had been around for decades, and even that was too much effort for most men.

I remembered once gently suggesting Jerry give it a try. He'd scoffed as if there was something inherently shameful or weak about the act of caring for your appearance. Never mind that I spent a full thirty minutes on my skincare routine every morning and evening in order to stay attractive-looking for him.

"How was it?" Angie prodded. "Did you talk to him? Did he remember you?"

"He did, actually. I was surprised."

"I don't know why. You two saw each other every day for two years. I should hope he'd remember you."

"Well, he did. We chatted a bit. He's just moved back to Chicago to be closer to his mother. His father recently passed away."

"God, he really is sweet. Is he married?"

"Divorced."

Her eyes narrowed. "Innnnnteresting."

"Is it?" I shrugged. "I'm divorced. I'd estimate half our graduating class is divorced, which is in line with average divorce rates in the U.S."

Angie rolled her eyes. "What I find interesting is that you managed to glean this particular piece of information from him."

"It came up organically. I wasn't grilling him."

"Sounds like you two had a lovely chat."

"We did, until I made a complete fool of myself." I winced at the memory.

"Uh oh. What'd you do?"

"I asked him to dinner."

"Oh no. Oh god."

"Oh god is right." I shook my head, grimacing. "I don't know what possessed me."

Angie gave me a sympathetic look. "Mike Pilota possessed you. You've always operated outside of reason where he's concerned. How'd he react?"

"Remember when I screwed up my courage to ask him out in high school?" I bit my lip and Angie nodded. "It basically went like that. Shock. Horror. Panic. Followed by immediate fleeing of the scene."

"Oh, sweetie. I'm sorry."

"Serves me right."

"No it doesn't. I'm proud of you. You took a chance, and that takes guts."

That might be true, but I certainly wouldn't be doing it again anytime soon. I'd learned my lesson about shooting for the stars.

CHAPTER SIX

MIKE

I flicked on the lights in my empty apartment with a mixture of relief and discontentment. I hadn't bothered to hang anything on the walls or do anything to make it look homey since I'd moved in, and it had a bleak, temporary look to it.

It had been a long, annoying day, and I had a headache that refused to go away. My boss at this new job was an arrogant bonehead ten years my junior who didn't know half as much about technology as he thought he did. He was always trying to wade in and get his hands dirty instead of staying out of the way and letting the IT staff do our jobs. His constant meddling and micromanagement slowed everything down, and then he'd turn around and gripe about how long it was taking to get tasks done. Our staff meeting today had been forty-five minutes of him complaining about problems he'd caused himself, either by interfering or by forgetting to assign tasks, and then accusing us of dropping the ball.

Even a trip to the gym after work hadn't done anything to relieve the band of tension radiating out from the base of my skull today. Usually a hard workout did the trick, but this time it had only seemed to make my headache angrier.

I toed off my athletic shoes and dropped my gym bag inside the door before stalking toward the small "kitchen." I used the term loosely. It was only large enough for a small refrigerator that dated from the Paleolithic, an equally ancient two-burner stove, and a sink with maybe a foot of counter space on either side of it.

I missed my old kitchen back in Columbus, which had boasted a dishwasher, small pantry, and enough space to move around comfortably. I wasn't exactly Bobby Flay, but I'd cooked occasionally when I lived there. I had three specialties in my repertoire: scrambled eggs, chili, and my mom's minestrone recipe. These days, however, I mostly stuck to frozen dinners for the sake of convenience.

Yanking the freezer door open, I surveyed my dinner options with disdain. None of it sounded appetizing. I selected a box at random and started it heating in the microwave. While my dinner was defrosting, I picked up my gym bag and carried it into my bedroom.

At least this place had a separate bedroom. It'd been a splurge I probably shouldn't have indulged in, but the thought of living in a studio at my age was too depressing to contemplate. Almost as depressing as the prospect of moving in with my mother.

After I'd emptied the dirty clothes out of my gym bag, I headed into the bathroom. This apartment building had been built around the same time as my parents' house, and it had the same medicine cabinet mirror as the one in my parents' master bathroom. I stared at myself in the pallid blue light cast by the fluorescent bulb above the mirror and ran my hand over my chin. My beard was in need of a trim, but I didn't have the energy to do it tonight.

Without the beard, I was the spitting image of my dad. Sometimes I'd catch a glimpse of myself in the mirror out of the corner of my eye, and it was like seeing a ghost. Especially now that I'd passed the age I remember my dad being when I was growing up.

I dismissed my haunted reflection by jerking the cabinet open and reached inside for the bottle of ibuprofen I kept there. Popping two pills in my mouth, I shut the cabinet and dry swallowed as I headed back to the kitchen. The microwave dinged as I leaned into the fridge for a beer. Once my dinner had cooled off enough to carry, I took it over to the desk that sat beneath the lone window in my living room.

More screen time probably wasn't the best thing for my headache, but all I wanted to do was zone out for a while and play some League of Magecraft, the MMORPG I favored at the moment. Slaying undead dragonkin with my paladin was the highlight of most of my days. Talk about sad, eh?

Before I started up my game, I did my once-daily check of Facebook and was confronted by a photo of my ex-wife Christine.

She'd changed the color of her hair to a lighter blonde. In the picture, she was at a restaurant holding a glass of wine, and I wondered who'd taken it and if she was seeing someone. She hadn't tagged anyone else in the photo, but it definitely wasn't a selfie, so someone else had been with her.

Our split had been amicable, so we were still "friends," both virtually and in meat space. Ostensibly, anyway. We hadn't actually spoken since I'd moved, but she had made a point of coming to my dad's funeral at Christmas, which I appreciated.

I searched my feelings for any jealousy about Christine dating, but there was nothing. I felt nothing. About her, about her life without me, about whoever had been with her at that restaurant. I was numb, which probably wasn't the healthiest response, but it was also how I'd felt about the last couple years of our marriage, so it fit.

As I reached for the mouse to scroll down my timeline, I noticed I had a new friend request. Usually these were from weirdos or bots, but I clicked it anyway, just to see. This one was from someone named Angela Sullivan Ellis, who didn't appear to be a bot, since we had forty-nine friends in common.

Curious.

All our mutual friends were people I knew from high school. The name Angela Sullivan was vaguely familiar, and I clicked through to her profile for a better look at her photo. Her jet-black hair triggered a memory, even with a prominent streak of gray in it. I vaguely remembered her now. Angie had been one of those goth, arty types who wore black lipstick and listened to The Cure. I hadn't known her well, but we'd had a couple classes together. I also recalled that she'd been friends with Dawn and had come into Pizza My Heart regularly to see her.

Curiouser.

It couldn't be a coincidence that Dawn's best friend from high school had suddenly decided to friend me on Facebook three days after I'd run into Dawn for the first time in thirty years.

Could it?

I accepted Angie's friend request, which gave me access to all the private posts on her Facebook page. There were multiple shots of Dawn's yarn store, and I gathered from the captions that she'd had a hand in decorating it.

There were also multiple photos of Dawn. Smiling proudly behind the counter in the store. Posing outside beneath the sign. Holding a glass of champagne at the grand opening party. There were other photos too, that she'd been tagged in. Pictures of various dinners and cocktails with check-ins at restaurants and bars around the city. Apparently, Dawn and Angie were still besties.

Curiouser and curiouser.

I clicked through to Dawn's profile, but it was locked down to friends only. The only thing I could see was her employment info: Owner at Mad About Ewe.

My mouse hovered over the friend request button.

Did I dare?

Our encounter on Saturday had ended awkwardly after I'd turned down her dinner invitation. She'd tried to hide it, but I could tell I'd hurt her feelings.

What would she think if I sent her a friend request now?

While I was deliberating, my computer blooped to let me know I had a new Facebook message. I clicked and found a message from Angie in my inbox.

> *Hi, Mike! I don't know if you remember me, but we went to high school together. Dawn mentioned she'd run into you this weekend and you'd recently moved back to town. I'm on the committee planning our 30-year reunion (can you believe it's been that long???) and I'm looking for volunteers to help out. Any chance you'd be interested?*

Everything about Angie's message confused me. Why would she think I'd want to volunteer for the reunion committee when I hadn't been to either of the two previous reunions? It didn't sound like the sort of thing I'd want to do. My interest in reconnecting with my high school peer group was minimal, and what the hell did I know about planning a reunion? Diddly-squat, that's what. Why would she want *me* on the committee anyway? Surely Angie was in touch with plenty of other people she could recruit to volunteer who'd be better choices than me?

But the part that stuck out to me the most was that Dawn had told Angie she'd seen me. What did that mean? I felt like it must mean something, but I wasn't sure what. I wasn't sure what I wanted it to mean either.

While I was deliberating, I got another message from Angie.

All you'd have to do is come to a few planning meetings, which usually happen over drinks at The Old House Pub on Milwaukee Ave. It should only take up 5-10 hours of your time a month, tops.

And then, a second later, she added:

Dawn will be there.

I stared at those four little words encircled in their own little blue message bubble. Why had Angie told me that? It sounded like an enticement. Like she thought I'd be more likely to say yes if I knew Dawn was doing it.

But how did she know that?

Because she was right. The prospect of seeing Dawn again made me want to say yes.

I waited, but Angie provided no additional information or clarification. The ball was in my court.

Sure why not, I replied. *When?*

After I'd hit Send, I clicked back to Dawn's Facebook profile and hit the Add Friend button.

Friend Request Sent.

CHAPTER SEVEN

DAWN

Mike Pilota sent you a friend request.

I'd received the notification a week ago but still hadn't responded. I'd just left it hanging there, unanswered. Ignored.

Out of spite? Perhaps a little. After he'd rejected me yet again, I had to admit I enjoyed the thought of Mike getting a taste of that same rejection for once. I liked to picture him sitting at home, futilely checking his notifications day after day, waiting for a reply that would never come.

I wanted him to know that I wasn't desperate for his attention and would not be begging for treats like a pet Labrador. I couldn't care less whether I ever spoke to Mike again.

Of course, it was just as likely he'd forgotten he even sent the request by now. There was no reason to assume he was in any way invested in my response.

I couldn't imagine why he'd sent it in the first place. Why now? Why would you send a friend request to someone you'd brushed off?

I hadn't even realized Mike was active on Facebook, which was probably just as well. It had saved me from years of pathetic cyberstalking. And it *would* be pathetic to be hung up on a man you'd had a childish crush on thirty years ago.

Good thing I wasn't.

I'd meant what I'd said about being done with Mike Pilota. Finito. Over and out. So long, and thanks for all the fish.

So it was annoying in the extreme when I walked into The Old House Pub and saw him sitting next to Angie. My steps, which had been confident and quick as I entered the bar, faltered as I recognized him.

How? Why? What the blazing hell was Mike doing here?

My eyes narrowed as they homed in on my best friend, the obvious answer to all my questions. She must have recruited Mike for her reunion committee. And I could guess why.

It was clearly some misguided attempt to force another reunion between me and Mike in the hopes that, against all odds, *this time* sparks would finally fly, and he'd realize his secret attraction to me which he'd been repressing all these years.

Did I mention Angie was a bit of a fantasist?

Obviously, there was no way any of that would happen. The far more likely scenario was that Mike and I would try our level best to ignore each other's existence while pretending there was no lingering awkwardness between us.

That was my game plan anyway. Mike could do what he liked.

Gathering a deep breath, I forced my feet to carry me to the table where Mike and Angie were seated. There were six chairs, and I set my sights on the one farthest from Mike.

Angie spotted my approach immediately and called out a greeting. Mike looked up, and our eyes caught and held for a charged second before I forcibly tore my gaze away to pin my best friend with an accusatory glare. Angie grinned back at me and shrugged, as if she knew exactly what she'd done wrong and didn't care one bit.

Before I could claim the chair diagonally across from Mike, he leapt to his feet. "Here, you probably want to sit next to Angie," he said, and held his own chair out for me.

I had no choice but to accept his offer at that point without looking like an ill-mannered ingrate. Mumbling my thanks, I draped my purse over the back of the chair and sat down.

To my consternation, Mike took the seat right next to me at the head of the table. He was so close our knees brushed as he scooted his chair forward, and I jerked my legs away from him as if I'd been zapped with electricity.

"It's good to see you again," he said in that warm, gravelly voice that used to make my limbs quiver like a gelatin mold on a mechanical bull. Fortunately, I was completely over my childish infatuation with him, and therefore impervious to his sexy man voice.

I looked up to find him smiling at me, his lips curved invitingly and framed by his neatly trimmed beard, and my heart gave a little involuntary jump in my chest.

Well, crud.

Perhaps I wasn't quite as over Mike as I'd hoped.

Swallowing, I tried to return his smile levelly. "Yes, I hadn't expected to see you again so soon."

"You can thank Angie for that. She talked me into volunteering for the reunion committee."

"Did she now?" I swiveled my head toward Angie.

She gave me another of her sorry-not-sorry grins. "When you told me Mike had just moved back to town, I knew he'd be perfect to recruit for the committee. Former homecoming king? It's a no-brainer."

"I don't know about that," Mike said with a sheepish duck of his head. "I didn't even go to the last two reunions."

"But now you're guaranteed to come to this one!" Angie's smile was broad. "It's a huge get for me."

Before Mike could respond, we were joined by a handsome-looking woman with a headful of springy black curls. "Greetings, everyone!" Her eyes lit up as they landed on me and then Mike. "Oh, fresh meat! Hello, I'm Yolanda Hamilton."

Both her name and her face were vaguely familiar. I reached back through my memory banks as I returned her smile. "I'm Dawn Botstein, formerly Czworniak. I think we had American history together."

Yolanda's smile became even warmer. "You know, I think you're right."

Mike had gotten to his feet beside me, and he extended a polite hand to Yolanda. "I'm Mike. Mike Pilota."

"Oh, I remember you, honey." She beamed as she squeezed Mike's hand. "We all knew who you were."

I noted with curiosity the way Mike's cheeks flushed above his beard and his eyes skated away, as if he were embarrassed to have been popular in high school.

Interesting.

As I contemplated this information, an extremely well-dressed man approached the table. "Well, hello there, Eagles! Who's ready to plan the banging-est reunion Taft High has ever seen?" He draped his arm around Yolanda as he kissed her cheek, and I recognized him as Deon Wilson, one of Mike's former compatriots from the varsity football team.

Yolanda confirmed my identification by squealing his name as she spun in his arms to give him an enthusiastic hug. "Deon! I'm so glad you decided to come back for more punishment!"

Deon's fashion sense was striking, and in direct contrast to the T-shirts and football jerseys I was used to seeing him in thirty years ago. His svelte frame was clad in an expertly fitted gray plaid blazer, gray dress shirt, navy blue tie, and slim pink slacks. He looked like he'd stepped right off the pages of a menswear catalogue. It was the sort of outfit clothing retailers always touted in their advertising despite the fact that until just now, I'd never actually known a man who dressed like that in his day-to-day life.

For a moment I wondered from their affectionate greeting if he was Yolanda's husband, but then I realized he was wearing a wedding ring and she wasn't. And then he moved around the table to Angie and greeted her with equal affection. "Hello, gorgeous. It's excellent to see you again. Congratulations on your little coup."

At that point I began to suspect he might be gay, based on the degree to which he was comfortable being physically affectionate with women who were not his partner—and how equally comfortable the two women seemed to be receiving his affection.

No one at our high school had been "out" that I knew of. I remembered a few kids who I'd guessed at the time might be gay, but in 1989, it wasn't safe for teenagers to be out of the closet. Not with gay slurs still commonplace in PG-13 movies, the

Moral Majority driving the political conversation, and the AIDS epidemic raging through the country unabated.

I never would have guessed Deon was gay in high school. But then I wouldn't have guessed anyone on the football team was. I realized now that was a remnant of my own narrow thinking. An assumption that athleticism was somehow inherently masculine and homosexuality was inherently feminine, which was obviously complete poppycock. Looking back on it, the way Deon had always seemed to be draped in cheerleaders probably should have been a clue. I'd assumed it was a sign of his sexual magnetism, but maybe they'd simply felt safer with him than with the boys who were trying to get into their pants.

Deon's eyes landed on Mike at the opposite end of the table, and his face split into a huge grin. "Jesus Christ. Mike Pilota, is that you?"

My eyes flicked to Mike, curious to observe his reaction.

He was still standing after shaking Yolanda's hand, and he grinned as Deon came around the table toward him. "Hey, Deon. Good to see you again." The two men met in a hearty, back-slapping embrace.

"My god, look at you!" Deon stepped back and gazed admiringly at Mike. "You look fantastic."

"You're looking pretty good yourself," Mike answered. "I like the chrome dome, Lex Luthor."

Deon reached up to rub his head, which was shaved completely bald, although a faint hint of darker shadow under his dark skin revealed where his natural hairline had receded. "Yeah, well, not all of us are as lucky as you." He reached up and tugged a lock of Mike's hair playfully. "Look at this mop."

Mike batted his hand away, and Deon turned his gaze on me, finally. "Hello! I don't think we've met." He smiled warmly as he extended his hand to me. "Deon Wilson."

"This is Dawn Czworniak," Mike said.

"Botstein," I corrected as Deon's hand enveloped mine. Even though it was my ex-husband's name, it had been mine for twenty-six years and was more familiar to me than my maiden name, which felt like it belonged to another person I could barely remember.

"Right, sorry," Mike muttered.

Once all the greetings had been made, Yolanda took the seat across from Angie, and Deon sat between them at the end of the table. Mike lowered himself back into his seat to my right, his knee once again brushing against mine.

"I like this," Yolanda said, looking from Mike's end of the table to Deon's. "Look at us, framed by two hunky football players."

Deon chuckled good-naturedly while Mike grunted and shifted in his seat.

"That only leaves one person we're waiting on," Angie said, casting a glance at her phone. "I wonder if we should start without her."

"I'm here!" a voice said, and I looked up to see my former nemesis approaching the table.

Gina Laird: head cheerleader, homecoming queen, and for seven months of our senior year, Mike's high school girlfriend. I'd hated Gina with a fiery passion that was likely undeserved. In truth, I hadn't really known her at all. All I'd known was that for a short time she'd had what I desperately wanted—Mike.

"Gina!" Mike looked surprised as he lurched to his feet.

"Mike! Oh my god!" Gina's face lit up as she threw her arms around him.

My eyes flicked to her left hand as they embraced, and my stomach sank as I noted the absence of a wedding ring. Belatedly, I reminded myself I wasn't supposed to care about Mike anymore, and therefore jealousy was uncalled for.

I gathered from the way the others greeted Gina that she'd been on the committee with them for the previous reunions. Angie introduced me to her, and she greeted me warmly and with no hint of recognition. Why would she recognize me? She'd only come into Pizza My Heart regularly to flirt with Mike.

Now that we were all present, Angie commenced the meeting. Fittingly, the music being pumped through the bar was all eighties hits. I wondered if she'd made a special request to the manager.

The first agenda item was the venue, which Angie, Deon, and Yolanda all had strong feelings about. Bossy Tess's choice of venue for the last reunion had gone over like a turd in a swimming pool, and they were determined to do better this time. Angie had already researched and identified three potential locations with availability in the fall, and it was now up to the rest of us to decide which one we preferred.

While the more experienced committee members wrangled over the finer points of chair rental and open bar charges, I quietly sipped the white wine I'd ordered and let my eyes drift to Gina sitting across the table from me.

She was stunningly beautiful for a woman of our age, but under closer inspection I could see all the effort that had gone into her youthful appearance. Certainly, Botox was responsible for the unlined smoothness of her forehead, and probably a shockingly expensive skincare routine to boot. Her lush, perfectly lined lips had almost definitely been augmented with collagen. Her eyelashes were as fake as her breasts, which had to be implants. Either that or she wore the best bra in the world. There was something else odd about her face, and I suspected cheek implants, or perhaps a face-lift. Possibly both.

And then there was her hair, which was just as shiny and blonde as it had been in her youth, but much smoother and longer now than the spiral perm she'd sported in high school. I guessed extensions, as well as a standing appointment for a Brazilian blowout.

All told, her appearance must have cost tens of thousands of dollars. I wondered what she did for a living, and how she afforded it. I certainly didn't stint when it came to my own beauty routine, but the kind of work Gina appeared to have had done was far beyond my means.

She was sitting on Mike's other side, and every so often she'd squeeze his arm in an attempt to draw him into the conversation. He didn't seem to mind the contact. I imagined their knees touching under the table and swallowed another mouthful of wine.

Regardless of how he felt about Gina's casual caresses, Mike didn't participate much in the venue debate. His one contribution was to ask why we didn't just hold the reunion in the school gymnasium. When the others explained that we weren't allowed to serve alcohol on school property, necessitating a dry reunion which would make it more difficult to recoup costs by selling drink tickets, he fell silent for the remainder of the meeting.

I didn't have much more to contribute than Mike. I didn't really care one way or the other, so when my opinion was solicited, I simply agreed with whatever Angie had just said. That was why she'd recruited me for the committee, after all. To consolidate support for her plans.

I hadn't even gone to the last reunion. The date had coincided with a planned family vacation to Hawaii. Even if I'd been in town, I wasn't sure I would have gone. The ten-year reunion had been an odd experience. I'd gone mostly out of curiosity, but had found the evening awkward and anticlimactic.

Most people had turned out to be exactly who I'd expected them to be. Our class had produced no celebrities or mega successes. Everyone had extremely mundane and commonplace jobs, except for Donal Larkin's twin sister Shannon, who'd joined the State Department.

There had been a lot of strained small talk with people who didn't remember me, as well as a few uncomfortable conversations with people I'd forgotten who remembered me well. One woman whose name and face rang no bell whatsoever had proudly produced her yearbook to show off the heartfelt note I'd written to her. There on the page, in my own handwriting, was a lengthy message I had no memory of writing, extolling our meaningful and abiding friendship.

The whole experience had been unsettling. I wasn't particularly looking forward to repeating it, but I supposed since I was on the reunion committee now I had no choice but to attend the thirty-year.

Eventually, an agreement was reached about the venue that seemed to satisfy everyone who was invested in the decision. Now that we had a venue, we also had a firm date for the reunion, and the next step was to spread the word.

Yolanda volunteered to take on the social media outreach, which I gathered she'd performed in the past. As she talked about the Facebook group she'd be setting up and inviting us all to, I remembered I still hadn't responded to Mike's friend request. I glanced his way and caught him looking at me. Our eyes locked and held for a pregnant moment before Gina leaned over to murmur in his ear, tearing his attention away.

I turned back to Yolanda with renewed determination to ignore Mike, listening as she encouraged us to post in the group frequently and start hyping the upcoming reunion date.

After that, we moved on to the topic of music. Deon offered to find a DJ, which everyone agreed to. By that point he'd made several references to a husband, which had confirmed my hunch about his sexual orientation. I figured if Deon's taste in music was anywhere near as good as his fashion sense, we'd be in capable hands.

With that, we'd reached the end of the agenda, and Angie adjourned the meeting. Deon came over to chat with Mike and Gina while we waited for the waitress to close out all our tabs. I tried to ignore them as I listened to Yolanda and Angie gab.

After a few minutes, Deon headed out, calling out a cheery goodbye and leaving Mike and Gina to talk on their own. I heard Gina's tinkling laugh and glanced toward them involuntarily, just in time to see Gina reach up and run her fingers through Mike's hair.

Well then.

I guess they were enjoying their mini reunion. Gina certainly looked happy. Mike was partially turned away from me, so I couldn't see his expression, but his body language seemed receptive to her.

Good for them. Maybe they'd be one of those second-chance love stories you heard about every so often. High school sweethearts who found each other again after thirty years. How sweet.

As nice as that sounded for them, I didn't feel the need to stick around and watch it unfold. As soon as the waitress dropped off my credit card receipt, I signed it, bid a hasty goodbye to Yolanda and Angie, and got out of there.

CHAPTER EIGHT
MIKE

I didn't give a damn about any of this reunion stuff. I had literally no opinion on the Fairfield versus the Kimpton as a venue for the big night. I'd never been to either hotel. I'd never even been to a reunion before. I was totally clueless about all this stuff.

What I did care about was that the meetup gave me a chance to see Dawn again. Not just see her, but really look at her. She spent most of the time turned away from me, listening to Angie and the others talk, so I was able to observe her without being observed doing so. My observation led me to a very important conclusion.

She was beautiful.

I admired how easily she smiled, and how comfortable she seemed in her own skin. That latter part was new. High school Dawn had never been half as self-possessed as this woman who sat beside me now. But then who was, at that age?

My own cockiness as a teenager had all been an act. An attempt to plaster over the cracks in my self-esteem and my fears about not being good enough. Looking back on it now, I respected that Dawn had never tried to put on a false front. Under the strict constraints of the high school caste system, she'd been authentically herself. Kind, sincere, a little bit weird—but the kind of weird you came by honestly, not the kind you put on for attention. She'd worn her heart and all her insecurities on her sleeve for all the world to see.

Nowadays she had a little more polish to her. Her clothes were bright and elegant. Flattering, but clearly chosen for comfort and practicality. She wore very little jewelry, except a simple gold necklace and a pair of dangly earrings that looked handmade.

Watching Dawn now, she reminded me of all the things I wasn't, and made me feel like an awkward, uncertain teenager again. It struck me as funny, because I never used to feel that way around her when we were working at Pizza My Heart thirty years ago. But I sure as hell felt it now.

Why hadn't I appreciated her more in high school?

Because you were an idiot, my subconscious supplied automatically.

Every once in a while, Dawn would shift in her seat or brush her hair back from her face, and I'd catch a heady whiff of her perfume. It was floral, but not like just any old flowers. She smelled like the kind of flowers that only bloomed deep in a mysterious woodland fairy realm.

Or maybe it was just jasmine, and I had an overactive imagination from playing too many video games.

Either way, it gave me a giddy rush every time I caught her scent, and I found myself leaning forward in the hopes of catching it again.

She didn't talk much during the meeting, except when her friend Angie asked for her opinion. When she did speak, Dawn's voice was warm and sweet, like someone had given a human voice to a cup of hot tea with honey.

I was totally smitten.

I wanted to get her alone and talk to her some more. I wanted to find out how life had treated her and what she'd been doing for the last three decades. I wanted to know her. I'd made up my mind. At the first opportunity, I was going to ask Dawn out on a date.

Unfortunately, there were two circumstances that threw a wrench in my new plans.

The first was that Dawn's demeanor toward me had chilled since our last encounter. I could guess why. I'd turned down her dinner invitation, and now she was feeling snubbed. She was still polite, but that was all she was. There was none of the warmth I'd sensed in her last week. Her eyes seemed to want to look everywhere but at me, and whenever our knees accidentally brushed under the table, she flinched away from me.

It was a setback, but I didn't consider it an insurmountable one. She didn't know why I'd turned her down. For all she knew, I wasn't interested in her. Hopefully when I explained that I'd actually had plans that night and was in fact very interested in going on a date with her, she'd warm up again.

The second, much more annoying wrench in the works was the unexpected presence of Gina Laird, my old high school girlfriend.

I hadn't thought about Gina in years, and I'd just as soon not have to think about her now. Talk about the exact opposite of Dawn. In high school, Gina had been just as shallow and fake as me, concerned mainly with appearances and maintaining her standing at the top of the social pecking order.

On the surface, we'd seemed like a perfect fit—the football player and the cheer-leader, homecoming king and queen—but the truth was, we'd never had much of anything in common. I couldn't say I'd ever particularly enjoyed spending time with her, and as soon as our senior prom was over and there was no reason to have a girl-friend anymore, I'd ended the relationship.

Gina didn't appear to have changed all that much over the last three decades. Every-thing about her was still calculated to attract, from her improbably long lashes to her glossy, over-plumped lips and body-hugging clothes. I detected more of a brittleness to her smile these days though, which never quite reached her eyes. But maybe that was just Botox.

I'd hoped to talk to Dawn after the meeting ended, but I was cornered by Gina and Deon. I liked Deon, so I didn't mind catching up with him, but I was afraid of missing my chance with Dawn.

After Deon made his goodbyes, Gina continued to monopolize my attention. "God, look at you! You're gorgeous. And this hair!" She reached up and ran her fingers through my hair before I could duck out of the way.

"You look good too," I said, trying to be polite. "You've been well, I hope."

"Oh, I've been fantastic! Couldn't be better." She let out a high-pitched laugh. "But tell me all about yourself. I'm dying to catch up. Are you married?"

"Uh, no. Divorced."

Her face lit up like this was the best news she'd heard all week. "Me too! What brings you back to Chicago after all these years?"

"I wanted to be closer to my mom after my dad passed."

Gina's nose wrinkled in sympathy as she squeezed my arm. "Aww, I'm sorry to hear about your dad. He was a sweetheart."

My dad was a lot of things, but a sweetheart wasn't one of them. As far as I could remember, he'd barely spoken two words to Gina the entire time she and I had dated. But I let the comment go, recognizing she was just trying to be nice.

Gina continued to engage me in conversation, asking me questions and chattering on about her kids, her plastic surgeon ex-husband, and her job selling diet supplements while I pretended to be interested. I itched to get away but couldn't figure out a polite way of extracting myself.

I glanced toward Dawn, longing to go talk to her, and saw her hug Angie goodbye before heading out the door.

Well, crap. There went my window of opportunity. Once again, I'd let Dawn get away.

Feeling defeated, I spent a few more minutes making desultory small talk with Gina before I finally managed to excuse myself and bid her goodbye.

When I got home thirty minutes later, I fired up my computer, intending to console myself by playing a little League of Magecraft before I hit the sack.

But then I saw the Facebook notification:

Dawn Czworniak Botstein accepted your friend request.

The bell on the shop door jangled loudly as I walked into Dawn's yarn store the following Saturday.

I was taking a risk. I didn't know for sure she'd be working today. But I hoped. It'd been a Saturday the first time I'd encountered her, so I had my fingers crossed that she'd be here again.

Just like last time, I felt every eye in the shop turn toward me. A couple of the customers browsing around the store did a small double take. I had the sense they didn't get a lot of men coming in here.

The same old lady was sitting in one of the chairs by the front window knitting. I gave her a friendly nod and her eyes narrowed with suspicion. *Alrighty then.*

My gaze went to the counter. A young woman in her twenties smiled at me from behind the register.

Damn. No Dawn.

Okay, well, in that case I'd just buy the first ball of plain yarn I saw and get the hell out of here.

"Dawn!" the old lady shouted. "Your good-looking gentleman friend is back."

I froze, my mouth falling open as I felt my face color.

Which was how Dawn found me when she emerged from a room in the back of the shop.

"Mike." She looked surprised to see me. Not quite like it was a pleasant surprise, but not like it was an unpleasant one either. Just plain surprised.

The sight of her twisted my insides into knots, but I forced my face to relax into a smile. "Hey, Dawn."

She was dressed more casually today, in jeans and a pink T-shirt with the store's logo on it. Her hair was pulled back from her face in a messy ponytail, and she reached up to push a loose strand behind her ear. "Is there something I can help you with?"

The girl behind the counter and the old lady were both watching us with interest, not even bothering to be subtle about it, and I suddenly felt self-conscious. I meant to ask Dawn out on a date, but I was uncomfortable posing the question in front of an audience in the middle of her place of business.

Fortunately, I'd devised a plan before coming in here. An innocent excuse to explain my appearance and hopefully get me a few moments alone with Dawn.

"Yeah," I told her. "I was wondering if you could point me to the basic supplies a beginner would need if they wanted to learn to knit."

Dawn's smile widened as she slipped confidently into her customer service persona. "Of course. What age is the beginner?"

"It's for me, actually."

That stopped her in her tracks. She hesitated as the surprise returned to her face. "You want to learn to knit?"

I cleared my throat. "Yeah. My mom hasn't showed any interest in that afghan kit I got her. And I thought maybe…maybe if I took it up too, I could sit next to her doing it while she was watching her TV shows and maybe it would…" I trailed off and scratched my head. "I dunno."

"Maybe it would inspire her to take it up again," Dawn suggested, her expression softening.

"Yeah, something like that." I shrugged. "I figure I'll be pretty bad at it, and if nothing else it'll probably get her to tell me what I'm doing wrong."

"And then the next thing you know, she'll be knitting."

I nodded. "Hopefully. That's the idea anyway."

"It's a good idea." Dawn smiled up at me, and I felt it shoot through my whole body, all the way down into my toes.

We stood there for a second, smiling at each other like a couple of idiots, until she shook herself out of it and set off across the store.

"Since you've got big hands, I'll set you up with bulky yarn and large needles to start." She stopped in front of a rack full of knitting needles of all types and sizes. "I recommend size tens," she said, spinning the rack as I caught up to her. "I like bamboo needles for beginners, because they've got a little flex to them and they're not as slippery as metal, so you're less likely to lose your stitches." She pulled a packet of needles down and handed them to me.

I accepted them wordlessly, since I didn't know shit about knitting needles. I didn't even know there were so many different kinds. Some of the ones on the rack seemed to be joined by a plastic cord, while others were shorter and came in packs of four and five. And then there were some that were just small curved bits of metal or plastic. The whole thing was mystifying to me.

"Now for the yarn," Dawn said, heading over to a wall of solid-colored yarns. "Wool is the easiest fiber to work with, but you want one that doesn't split too much when you're just starting out. This Plymouth Encore Chunky is nice for learning on. See any colors you like?"

I stared at the dozen different colors of yarn, frozen in indecision. "It doesn't really matter, I guess. This is just for practice, right?" I wasn't intending to make anything with it. I just figured I'd mess around a little bit to try and get my mom interested. If it worked, there wouldn't be any reason to keep going with it, so whatever I bought would just go to waste.

"If it helps you choose, I find it easier to see what I'm doing with the lighter colors," Dawn said. "The dark yarns can be a little bit tricky if you don't have a lot of light— or if you have bad eyes like me." She let out a self-deprecating little laugh and smiled at me again.

I loved the way her green eyes danced when she smiled, and the way the skin around them crinkled. She had deep laugh lines, like someone who smiled a lot. The sight of them sent another rush of warmth through my body.

Turning to the yarn again, I selected a light green that reminded me of the color of Dawn's eyes. It was soft and squishy under my fingers. I liked the way it felt when I squeezed it.

"Good choice," she said. "Now you'll just need a good instruction book for beginners, and you'll be off to the races."

I followed her to the books section and watched as she deliberated over them, tapping her index finger against her lips. She had lovely, soft lips, and I couldn't help wondering what it would be like to kiss them. I hoped she'd let me find out, but I still hadn't figured out how I was going to ask her out. Everywhere we went in the store, we were being overheard by someone. I'd started to regret the impulse that had led me to do it here.

"Oh, this is a good one!" She stooped to pull a book off the bottom shelf and held it out to me. "It's got lots of helpful illustrations and covers all the basics you need to get started."

"Sounds good," I said, taking it from her and flipping through the pages. The illustrations inside made about as much sense as quantum physics. "Is it the sort of thing you can learn from a book? Or do I need to sign up for a class or something?"

"That depends on you. It's possible to learn from a book, but I think most people find it helpful to have a friend or a more experienced knitter get them started. We do offer a beginner's class once a month, if you'd like to sign up for our next one in two weeks. There are also websites I can point you to with helpful videos to demonstrate the techniques."

"I guess I'll try and muddle through on my own."

"I could always..." She hesitated, pressing her lips together, and I saw two spots of color tinge her cheeks.

"What?" I prompted, eager to know what she'd been about to suggest that had made her flush.

Her lashes shadowed her cheeks as she lowered her eyes. "I could give you a quick lesson to get you going. Right now, I mean—if you have time."

"You'd do that?" I tried to keep the excitement out of my voice.

Be cool. Be normal. Don't scare her.

She gave a small shrug. "Sure. If you'd like."

I couldn't control my grin. "I'd like that a lot."

CHAPTER NINE
DAWN

"Y"ou sure I'm not taking you away from anything else you should be doing?" Mike asked as he followed me.

"It's fine," I assured him, grabbing a pair of reading glasses off the counter as I headed to the couch by the front window. Chloe was here to handle the register and help the other customers. I'd assigned myself the task of reorganizing the stockroom today, and it wasn't a job I was in a hurry to get back to. I'd much rather be helping Mike.

What a surprise he'd turned out to be. First coming in to buy a gift for his mother, and now here he was determined to learn to knit himself, in the hopes of inspiring her to take it up again. I couldn't think of many men who'd do as much. Which was perhaps more of a sad commentary on his brethren than a compliment to him.

"This is Linda, one of my VIP customers," I said to Mike as we joined her by the window.

Natural light was beneficial to handiwork, which was why I'd put my group seating area in front of the store's only window. I also liked the idea of passersby looking in and seeing people sitting together knitting and crocheting. I hoped it would make the store more inviting.

"Linda, this is Mike, an old friend from high school." I felt an odd nervousness about claiming Mike as my friend. I never would have been so presumptuous in high school, even though, by any normal definition of the word, that's what we were.

Mike greeted Linda and she responded with a curt nod. Obviously, she remembered his previous visit to the store, and I suspected she might be holding a grudge against him on my behalf.

I sat on the couch closest to the window and gestured for Mike to join me. It was a bit gray outside today, so we'd need all the light we could get.

"How do you get to be a VIP customer?" Mike asked as he sat down beside me. His heavy frame caused the couch to dip, and me to tilt toward him involuntarily. My shoulder pressed against his arm, and a tingling warmth shot through me.

I hastily scooted away, putting a few inches of space between us, although I knew from experience that beginner knitting lessons required a degree of closeness. Soon we would be passing the needles back and forth, heads bent together as we peered down at the work, and some touching would be inevitable.

My mouth felt dry at the prospect. I'd been hesitant to offer Mike a knitting lesson because I'd been afraid of being shot down a second time. But he'd seemed genuinely excited to take me up on this proposition, and now I just hoped I could retain my dignity.

"Linda comes in almost every day," I told Mike.

"Something to aspire to," Mike said, smiling at me with his eyes. Thank god I was sitting down, because those eyes of his made me weak in the knees.

I cleared my throat and held my hand out. "I'll take the yarn, and you can open up that package of needles."

Mike passed me the yarn, and I slipped the label band off while he took the needles out of their plastic pouch. Once Mike had the needles out, I explained how to find the yarn end in the skein. Then I passed it to him and instructed him to make a slip knot on one of the needles, which he did easily. After that it was time to teach him how to cast on.

I took the needle from him, suppressing the urge to shiver as our fingers touched for the first time. We were working with our hands, and there would be quite a lot of touching before the lesson was through. I needed to keep my reactions under control.

Mike was here as a customer, not a sex object. It was important our interactions remained professional.

After demonstrating the proper hand position for the long-tail cast on, which was a bit like a cat's cradle, I cast on a few example stitches. Mike watched me intently, leaning in close enough that our shoulders pressed together, and I felt the tickle of his breath on the backs of my hands.

When I sensed he'd gotten the gist of it, I handed him the needle and let him try.

"Am I holding it right?" he asked, attempting to imitate me.

"Yes, that's it exactly."

"And then the needle goes under here…" His lips pressed together in a frown of concentration as he picked up the strand of yarn running across his palm.

"That's right," I said, encouraging him.

"I'm afraid that's as much as I can remember. Where does it go next?"

I laid my right hand over his—determinedly ignoring the tingling sensation that went shooting up my arm at the contact with his skin—and guided it through the motions, wrapping the yarn around the needle and dropping the loop off his thumb. His hands were large and strong, but surprisingly pliable in mine.

"Sorry," he muttered when the yarn snagged on one of his calluses. "My hands are rough."

"It's fine," I muttered back, swallowing down the urge to stroke my fingers over those rough calluses as I showed him how to tighten the cast-on stitch. "Now you do the next one."

Removing my hands from his, I watched him go through the motions again, uncertain and a bit clumsy, but eventually figuring it out on his own. "You've got it," I said when he'd completed his first solo cast-on stitch. "Now keep going until you've got twenty stitches on the needle."

I sat back, putting a little distance between us again, and caught Linda staring at us. When my eyes met hers, she gave me a knowing little smile. I lifted my eyebrows in silent inquiry, and her smile widened mysteriously as she turned her gaze back to her own work.

"This is kinda cool," Mike said. "There's a satisfying sort of rhythm to it once you get the hang of it."

"That's why people enjoy it," I said. "It's very relaxing. Almost meditative. And then of course there's the sense of accomplishment from making something with your hands."

"I could see that."

"I've always thought it was sad that boys in this country aren't encouraged to do handicrafts more, because they can be very therapeutic. But we've developed this ridiculous idea that the hearth arts are feminizing and anything feminine is inherently weak, which prevents men from pursuing them."

"Like how the girls all took home ec and the boys took shop class," Mike said.

"Exactly," I said. "Although they've done away with home ec and shop at most schools these days. But you still see it in scouting. Boy Scouts learn wilderness survival skills, while in Girl Scouts it's often more about cooking and sewing and selling cookies."

Mike frowned at his yarn. "It never even occurred to me when I was a kid to ask my mom to teach me how to knit. I remember she taught my sister, or she tried to, anyway. I learned how to change the oil in my dad's car instead, which isn't nearly as much fun."

"It's arguably a bit more useful I suppose."

"Yeah, but no one really changes their own oil anymore, do they? I wouldn't have minded learning something like this. I never developed any hobbies—except video games, which don't really count."

"Do you enjoy them?" I asked.

"Yeah." He shrugged. "It's a fun way to pass the time anyway."

"The whole point of a hobby is to be pleasurable, relaxing, and rewarding," I told him. "So if playing video games feels that way to you, it totally counts as a hobby."

"I'm not sure about rewarding," he said, "but it's definitely the other two."

"Not everyone is naturally artistic like Angie. Those of us who aren't as creative need to take our hobbies where we can find them, whether that's doing crafts, or playing video games, or whatever else interests us. Running, watching movies, fantasy football. Anything can be a hobby if we invest enough of ourselves in it."

Mike smiled to himself as he squinted at the yarn on his needle. "Fantasy football's just Magic: The Gathering for wannabe jocks."

I laughed. "I never thought of it that way, but I suppose it is." My sons had both gone through a Magic the Gathering phase in high school. Much like fantasy football, I'd never understood the rules well enough to play, but I could appreciate the similarities, having observed my boys talking about both.

"I think that's twenty," Mike said, holding out his needle for inspection.

"Very well done." His cast-on stitches weren't as even as an experienced knitter's would have been, but they had improved as he went along.

I didn't bother double-checking the count like I would with my own work. Since we'd just be doing a plain garter stitch for practice, it didn't matter how wide it was.

"Now it's time to bring your second needle into the mix," I told him.

This was where it started to get a little more difficult. I took the needle with the cast-on stitches from him and showed him how to hold it in his left hand with the working yarn to the right and the empty needle in his other hand. Then I demonstrated how to insert the empty needle into the closest stitch, loop the working yarn around it, and slide it back out, capturing the new stitch we'd made while carefully dropping the old stitch off the left needle.

Like I said, this part was tricky. And not for the faint of heart. If you dropped the wrong stitch at the wrong time, all your work could unwind.

I did a few example stitches, working slowly, as Mike leaned in close to observe. He smelled strongly of soap today—something fresh and bracing that reminded me of Irish Spring—but with a lingering hint of baked bread, just like I'd smelled on him before.

What was that about? Was he a secret bread baker? Or did he stop in at a bakery for breakfast every day? I wanted to ask, but I couldn't very well comment on his odor without admitting I'd been sniffing him, and I was far too embarrassed to admit that.

Whatever the reason for it, he smelled positively scrumptious. It took all my willpower not to bury my face in his beautiful salt-and-pepper hair and inhale a big whiff. Which would be quite easy to do, as close as he was. He'd leaned in so close that his head was practically next to mine. All I'd need to do was turn my face a little to the side and I'd be nuzzling his hair.

As I was waging this battle of wills with myself, Mike leaned in even closer, lowering his head, and his beard brushed against my upper arm. The soft, prickly bristles sent a shower of electric sparks shooting through my body, and my hands trembled, nearly causing me to drop a stitch.

I recovered quickly and passed the needles over to him. "Your turn," I said, my voice coming out slightly froggy.

He took the knitting from me with painstaking gentleness, as if it were a bomb that might blow up in his hands.

"You can do it," I told him. "Don't worry if you mess up. I can fix it if you lose a stitch."

He still looked apprehensive, so after a moment's hesitation, I gave his shoulder an encouraging pat. It was the sort of innocent gesture I might make for any of my students, but most of my students didn't possess deltoids the size of a volleyball and the density of a brick. I pulled my hand away quickly, before I succumbed to my overwhelming urge to squeeze Mike's remarkable muscles.

He nodded in response, seemingly oblivious to my inappropriate drooling, thank god. Deep furrows sprouted in his brow as he tried to position the needles in his hands the way I'd shown him.

Leaning over, I guided the working yarn around his pinky and over his index finger for him. Unfortunately, this required me to touch his calloused hand quite extensively, which in turn caused me to imagine how those rough calluses would feel on my body. My ex-husband had always had the soft hands of a doctor. I couldn't remember ever being touched by hands as rough as Mike's, and I suddenly felt as if I'd missed out on something important in my life.

I cleared my throat, leaning away again as I felt my cheeks heat. "There. That'll give you a little more control."

I watched as Mike attempted his first knit stitch, giving him small corrections and encouragement where appropriate. I'd taught him English-style knitting rather than Continental, both because he was right-handed like me, and because I guessed it was the way his mother had learned to knit. It took a few false starts, but he eventually completed his first stitch successfully.

"You did it!"

"Whew." He blew out a long breath, his shoulders slumping as he released the tension he'd been holding in them. "It looks a lot easier when you do it. Your fingers are so small and graceful. Mine are as ungainly as a pack of Oscar Mayer wieners."

I laughed to hide my blush at the compliment. "You'll get the hang of it. This was just your first stitch. Now try number two."

He looked pained. "Do I have to?"

"Yes. You can do it." Before I realized what I was doing, my hand had reached out and squeezed his leg. Once again, I was dazzled by the size and density of his muscles. His quadriceps were the size of a tree trunk and straining the seams of his well-worn jeans.

I snatched my hand back before it could make further inappropriate explorations, and I caught Linda watching me again with another little smile on her face.

"Linda," I said, hoping that by drawing her into the conversation I could remind myself to behave, "when did you learn to knit?"

"My mother taught me when I was a girl," Linda replied as her needles clicked with the perfect rhythm of a metronome. She was one of the fastest knitters I knew. "Had me knitting pot holders and washcloths at seven years of age."

"That's exactly how I learned too." I glanced over at Mike to check his progress before returning my attention to Linda. "If I had to guess, I'd say you're a few years younger than my mother was."

Only now did it occur to me I'd never asked my mother how she'd learned to knit. I'd assumed her mother had taught her, but we'd never talked about it. Of course, I'd had no thought of opening this shop when she died ten years ago. It was only after her death that I really got into knitting again, after I'd gone through her belongings and found all her abandoned knitting projects stashed in a closet. A lifetime's worth of unfinished sweaters and scarves left behind.

I suppose my renewed interest in knitting had been a tribute to her. A way of coping with the loss of someone who'd been there every day of my whole life and was suddenly gone. Which meant this store was a tribute to her as well.

"Everyone knit during the Second World War," Linda said. "My mother told me she knit care packages for Britain during the Blitz, then socks and sweaters for the troops after Pearl Harbor and while my father was stationed in Italy. Even boys learned to knit to support the war effort. Some of the men who were left at home did too. I remember my grandfather could knit."

Mike made a noise of frustration as one of his stitches slipped off the needle.

"That's fine." I reached over and pinched the wayward loop between my thumb and forefinger, then placed it back on the needle for him. "Try again."

He started his stitch over, but the error had gotten in his head and thrown off the comfortable rhythm he'd only just started to develop.

"Not there," I cautioned him when he started to insert the needle incorrectly. "Stick it in here." I'd leaned in close to point out the proper loop and caught another heady whiff of Mike's delectable soap and baked bread scent. Our increased nearness, combined with the double entendre of the instruction I'd just given him, caused my cheeks to heat anew.

I didn't usually face this kind of problem while giving a knitting lesson. I wasn't twelve anymore, so the sexual innuendo of telling someone what to do with their long, pointy object didn't even register most of the time. Of course, most of my students were women or young girls, not hunky, muscular men I was borderline obsessed with.

There had been a few men in the classes I'd taught, but never any I'd been attracted to like this. I thought about my best-looking male customer, Nico Moretti, and wondered if I would have behaved this shamefully if he'd come to me for crochet lessons. It was difficult to imagine, since he was both fifteen years my junior and happily married to a woman I knew and liked quite a lot. Never once, for instance, had I been tempted to cop a sniff of Nico when he came into the store, as I'd now shamefully done to Mike multiple times.

As soon Mike inserted his needle into the correct loop, I leaned away from him again, chastising myself for my unprofessional behavior. I needed to get myself under control if I was going to be seeing Mike regularly. The last thing I needed was a replay of my teenage years, when I'd spent hours styling my hair and putting on drugstore makeup every day just to be ignored by a boy who wasn't the least bit attracted to me. I knew better now. For one thing, I'd sooner put mud on my face than drugstore makeup. But for another, I had a better sense of my own worth, and I didn't plan on wasting my time pining for a man who clearly wasn't interested.

I was quite happy alone, and I could continue to be happy without the romantic notice of Mike Pilota.

He finished another stitch and blew out a breath between his teeth. "I'm terrible at this."

"No, you're not," I assured him. "Everyone struggles at first. Your fingers just have to learn the movements until muscle memory takes over. It takes practice."

"You're very patient." His voice had softened, and I glanced up to find him looking at me.

I quickly dragged my eyes away from him, shrugging off the compliment. "I've taught a lot of knitting classes. Trust me, you're far from my worst student."

"You're just saying that to be nice."

"I'm not. It's difficult for everyone at first. I hope your mother appreciates the effort you're going to for her."

He grunted. "I wouldn't count on it."

"How's she doing?" I asked, letting myself look at him again.

He frowned as he struggled with his next stitch. "Not great, I don't think. She just sits on the couch all day watching TV and barely leaves the house. I can't seem to get her interested in…anything, really."

I felt a surge of sympathy. "It must be hard when someone's been your partner for that long and then suddenly they're gone. My parents had been divorced for nearly twenty years when my mother passed away, so it wasn't the same thing, but even so…" I remembered the look on my father's face at my mother's funeral, and how he'd seemed to retreat into himself afterward. "They were married for nearly twenty-five years before that, and my dad took it hard when she died. He only outlived her by another two years, and I always felt something in him had died with her."

"I'm sorry about your parents," Mike said.

I offered him a soft smile. "I'm sorry about yours. I hope you can get your mother interested in knitting again."

"Me too." He finished the last stitch in the row and held it up proudly. "Hey, look at that. I did it."

"You did. Congratulations."

"Now what?"

"Now you flip it over and start again from left to right." I helped him reposition the knitting in his right hand, holding the yarn to the back, and showed him where to insert the needle for his first stitch of the new row.

After he'd successfully knit a few stitches into the second row, he paused and looked over at me. "Tell me the truth: are all your customers offered private lessons with the proprietor?"

"No." I swallowed thickly under the weight of his steady regard. "Only the old friends."

His bottomless brown eyes seemed to stare straight into my soul, as if he could tell exactly what I was feeling—and what I'd always felt when I was around him. My cheeks started to burn, but this time I couldn't look away. His gaze was like a tractor beam, and I was helpless in its pull.

"I need to take a whiz," Linda announced, standing up and depositing her knitting on her chair before disappearing into the back.

Her sudden declaration broke the spell, and I dragged my eyes down to my lap, willing my heart to stop throbbing as I blew out a long breath. I was seated so close to Mike our arms were touching, and I felt his muscles shift, solid and warm against mine, as he lowered his knitting.

"I think I've got the gist of it," he said. "I can probably stumble through from here with that book you recommended."

I nodded, unable to look at him. My emotions were a muddle of disappointment that our lesson had come to an end and embarrassment that he'd undoubtedly noticed the attraction I'd failed to keep in check. I'd probably made him uncomfortable. Once again, I'd driven him away by allowing my feelings to show.

Mike's thumb ran over the row of stitches he'd made. "I really appreciate all your help. I definitely never would have figured it out on my own."

I busied myself brushing wool fibers off my pants leg. "It was my pleasure. If you run into any trouble, you can always come back for more help. That's what we're here for."

"Can I take you to dinner tonight to say thank you?"

I froze, convinced for a second that I'd misheard him.

But no. He'd definitely said it.

Mike Pilota had asked *me* out.

I sucked in a breath and swiveled my head to look at him. His expression was neutral, waiting for my answer, but underneath I was positive I detected a hint of uncertainty. As if he were actually nervous to ask me out to dinner. As if he were afraid I'd say no.

"I'd love to," I blurted, and felt my heart swell when he broke into a relieved smile.

We were going on a date! I wanted to squeal or scream or jump up and do a victory dance.

Then reality struck, and I cursed the bad timing.

"But I can't tonight." Of course he'd picked the one night on my otherwise empty social calendar when I actually had something to do.

He nodded and looked back at his knitting, but not before I glimpsed his disappointment.

"I'm having dinner with my sons tonight," I explained. "Otherwise I would."

Mike looked back at me. "Are you free next Friday?"

"I am." My face hurt with the effort of holding back the excitement whirling in my stomach.

"Can I take you to dinner then?"

"Yes," I breathed out giddily. "I'd love that."

CHAPTER TEN

MIKE

O n Sunday, I went over to Mom's house like usual, only this time I took my knitting needles and yarn in the tote bag Dawn had given to me. It was made of black canvas and had the store's logo on it. *"A gift for being a VIP customer,"* she'd said with a sly smile. I felt a renewed rush of happiness every time I looked at it.

"Hey, Mom!" I called out cheerfully as I let myself in the front door.

"Is that you, Mike?" she called back from the living room.

"Yeah, it's me." I wasn't going to let her get to me today. Nothing could puncture my good mood after my encounter with Dawn yesterday.

My mom was sitting on the couch in front of the TV like usual, and barely looked up when I came in the room.

"How you doing?" I asked, stooping to kiss her cheek.

"Same as usual." She wrinkled her nose as she batted me away. "I don't like the feel of that beard of yours."

"I know, Mom." She'd always hated it whenever I had facial hair, and never hesitated to let me know how much. Granted, some of my facial hair choices over the years were pretty regrettable. The nineties had been a particularly embarrassing decade, between my goatee, my brief flirtation with a Van Dyke, and my truly unfortunate experiment with a soul patch. What could I say? I'd really liked Pearl Jam in my twenties.

Dad had always been clean-shaven, so that was the way Mom liked me best. Which might have something to do with my lifelong affinity for facial hair. I'd been rebelling against my dad's ideas about what kind of man I should be ever since I left home. Even now that he was gone, I felt myself chafe at Mom's reinforcement of Dad's status quo, and had to remind myself not to let it bug me.

I set my tote bag on the end table at the far end of the couch and headed into the kitchen. There weren't as many dishes stacked around the sink today. At first I thought maybe Mom had been doing more cleaning up, but a check of the refrigerator and freezer showed the truth: she hadn't been eating much.

"You feeling okay?" I asked, wandering back into the living room.

"I'm fine." Her eyes never left the TV screen.

"It looks like you haven't been eating."

"I've been eating."

I crossed my arms, glaring down at her. "What'd you have for dinner last night?"

She still refused to look at me. "Microwave popcorn."

"Mom, you need to eat."

"I eat."

"You need to eat real food. From all four food groups, just like you taught me when I was a kid."

"I wasn't hungry."

I recognized the stubborn set to her jaw and gave up, heading back into the kitchen to start my weekly cleaning. All told, it took me about an hour and a half. Most of the house didn't get used at all, so it didn't take much effort to keep it clean.

I still had hopes that one of these days my mom would start doing it herself again. We hadn't really talked about the fact that she was letting things slide. I'd tried, but she always shut me down.

When I first started coming over every week, after I moved back to Chicago, I'd been shocked at the state of the house. My sister had been trying to do what she could, but she couldn't keep up with her own family's needs *and* mom's *and* work a full-time job. She'd floated the idea of hiring a house cleaner for my mom, but I figured I could save us the money and do it myself. It was why I'd moved back here, after all, to pitch in.

Of course, the first time I'd offered to clean my mom's house for her, she'd balked at the suggestion, insisting she didn't need help. The following week when the place was still a mess, I'd raised the subject again, and again she'd insisted she didn't need me cleaning up for her.

So I just started doing it without saying anything, and she let me. But we never talked about it. We never talked about a lot of things.

Once I was done with the cleaning and had a load of laundry going downstairs, I went into the living room and sat down next to her on the couch. First I had to move a stack of old newspapers and catalogs out of the way to clear a space for me.

Mom looked over at me, surprised. Usually when I sat down in here, I sat in one of the armchairs so I was facing her.

I reached for the tote bag I'd left on the end table and got out my knitting needles and yarn.

"What's that?" she asked, still watching me in surprise.

"I'm learning to knit."

"Why?" It was hard to miss the scornful tone in her question.

"I thought it'd be fun," I said simply.

"*You* thought knitting would fun? Just like that? Out of nowhere?"

I shrugged. "When I went into that knitting store a couple weeks ago, it got me interested. So I decided to go back and ask them to set me up with a starter set so I could learn."

She eyed the sad collection of stitches on my needles. "You learned all on your own, did you?"

"Well, no," I admitted as I tried to remember how to insert the needle for my first stitch. "The woman working at the store gave me a lesson to get me started." I didn't see any reason to mention Dawn to my mother. She was unlikely to remember her, and I didn't want her thinking this was just some a ploy to get closer to a woman.

Even if that's what it was.

Really, it was a ploy to get closer to two women—Dawn *and* my mother. Two birds with one stone, so to speak.

"I figured if I needed help, I could always ask you." I dared a sideways glance at my mom and was pleased to find her still watching me.

She made a derisive sniff. "As if I can still remember how."

I was finding it difficult to remember as well. Especially with my mom sitting beside me, judging my every move. For a moment, I was overwhelmed by my fear of making a mistake, my mind a total blank as I tried to recall the first step.

I had to remind myself that the entire point of this exercise was to get my mom engaged, and nothing caught her interest more than a mistake. If she saw me doing it wrong, she wouldn't be able to resist correcting me. That was my hope anyway.

Rolling my shoulders to release some of the tension that had built up just in the short time I'd been here, I cast my mind back to yesterday, when I was sitting beside Dawn in her cozy little shop. Our shoulders pressed together. Her soft, dexterous hands guiding mine. Her voice sweet and encouraging. The flowery scent of her perfume teasing me every time she leaned in close.

Conjuring a memory of Dawn caused my fingers to find their confidence again. Almost by instinct, they completed the steps to knit a new stitch.

She was an excellent teacher. I'd been impressed how much in her element she seemed running that store. I was also a little envious, to be honest. She appeared to have found her calling in a way I never had. It must be nice to have something you cared about that much driving you. Something you enjoyed doing. Something that gave you a sense of accomplishment and purpose in the world.

As I fell back into the rhythm of knitting, I dared a glance at my mother again. She'd returned her attention to the television.

"How long's it been since you last did any knitting?" I asked, trying to engage her in conversation.

"I don't know," she replied. "Long time."

"I remember you knit that blanket we used to keep on the back of the couch. Remember that? Whatever happened to it?"

"Moths got at it. I threw it out."

"That's too bad. It must have been a lot of work to make it."

She didn't say anything. Her attention was fully consumed by her TV program.

"Hey, Mom?"

"What?" she said without looking at me.

"How'd you learn to knit?"

She glanced away from the TV long enough to frown at me. "Why?"

I shrugged. "The women at the store were talking about how they'd all learned to knit from their mothers."

"That's how I learned. That's how all the girls learned back then."

"I remember you teaching Kelly when we were kids."

"She never took to it. Didn't have the patience."

I lifted my eyes from my needles and caught her watching me. She quickly looked away, pretending to be engrossed in the TV again.

"Did Grandma Helen knit for the troops during World War II?" I asked.

"I don't know. I was too young to remember the war."

"She never mentioned it?"

"She didn't like to talk about the war."

My mother's father had died at the Battle of the Bulge when she was only four years old. The man I'd known as Grandpa Frank was her stepfather. She'd told me once she didn't remember her real father at all. I'd only ever seen one picture of him, looking nervous and way too young in his brand-new army uniform before he shipped out for Europe.

Sensing this line of inquiry was a dead end, I changed tack. "Why'd you quit knitting anyway? You used to do it all the time when I was a kid."

"I don't know. Just lost interest. Found better things to do."

"Seems like it'd be perfect for something to do while you watch TV."

"I don't need anything else to do. Watching TV is interesting enough for me."

All my attempts at starting a conversation with my mother were going over like a lead weight, and I was growing progressively tenser as a result. My fingers started to lose the plot as my frustration increased, and one of my stitches got away from me and slipped off the end of my needle.

"Shoot," I muttered as I tried and failed to save it.

"Not so easy, is it?"

"No," I replied. "I lost a stitch. Can you help me get it back on the needle?"

My mother shook her head at my attempt to hold it out to her. "You're on your own."

"Just a little help, Mom."

"I can't remember how."

I was starting to get pissed at her obstinacy. "Maybe if you looked, it'd come back to you."

"Don't have my readers."

I knew for a fact they were sitting on the table next to her. "Come on, Mom, they're right over there."

"I'm trying to watch my show."

"Is this really how you want to live the rest of your life?" I snapped, letting my temper get the best of me.

She turned a bitter look on me. "What do you want from me?"

I sighed, regretting my outburst. "I don't know. For you to join the living again. I'm worried about you."

"I'm fine."

"You're not fine, Mom. I don't know what you're going through because you won't talk to me about it, but you're definitely not fine."

"You think I should be happy?" she shot back.

"No, of course not."

She turned back to the TV. "Leave me be. Let me live my life the way I want."

"I think you should see a doctor."

Her mouth set in a hard line. "I'm not sick."

"I think you're depressed."

She directed another angry glare my way. "My husband died. Of course I'm depressed. You think the doctor's got a pill that can cure that?"

I kept my voice soft, trying to reason with her. "It's not healthy the way you're living here, all alone. Never leaving the house. Barely even getting off the couch. You need to get some help."

"I don't need you treating me like a child. I'm still capable of making my own decisions."

I gave up. It was pointless to keep badgering her if she didn't want my help or advice. She was right—she was an adult capable of making her own decisions.

If this was really how she wanted to live her life, so be it.

CHAPTER ELEVEN

DAWN

"You can wait in here, Ms. Botstein." The nurse opened the door to an office down the hall from the exam room I'd just exited and gestured for me to enter. "Dr. Norman will be in to speak with you shortly."

I'd never set foot in my doctor's actual office before. The fact that I was being invited into the inner sanctum now filled me with apprehension. Too many scenes in too many movies and television shows had conditioned me to expect that only the worst sort of news was delivered in the relative comfort of a doctor's private office.

My blood work hadn't shown anything definitive, so I'd been scheduled to come back in for a vaginal ultrasound. The ultrasound tech had been frustratingly cagey while performing the procedure. My head spun with questions as I seated myself in one of the chairs across from Dr. Norman's desk to wait.

The office could have been a television set, it was so generic. Bookshelves full of medical texts hulked along one wall while Dr. Norman's framed diplomas shared space on another with pictures her children had drawn. A potted palm—fake, I realized upon further inspection—sat beside the room's one window.

I fidgeted as I waited, crossing and uncrossing my legs, unpleasantly aware of the medical lubricant between my legs as my mind ran through a list of worst-case scenarios. I'd intentionally avoided looking up my symptoms on WebMD. Jerry's rants about patients who filled their heads with misinformation and worked themselves into a panic consulting "Dr. Google," as he derisively called it, had sunk in enough that I'd talked myself out of the urge. But now that I sat there with no real information and a million questions, working myself into a panic anyway, I wished I had done some research.

In the past, I'd always turned to Jerry when some scary medical situation loomed. It had been handy to have a doctor in the family during my parents' final illnesses and the various minor medical problems that had cropped up with me or the boys over the years. Jerry had always answered my questions in a straightforward, no-nonsense manner that I'd found reassuring. Information calmed me, while the absence of it threatened to send me into a tailspin.

But now I was on my own. An independent single woman who handled things for herself. There would be no running to Jerry for help anymore. Not if I could help it.

Unless…

I supposed in the event of very bad news, I would need to tell him what was going on. I'd have to tell the boys, and they'd want to talk to him about it. Which meant I should tell him before they did, to prepare him. Divorced or not, we were still family. Brandon and Zach tied us together, and always would.

But I was jumping the gun. There was no reason to go there yet. I didn't know what was wrong with me. It could still turn out to be nothing.

I looked around Dr. Norman's office again and decided nothing was very unlikely. I wouldn't be in here for nothing. Nothing news was delivered in the exam room, or over the telephone by a nurse. I'd received enough nothing news over the years to know.

This was different than nothing.

But it could turn out to be something manageable. Something I could deal with on my own. Something that wouldn't turn my entire life and the lives of my family upside down.

I heard the door open, and Dr. Norman walked in. She gave me one of her crinkly smiles as she greeted me and apologized for the wait.

I sat quietly with my hands folded in my lap as she settled herself into the desk chair across from me. And then I listened numbly as she began to explain that something atypical had shown up in my ultrasound, and therefore, the next step was to schedule a biopsy.

The word turned my bowels to jelly.

Biopsy.

That meant cancer. Or at least the possibility of cancer. Enough of a possibility that an invasive procedure was warranted.

"What is it you think is wrong with me exactly?" I asked.

I saw her hesitate. Doctors were always so reluctant to be pinned down into giving opinions or making guesses before they had all the facts. "It might be a fibroid," she said. "Although it doesn't fit the typical profile of a fibroid. Another possibility is endometrial cancer, which is why I'd like to do the biopsy."

I sat very still while this news sank in.

Cancer.

I had cancer—or might have cancer.

I'd always heard in such moments your life flashed before your eyes, but my brain seemed to have shorted out. I couldn't move past the word *cancer*. It flashed like a giant, blinking neon sign in my head, pulling focus from everything else.

"I don't want you to be alarmed," Dr. Norman said gently. "As cancers go, endometrial cancer is quite treatable, and there's every reason to believe we've caught it very early."

I swallowed, struggling to find my voice again. "What does the treatment involve? If it is cancer, I mean."

"That would be up to your oncologist to determine. But the most common treatment is surgical removal of the uterus."

"I see."

So a hysterectomy. Bye-bye fertility and menstruation, hello early menopause.

Even though I'd been welcoming the change just a few weeks ago, it didn't sound quite as appealing now. It was one thing for it to happen naturally, but another entirely to have one of your organs—the one where your children had been conceived and nurtured—removed from your body.

"But first we need to do the biopsy," Dr. Norman said. "That will give us a better idea of what we're dealing with, and if it is cancer, whether or not it's spread."

She went on to describe the procedure, which would be performed here in the office without anesthesia. I'd even be able to drive myself home afterward. Easy-peasy.

"I'd like to schedule it as soon as possible," she said. "How does Friday sound to you?"

Friday was only four days away.

It was also the day of my date with Mike. No way was I missing that. I'd waited thirty years to go on a date with him. Not even cancer would stop me.

"Friday's fine," I said.

Biopsy or no, I was going on that date.

CHAPTER TWELVE
MIKE

I'd thought I was nervous about my date with Jessica a few weeks ago, but that was nothing compared to how nervous I was about my date with Dawn. I agonized over what shirt to wear, the fact that I hadn't had time to get my car cleaned, and what restaurant I should take her to.

I was kicking myself for wasting Taj's on Jessica. Now I couldn't take Dawn there unless I wanted to revisit the scene of my last date. Which I definitely did not. It also seemed tacky to take a different woman to the same restaurant. I recalled what Jessica had said about people who dated a lot having a game plan they followed. *Down to a science*, she'd said.

I didn't want to be a guy with a dating game plan. I didn't want to treat my date with Dawn like a science experiment.

I just wanted her to like me and have a good time. I wanted her to want a second date with me.

So I'd picked an Italian restaurant—after first texting Dawn to confirm she liked Italian food. At least I'd learned something from my last experience.

Dawn and I had texted back and forth a few times this week. First about the restaurant, which led to a whole conversation about the best places to get Italian food in Chicago and which old favorites had closed since I'd lived here last. Then she asked me how my knitting was going, and I responded with a meme I'd found of a woman holding a giant snarl of yarn that said "Try knitting, they said. It relieves stress, they said." Dawn sent back a whole row of laughing emojis and a Ryan Gosling meme that said "Hey girl, knitting mistakes are no big deal."

It gave me a goofy thrill to see those laughter emojis. It wasn't quite as good as hearing her laugh in person, but knowing she was out there hopefully smiling at her phone because of me was a damn good feeling.

All week after that I'd scrambled for my phone like a teenage girl every time I got a notification, hoping it was a new message from Dawn. This morning I'd texted to ask how her day was going and tell her I was looking forward to tonight. She never answered, but I wasn't letting that get into my head. She was probably just busy at the store.

On my way home from work, I contemplated stopping off to buy flowers. But it felt a little too old-fashioned—or desperate, or something—and I talked myself out of it.

When I got home, I discovered the blue-striped shirt I'd wanted to wear was missing a button, which threw off my whole wardrobe plan. I really liked the way I looked in that shirt, and I couldn't decide if Dawn would like me better in solid gray or blue checks. I didn't have a lot of time to stand there deliberating, but I really wanted to look good for her. At least I'd had the foresight to groom my beard last night.

Traffic was predictably a bitch, but to make matters worse, one of the signal lights between my place and hers was stuck blinking red, which added an extra ten minutes I hadn't accounted for to the drive. So by the time I pulled onto Dawn's street, I was late.

She lived in Lakeview, in a beautiful brick house that probably appraised for more money than I'd made in the last ten years. Staring up at it, I felt my stomach sink. Dawn's ex-husband must have been loaded.

What was I doing here, thinking I had anything to offer a woman who lived in a house like that? Who was I kidding? I was way out of my league.

But I was here now, and she was expecting me. It was too late to back out. I'd just have to make the best of it and see how the chips fell.

I pushed open the gate and made my way up the short walk, past a compact lawn edged with tiny box hedges and beds of snapdragons, sweet peas, and pansies. It had been an unseasonably warm April for Chicago, and the grass was already starting to green up a little.

I'd forgone the blazer tonight in favor of a black bomber jacket. Even though the temperature had dropped into the fifties at sundown, I found myself sweating as I climbed the half-flight of steps up to the house. After taking a second to gird myself, I lifted my hand to knock on the black-paneled door.

Dawn answered promptly, and I sucked in a breath at the sight of her. She'd dressed up for tonight—for me—in a floral wrap dress that hugged her hips and showed off a tantalizing glimpse of cleavage. The sexy black knee-high boots she'd paired it with reminded me of Catwoman's costume and had me imagining Dawn in a skintight leather bodysuit before I pushed the distracting thought away.

"Hi," she said. She didn't sound pissed exactly, but there was something guarded about her expression, and I knew it was probably because of my lateness.

"Hey," I managed, my voice coming out way huskier than I intended.

"I was starting to wonder—"

"I'm really sorry," I offered hastily. "Traffic, you know?"

She gave me a nod and a tight-lipped smile. "Let me just grab my sweater, and I'll be ready to go."

As she ducked back into the house, I caught a glimpse of shiny hardwood floors and white-paneled walls before she reappeared with her purse and an aquamarine sweater draped over her arm. I waited while she locked the front door behind her, then helped her put her sweater on.

"You gonna be warm enough?" I asked as I followed her down the steps. It wasn't a very heavy sweater, and I worried the wind would go right through it.

"I'll be fine," she said, giving me another tight-lipped smile, and I couldn't help feeling I was already doing this all wrong.

I gestured to my eight-year-old Jeep Cherokee and quickened my steps to open the passenger door for her. It wasn't very impressive looking with its dented fender and the layer of dirt and mud that had built up over the last month. "You look beautiful, by the way," I said, trying to steer things back on track.

She glanced at me shyly, and I saw her smile reach her eyes finally. "Thank you. You look very handsome."

As I walked around to the driver's side, I broke into a grin. Maybe this wasn't a complete disaster after all.

We made polite small talk in the car on the way to the restaurant. When she asked me what I did for a living, I tried to explain my network administrator job without putting her to sleep.

"I think it'd be lovely to work for the library," Dawn said. "I love libraries, although now that I think about it, I haven't been to one in years. Not since the boys were young."

"It's not bad," I said. "I get to visit a lot of different branches." I didn't mention that a big part of my job was scrubbing porn and malware from porn websites off the free public computers. Libraries tended to lose some of their charm when you realized how many patrons were getting their rocks off watching smut in full view of everyone. "How old are your boys?"

"Brandon's twenty-three and Zach's twenty."

"So out of the nest, then?"

I saw her nod out of the corner of my eye. "Brandon's got an apartment with a couple law school friends, and Zach's in the dorms at UChicago."

"Good for them." Of course Dawn's kids would be high achievers. She'd always been smart as a whip, and they'd clearly had a comfortable upbringing, judging from her house. "Was it hard for you when they moved out?"

"Not really. I mean, I miss them, obviously, but I kind of love having the house to myself now." She gave a stilted little laugh. "That probably makes me sound like a terrible mother."

I glanced over at her and smiled. "Not at all. I think it's healthy that you can let your kids go live their own lives while you enjoy yours."

"You never had kids?" she asked.

My fingers tightened on the steering wheel. "Nope. Wasn't in the cards."

My first marriage hadn't lasted long enough for it to be an issue. But my second wife, Christine, had wanted kids bad. We'd tried for five years. After a while, the endless doctor's appointments, expensive fertility treatments, and repeating cycle of stress and disappointment had worn us both down.

"I'm sorry," Dawn said. "If it was something you wanted, that is."

I'd never felt that strongly about kids, to tell the truth. I'd only wanted them because Christine had wanted them. She was devastated when we finally admitted it was time to give up. I'd tried to be supportive and understanding, but I don't think she ever forgave me for not being more disappointed.

My right shoulder twitched into a shrug. "It is what it is."

We both fell silent for the last few minutes of the drive. I managed to find a parking space a few blocks from the restaurant. The wind was bitter coming off the water, and Dawn pulled her sweater tight around her as we trekked down the sidewalk.

"You want my jacket?" I offered, trying to be a gentleman.

She gave me a thin smile and shook her head. "I'm fine. We're almost there."

If she wanted to suffer in silence, there wasn't much I could do about it.

I thought about putting my arm around her and pulling her up against me to shield her from the wind a little but decided that might be too forward. It was only our first date after all, and so far I wasn't getting great vibes from her. She wasn't smiling as much as she usually did, and I detected creases of tension around her mouth. I couldn't figure out if she was just having an off day, or if it was me making her tense, but I vowed to up my game.

Once we reached the restaurant and the hostess led us to our table, I hefted the wine list, which was heavier than my high school world history textbook. "Do you want to get a bottle of wine?" I asked, feeling an uncomfortable sense of déjà vu.

"Actually, I'd prefer a martini," Dawn said. "If that's all right."

"That sounds great," I said, putting down the wine list in relief.

"Hendrick's martini, extra dirty with three olives," she told the waiter when he appeared to take our drink order.

"Make it two," I told him, impressed that she knew exactly what she wanted. I'd never been a big cocktail guy, although I enjoyed a good martini or old-fashioned now and again. Mostly for special occasions. Day to day I tended to default to beer simply because it was easier and cheaper.

I wondered if Dawn was a regular "martinis after work" kind of person. It was something I could picture the woman who lived in that nice big house doing, but I hadn't quite reconciled the sweet, mousy Dawn I knew back in high school with the elegant woman sitting across the table from me.

As we perused our menus, I took the opportunity to peer at Dawn properly. She'd matched her bright lipstick perfectly to the flowers on her dress, and she was wearing more eye makeup and jewelry tonight than the previous times I'd seen her. Diamond studs sparkled in her ears, a few understated gold rings bedecked her fingers, and a gold cuff bracelet adorned one wrist.

She'd dressed up for tonight, which made me think she'd been looking forward to it as much as I had. But as she concentrated on her menu, her usually pleasant expression settled into a frown. And was it me or was she looking a little pale under all that makeup? It reminded me of when Christine used to get headaches from the fertility drugs.

Dawn glanced up and caught me looking. "Something wrong?" she asked, and I realized I must have been frowning.

I shook my head and flashed a smile. "Just admiring the view."

The smile she offered in response was muted, increasing my suspicion that something was off with her tonight.

I considered asking her about it but was afraid that might be prying. We didn't really know each other well. I also didn't want her to know I'd noticed anything wrong, if she was trying to hide it. She might think I was having a bad time, which I most assuredly wasn't.

I was saved the trouble by the return of the waiter with our drinks. He inquired if we'd decided on our entrées, and Dawn nodded and ordered the chicken marsala. I ordered the chicken parmigiana, which was supposed to be one of the restaurant's specialties, and the waiter retreated again, taking the menus off our hands.

Now that we were alone, I decided it was time to start getting to know each other better. There were a lot of blanks to fill in over the last thirty years.

"So tell me what you've been up to since high school. Last I heard you were heading to Northwestern."

"That's right." She nodded as she sipped her martini. "I majored in art history, which in retrospect probably wasn't the most practical choice." She gave a little shrug. "I met my ex-husband, Jerry, my senior year there. He was a doctor doing his fellow-ship in pulmonology and critical care."

That explained the house, I thought to myself. A doctor's wife—or a doctor's ex-wife. She'd mentioned when we first ran into each other again that she'd used the proceeds from her divorce settlement to open the store. If she got that house *and* enough capital to start a new business, this Jerry guy must be loaded.

"We got married shortly after I graduated," she continued. "I worked in marketing for a few years, planning trade shows booths mostly. I didn't really like it that much, so I quit when Brandon was born and became a full-time mom."

"Did you like being a full-time mom?"

"I did. I loved being a mom. I thought it was all I needed, but then of course your kids grow up and don't need you so much anymore, and your life starts to feel a little…" She trailed off as she stirred the olives around in her martini.

"What?" I prompted.

She shrugged again. "Empty, I guess. Jerry's work was all-consuming, and for a long time I was content to be his support system and take care of the kids. But after a while, I started to realize I didn't have anything that was just for myself. There was nothing I was passionate about the way he was passionate about being a doctor."

It reminded me of myself, only without the kids in the equation. "But now you have the shop." If Dawn could find a new passion this late in life, maybe there was hope for me yet.

Her expression brightened. "I do. After all these years, I've finally got something I can feel proud of that I built for myself."

I loved the way she looked when she was talking about the store. She got this spark in her eyes, and it was like her whole face opened up. I felt another pang of envy as I admired her. I wished I had something in my life that gave me that kind of energy. But I was happy for her that she'd found it for herself. Maybe my thing was still out there somewhere. Just waiting for me to wake up and find it.

"What about you?" she said, picking up her martini glass. "You went off to Ohio State, and then what?"

I shifted in my seat, reluctant to talk about my past, as always. "Started out in sales. Picked up enough computer skills along the way that I transitioned into network support. I worked for the school district for ten years before I moved back here."

She nodded as she reached for a piece of the garlic bread a busboy had just dropped off at the table. "And you were married at some point? Twice, I believe you said."

"That's right." I cleared my throat. "First time when I was twenty-six. That one only lasted a year. Second time around I was in my thirties. Christine and I split up a little over a year ago."

"I'm sorry," Dawn said.

I shrugged. "We had a good run. Wasn't meant to be."

I didn't like the turn the conversation had taken. I wanted to know all about Dawn, but I didn't want to talk about myself in equal measure. Unfortunately, there wasn't any way to ask about her past without opening myself up to questions about my own.

"Do you like your work?" she asked.

"No." I realized I sounded abrupt and grimaced. "It pays the bills, but that's about all I can say for it."

"You ever think about doing anything else?"

"I don't know what I'd do." More importantly, without a degree, I didn't know what kind of job I'd be able to get. These days, they wanted you to have a bachelor's just to work at Starbucks. My experience and good track record were the only things keeping me employed, which meant I was pretty much stuck.

I didn't say any of this to Dawn. I was embarrassed to admit I hadn't finished college. Compared to her rich doctor ex, I wasn't much of a catch.

We fell into an uncomfortable silence after that. I could tell she wasn't having a very good time, but my powers of conversation failed me. I didn't know what to say. I was too nervous, I guess.

Despite my best efforts, I was pretty sure I was blowing it.

CHAPTER THIRTEEN
DAWN

I should have canceled my date with Mike tonight.

The biopsy today had left me sore and crampy, but the bigger problem was that I was completely distracted. I wouldn't get the results until Monday or Tuesday, which meant I was facing three to four days of waiting and wondering if I had cancer. It was all I could think about.

I was *on a date with Mike* and I should have been over the moon with happiness, but instead I couldn't stop thinking about cancer and hysterectomies and worrying that I'd need chemotherapy or radiation, that despite Dr. Norman's optimistic outlook, the cancer had been secretly spreading through my body and my fate was already sealed.

Mike had been making a valiant effort to be a good date, but I knew I was a terrible companion tonight. This was probably my one and only chance with him—a chance I'd waited thirty years for—and it was slipping away from me, and I couldn't even muster the will to care all that much.

What was the point? Chances were good the only new relationship in my future was with an oncologist. Fate was a real bitch.

I certainly wasn't going to drag Mike along on my cancer journey after one measly date.

He'd undoubtedly reconsider his interest fast enough once he knew the score. I couldn't imagine any man voluntarily taking on damaged goods like that.

Mike seemed like a really nice guy, actually. He might even be the sort who'd feel duty bound to stick by me out of some misplaced sense of guilt.

I definitely couldn't allow that. The last thing I wanted was his pity. I wasn't going to become an obligation he hadn't asked for. That would be even worse than not having him at all.

"You want another?" Mike asked when I finished my martini.

I shook my head reluctantly. "No, I'm good." As much as I could use the social lubricant tonight, I probably shouldn't even have had the one. Alcohol was an anticoagulant, and I'd had a minor medical procedure today. Plus I'd taken some anti-inflammatories earlier. Jerry would scold me for throwing a martini on top of ibuprofen.

I pushed my food around on my plate, trying to summon the will to eat. Normally I loved chicken marsala, and it was very good here. But I didn't have much of an appetite.

"Do you not like it?" Mike asked, gesturing at my plate.

"No, it's great." I forced myself to take another bite to prove how great it was. It was like chewing a wad of paper towels. I swallowed and reached for my water glass, wishing I'd saved some of my martini to wash it down. "How's your chicken parm?"

"Fantastic. Want a bite?"

"No, but thank you." It looked delicious, but I wouldn't be able to appreciate it, and with all those muscles Mike could probably use all the protein he could get.

I saw a fleeting look of...annoyance? Disappointment? Something flashed across Mike's face before he looked down at his plate again. I could tell he wasn't having a very good time. He probably thought I didn't like him, which was so far from the truth I could laugh, if I'd been in any kind of mood to laugh.

I resolved to make more of an effort. It wasn't fair to him. He shouldn't have to put up with me being such a wet blanket.

"How's the knitting going?" I asked, figuring that was a safe subject. He hadn't seemed very game to talk about his job, and any questions about his past seemed to lead back to his failed marriages, which wasn't a great topic either.

His scowl told me knitting wasn't as pleasant a subject as I'd hoped.

"That bad?" I couldn't help smiling a little. His frustration was familiar to me.

"I messed it up. Dropped a stitch and now I can't figure out how to move on."

"You could ask your mom for help. She can probably fix it for you." It was a simple fix, but one that could be a real obstacle for beginners if they didn't know how to overcome it.

His scowl deepened. "I tried. She wasn't any help."

I sensed from his tone there was more to the story, but he didn't elaborate. "You could always bring it into the shop, and we'll be more than happy to help you," I offered.

He gave a half-hearted nod as he stabbed a piece of chicken parm with his fork. I guessed he wouldn't be bringing it into the shop. After tonight, I couldn't really blame him if he never wanted to see me again.

"How's your mother doing?" I asked, trying again to jump-start the conversation.

"Not great."

I waited, but again, he didn't elaborate. "I'm sorry," I said finally.

He shook his head. "I don't want to talk about it."

Well, this was going great. I seemed to have infected him with my foul mood. Or maybe he'd realized over the course of the night that he didn't like me after all.

We sank into a dull silence as we finished our meal. When the waiter finally brought the check, I offered to split it, but Mike wasn't having it.

"It's supposed to be a thank-you dinner," he reminded me. "For teaching me to knit."

I relented without further argument, thanking him for the meal. He grunted an acknowledgment as he shrugged into his jacket, and I followed him to the door.

It had gotten even colder outside while we were at dinner. As I stepped out onto the sidewalk, a sharp gust of wind blew right through me, and I clutched my sweater tighter around my shoulders.

Halfway to the car, Mike glanced over at me and frowned. He'd been doing quite a lot of frowning as the night wore on. He had a very attractive frown—it made him look like a big, grumbly bear—but it wasn't a good sign of how the evening was going.

"Here," he said, stopping and taking his jacket off. "Put this on."

"I'm fine," I tried to insist.

"You're freezing," he growled. "Put it on."

If I thought his frown was attractive, it was nothing compared to his growly voice. Powerless to resist his command, I let him help me into his jacket. It was warm with his body heat and it smelled like the cologne he was wearing tonight. I'd only caught faint whiffs of it earlier, but now it enveloped me like a comforting fog, leaving me giddy and flustered. I imagined this was what it would be like to be hugged by Mike. Or at least this was as close as I'd probably ever get to it.

"Better?" he asked, and I nodded.

"Yes, thank you."

He shook his head, his voice gently chiding. "Lived here all your life and still don't know how to dress for the weather."

"I don't know what I was thinking." I hadn't been thinking very clearly earlier, but I couldn't tell him why. Well, I *could* tell him. Nothing was physically preventing me. But I didn't want to. I wanted Mike to exist outside the grim reality I was facing, like a little pocket of happiness separate from everything else. A pure, untainted memory I'd be able to cling to if things got bad.

In the car, we fell into another silence. I stared down at the backs of my hands, the skin crepey and spotted with age no matter how faithfully I moisturized them. Then I thought about that photo of Mike's ex-wife I'd seen on Facebook. How beautiful she looked standing beside him in her bikini. How vital and full of life. She must be younger than me. Not excessively so, but…enough.

Involuntarily, my hand pressed against my own poochy midsection, the skin sagging and crisscrossed with stretch marks after two pregnancies. I hadn't worn a bikini since my twenties. That woman—Christine—that was the sort of woman Mike was used to, the kind of woman a man like him deserved. Long legs, smooth blonde hair, perfect tanned skin. Not a short, middle-aged frump whose freckled skin was going over to age spots.

He parked his car in front of my house and got out to walk me to the door. He really was an old-fashioned sweetheart. Too bad I'd probably never see him again after tonight.

I stopped at the top of the steps, clutching my purse, and turned to thank him for a lovely evening, fully prepared to be bid an unceremonious goodnight.

"Listen," Mike said, waving away my thanks. "I know something's been weighing on your mind tonight." His eyes burned into me with a keenness that made my stomach clench. "I hope you'd tell me if it had something to do with me."

"It's nothing at all to do with you," I rushed to assure him.

He nodded. "I guess you don't want to talk about it…?" He let the implied question hang in the air between us.

"I'm sorry," I said. "I know I've been terrible company tonight."

"You've been great, I just got the sense you weren't quite yourself, is all."

"I'm not feeling very well, to be honest. I probably should have canceled, but I was really looking forward to tonight."

One side of his mouth curled into a sexy almost-smile. "You were looking forward to it?"

"Yes. Very much."

"Me too." His eyes seemed to sparkle under the streetlights. "I'm sorry you're not feeling well."

"I'm sorry I wasn't more fun."

"I don't need you to be fun. I'm just glad I got to see you. But I wish you hadn't forced yourself to come out when you weren't feeling up to it."

I appreciated that he didn't ask what was wrong. I further appreciated that he apparently wasn't writing me off after one bad date. But most of all, I appreciated how breathtakingly good-looking he was—by far the most handsome man I'd ever been on a date with. This time when I smiled, it wasn't at all forced. "I'm feeling a little better, actually."

"Glad to hear it."

The way he looked at me made me feel so…seen. Noticed in a way I wasn't used to being noticed by anyone, much less an attractive man.

But surely that was just my mind playing tricks on me. The heat I thought I could see in his gaze had to be a figment of my imagination. I tried to school my features as my skin tingled in anticipation of his touch—a touch that would certainly not be coming.

"Dawn…" He hesitated, his frown returning.

"Yes?" Despite my better judgment, I found myself leaning toward him, caught in the intensity of his eyes. I wanted so badly to reach up and smooth away that frown, but I didn't dare.

He touched his fingertips to my cheek. Just the lightest of feathery touches, but it jolted through me with a shock of desire. Though I tried not to react, my sharp inhale sounded ragged and a little bit desperate.

His eyes widened slightly at my response to his touch. Then the heat in them seemed to increase a thousandfold. This was no figment of my imagination. The way he was looking at me unraveled me like a ball of yarn dropped down a flight of stairs. I couldn't feel the cold anymore. I was burning up. The air was charged with so much potential energy, I thought I might explode.

He leaned closer, and I held my breath, caught on a knife's edge.

"Can I kiss you?" His voice was soft and gravelly, and the words shot straight through my heart.

I felt dizzy. I opened my mouth, but I was afraid if I let myself speak it would come out as a sob, I was so wildly desperate for that kiss. So I nodded my answer, a rough jerk of my head, as my mind silently screamed *yes, yes, yes!*

His mouth curved into one of his beautiful smiles as his fingers slid down my jaw to tilt my head back. The scent of his cologne clouded my senses, forever etched into my memory and this moment.

He kissed me the way he seemed to do everything: calm, thoughtful, and sweet. The first kiss was just a prelude. A light touch of his lips, experimental and inquisitive. A promise of things to come.

The second kiss followed close on its heels but with more urgency. His lips were deliciously firm as they pressed against mine. Still chaste, our mouths still closed, but with enough heat to make me want more. It shot through me like a Fourth of July fireworks display, lighting up all my nerve endings, including some that had been dormant for years.

I leaned into him, my hands coming up to rest against his broad chest. Our heads tilted in perfect mirror unison, and he kissed me for the third time.

This one was deeper, harder, and slower. His tongue teased me, flicking against my lips like he was tasting me. I made a raw sound in the back of my throat, and he grunted in response. His tongue slipped inside my mouth, and I rose up on my toes, angling for more. One of his hands cupped the back of my head; the other glided down my neck. Our breaths mingled, hot and ragged, as our mouths slid together, tongues dancing, his beard scraping against my lips with the most wonderful sort of friction.

I couldn't get enough. My hands moved over his chest, over the impossibly firm muscles there. I'd never felt anything like it. I'd never experienced anything even close to this.

His kiss pulled me apart and then put me back together again. My body and my mind felt wholly alive for the first time in years. It was both exhilarating and terrifying. For that one long, achingly close, trembling moment we were perfectly in sync. Breathing and moving as one. Drinking each other in.

It reminded me how much I used to like sex when I was young. Before it became rote and predictable, then later an obligation and a source of guilt, intertwined with all the things I hadn't wanted to admit were wrong with my marriage.

The feelings Mike inspired in me were primal, raw, and spontaneous in a way that surprised me. I hadn't known I could still be any of those things.

I wondered what it would be like to have sex with him. I wanted to know, desperately, but I was afraid. He was like a tempting pool with dangerous riptides. If I let myself go in too deep, I knew I'd be pulled under.

My breath hitched, and I let out a ragged gasp. Mike broke off the kiss—not abruptly, but tenderly, leaving a string of featherlight kisses along my jaw before resting his forehead against mine. His fingers tightened in my hair. The hand on my neck slid over my skin, warm and solid and roughly calloused.

He was a gentle giant. A soft mountain of a man. The sort you could lose yourself in completely. I breathed out a sigh, wishing this moment could last forever. I wanted so badly to shelter in his embrace and let him ease away all my cares. Use him to hide from reality and the whole rest of the world.

I could invite him in. It would be that easy. I sensed, as unbelievable as it seemed, that if I asked, he'd say yes.

I could have him.

Tonight.

Right now.

All I had to do was reach out and take what he was implicitly offering.

Fear splashed over me like a bucket of cold water. My protective instincts kicked into gear, and I felt my defensive walls go up—a little late, but better late than never.

It wouldn't be fair to him, I reminded myself. Not when there was so much uncertainty in my future. What kind of relationship could I hope to start now? In the midst of biopsies and worry and the giant gaping chasm with a big sign over it that read *CANCER* in bright neon letters with a flashing question mark.

If I was going to do this, I wanted to do it right. And there was no doing it right until I'd faced whatever lay in store for me and come out the other side—whatever that might mean. Maybe then, and only then, could I consider inviting Mike into my life.

He drew back, his eyes boring into mine. Searching and seeing. Seeing too much, probably. His cheeks were flushed, his lips pink and swollen.

I did that, I thought with a perverse surge of pleasure. He was sexy as hell, the sort of man who probably kissed women all the time, but tonight he'd kissed *me* and liked it. I clung to the thought, wrapping it up tight and holding it close to my heart. Mike *liked* me. Against all odds, this beautiful hunk of a man was attracted to me.

"Can I see you again?" His voice was soft and a little hesitant. It almost broke my heart in two.

I opened my mouth, wanting so badly to say yes, then snapped it shut. My eyes dropped to the ground, focusing on his feet. He wore leather oxfords. Comfortably worn in but immaculately cared for.

I swallowed thickly. "I'd like that, but I'll have to let you know. I've got…some things going on. I'm not sure when I'll be able to." I dared a glance and saw him nod, his expression unreadable.

"I can wait." He reached up, trailing his index finger over my cheek before tucking my hair behind my ear. "Whenever you're ready, just let me know."

I bit down on my lip, and his dark eyes went even darker. It made me want to grab him and drag his mouth back down to mine.

But I held strong. My better instincts were in control now. I could do this.

"I will." Choking down my regret, I gave him a smile that was probably a little too bright. "Thank you for tonight. It was wonderful." I meant every word.

"It was my pleasure." He waited while I fished my keys out of my purse and unlocked the door. Then he bent to brush a kiss against my cheek before striding down the steps toward the street.

I watched him go, drinking in as much of him as I could.

CHAPTER FOURTEEN
MIKE

I texted Dawn Saturday morning after our date, because I was a goddamn gentleman. Also because I wanted to make sure there was no room for misinterpreting my level of interest.

Mike: Are you feeling better today?

Dawn: Yes, much. Thank you for last night.

I considered what I wanted to say next. There was always a risk of sounding either too needy or too wishy-washy in these sorts of conversations, especially over text. I decided to go for the direct approach. I wasn't into playing games with women. When I liked them, I told them so.

Mike: I had a great time with you.

Dawn: Me too.

My heart did a loop-the-loop at that *me too*, and I smiled as I typed my reply.

Mike: I hope we can do it again when you're ready.

I had a pretty strong hunch she wanted that too. Her behavior last night could be interpreted as a brush-off, but I didn't think that's what it was. I'd seen how bright her eyes were after our kiss, how her cheeks had been flushed with pleasure. She'd enjoyed it. I could tell. Not to be immodest or anything, but I knew how to kiss a woman. She'd enjoyed the hell out of it.

But something had made her pull away at the end. I'd felt it when she'd stiffened in my arms. Before that she'd been really into being kissed, giving as good as she got. So much so that we'd both gotten a little carried away for a minute.

I closed my eyes, remembering the sweet taste of her mouth, her small, warm body pressed against mine, her hands wandering over my chest. My pulse raced at the recollection of the thrill that had shot through me. I hadn't felt anything like it for ages. That flare of glittering excitement had melted some part of me that had been frozen for a long time.

The sensation wasn't exactly comfortable—it was more like the pins and needles you get when one of your limbs has fallen asleep and starts waking up again—but I craved more of it. If one little kiss from Dawn could make me feel this alive, imagine what else she could do to me.

I wasn't alone in feeling something either. I'd seen how her face had lit up when I asked if I could see her again. Her little smile, like the sun peeking over the horizon. Just like her name. Dawn. My favorite time of day, when the world was all promise and anticipation, when it was easy to believe anything was possible.

And then how she'd blinked a little too hard, and the slight slump in her shoulders when she'd turned me down. She'd tried to school her expression, but I'd seen it. She was disappointed. She hadn't wanted to put me off.

In fact, I was pretty sure she'd been on the verge of inviting me inside that pretty house of hers. My dick twitched to life, letting me know its thoughts on the possibility as I imagined taking Dawn into her elegantly furnished bedroom, laying her down on what were undoubtedly expensive, high thread count sheets, and fucking her until she came calling out my name.

Something had made Dawn push me away, and whatever that reason was, I needed to root it out at the source and destroy it.

I wanted to see her again. I needed it. Craved it, in a way I hadn't craved anything but sleep in a long time.

I felt like I was finally waking up again.

I texted Dawn again on Sunday. She hadn't responded to my last text yesterday about seeing her again, but I didn't let that stop me. On my run that morning, I stopped to snap a picture of some yarn graffiti I'd spotted. Someone had knit a multicolored sleeve for one of the bike racks in my neighborhood, and I sent her the photo.

I never noticed stuff like this until you came back into my life, I wrote along with it.

She replied right away to tell me about some of the local yarn bombers she knew from the store, and to send me an article from the *Tribune* about a group in Highland Park.

I took it as a good sign. She wouldn't have replied so enthusiastically if she didn't want anything to do with me, right? So I kept texting her all kinds of random stuff— little things that made me smile or made me think of her, or things I thought she'd like. Jokes, pictures, random facts. Anything I could think of to keep the conversation going.

It worked. We texted back and forth all day, and I wasn't always the one initiating our exchanges. She texted me a running commentary about the customers who came into her store. We had a virtual laugh together about the woman who touched every single skein of yarn in the whole store before leaving without buying a thing, and the woman who came in trying to find a yarn color that perfectly matched her husband's skin tone.

She's definitely making a voodoo doll of him, right??? Dawn wrote.

I hope so, I replied. *That's the least disturbing possibility I can imagine.*

Now it was Monday, and I was at work, and the temptation to check my phone every five minutes was almost overwhelming. But I needed to resist. My boss, Rich, was prowling around the office this afternoon, looking for something to complain about, and he didn't like it when he saw us on our phones.

I tried to concentrate on the ancient Wi-Fi router I was attempting to coax back to life. This was the second time it had gone out, and I was afraid it might be beyond my powers of resuscitation. The city library budget was tight—library budgets were always tight—and replacements didn't come easy. I was under orders to fix it, and that's what I intended to do, if at all possible.

I'd been at it for most of the afternoon already, but there were still a few more things I could try. I didn't plan on giving up until I was sure I'd made every attempt. Otherwise, I'd have to tell Rich I couldn't do what he'd asked, and he'd make it seem like my fault that I couldn't magically make an old-ass piece of equipment work forever.

I squinted at the results of the latest batch of diagnostics on my screen, looking for clues as to the source of the problem, but I was soon jarred out of my concentration by the sound of footsteps coming up behind me.

"You still working on that same router?" Rich said in his smug, sneering voice.

"Yep," I replied without turning around.

"I only expected it to take you an hour, tops. What's the problem?"

"The problem is this equipment is ten years old, there are about a million things that could be wrong with it, and I've got to check every single one to rule them out." I swiveled my chair and gazed up at him blandly. "But if you think you know how I can get this done any faster, I'd be glad to learn from you."

Rich was a little pip-squeak of a dude who wasn't all that much taller than me when I was sitting down. I suspected his overbearing managerial style was his way of over-compensating for his unimpressive physique, and I further suspected he felt threatened by my size, which only made him overcompensate more. So I always made sure to keep my voice mild and calm and my posture relaxed and unthreatening when I was interacting with him. But that didn't mean I had to take his crap lying down.

I gave him a shit-eating grin, knowing full well he couldn't fix the damn router himself. He might have a management degree and a stack of expensive certifications to his name—all framed and hanging on the wall of his office—but none of it was worth the paper it was printed on. He was a technical lightweight ten years my junior who didn't have one tenth my experience or know half as much about networking and security as the people he was supposed to be managing.

I kept my features schooled as I saw him stiffen in response to my mildly phrased challenge. "Well...uh...I'm not going to do your job for you," he sputtered. "The best way to learn is solving problems yourself."

"That's absolutely true," I agreed, knowing he'd probably never solved a technical problem on his own in his whole damn life—and certain the irony was completely lost on him.

"Just hurry it up. And stay on task. I don't want to see you wasting time over here."

I smiled even wider as I felt my temper flare. "You got it."

As soon as his back was turned, I mouthed the word *dick*. I'd only been in this job three months and I'd already lost most of the fucks I'd had to give.

I watched as Rich made his way across the office and disappeared in the direction of the men's room. As soon as he was out of sight, I slipped my phone out of my pocket.

My mood brightened when I saw I had a new text from Dawn. She'd sent me a funny gif of a dog licking a lemon. *Hope your Monday's going okay*, she'd written.

I smiled to myself as I considered my reply. I could play it coy and find a funny gif to send her in response—or I could tell her how I felt.

I miss you, I typed and hit send before I could think better of it.

There was no denying it. I was a complete goner for this woman.

I was screwed. Absolutely screwed.

And I loved it.

CHAPTER FIFTEEN
DAWN

"**H**appy birthday, dear Daaaa-awwwwn! Happy birthday to youuuuuuu!"

I tried to smile at my friends and coworkers as they serenaded me. Birthdays had never been my favorite, but since my divorce they'd become even more depressing.

After twenty-plus years of marriage and two kids, I'd grown accustomed to waking up to a house full of family wishing me well on my special day—even though Jerry almost always had to work late and in their teenage years the boys' schedules were so busy there wasn't a lot of room for family celebrations. Still, it was better than waking up alone in an empty house with only your Boston fern to wish you happy birthday.

On top of that, birthdays these days made me miss my parents. I'd mostly gotten used to not having them around anymore, but my birthday always got me thinking about my childhood and feeling their absence extra sharply.

"Make a wish!" Angie said as Chloe came forward with a cake covered with candles. Not the full forty-eight, thank god, but enough to make an impressive display.

At least this year I knew exactly what to wish for. I still hadn't heard from my doctor's office with my biopsy results, so I closed my eyes and sent up a silent prayer for a clean bill of health before huffing and puffing all the candles out.

Forty-eight years old—emphasis on the *old*. And yet in my heart I still felt like a young girl. Where had the years gone?

"Do you not like the cake?" Chloe asked, noticing my half-hearted attempt to look happy. "I wasn't sure if I should get the chocolate icing or vanilla."

"No, it's perfect!" I assured her hastily. "You know how much I love chocolate."

"Don't mind her," Angie said, well versed in my annual birthday funks. "She's one of those freaks who hates birthdays."

"How can you hate birthdays?" Chloe wondered as she set the cake on the table next to the coffee maker and got out paper plates and plastic forks. "You get cake and lots of attention and everyone sings to you and makes a big fuss."

"You've just answered your own question," I grumbled. "Except for the cake. It's the only good part of the whole deal."

"Just wait until you're older," Angie told the twenty-something Chloe. "The advancing of the sands of time gets a little less thrilling as you approach forty."

"Well, when you're as old as me, you'll realize that every day is worth celebrating," Linda said, cutting herself an enormous corner piece of cake.

I felt my phone buzz in my pocket and fumbled it out to check the screen. I'd been jumpy as a frog on hot pavement while I waited for news from my doctor. Both my sons had called to wish me a happy birthday today, and I'd practically pulled something scrambling for the phone each time.

It was just a text from Mike. He'd been texting me every day since our date last week. Not being pushy, which I appreciated, just checking in and letting me know he was still interested. Under ordinary circumstances I'd be over the moon, but it was hard to rejoice too much with a black cloud of uncertainty hanging over my head.

For now, I appreciated the distraction. He'd managed to make me smile more than once over the last several days with his cute pictures and amusing commentary.

As I considered my response to Mike's latest witty observation about one of his coworkers, my phone started ringing in my hand.

It was my doctor's office. Finally.

I went into the store's bathroom and closed the door before answering it.

As I stood there next to the toilet in the cramped space Angie had tried to brighten up with shabby chic decorations, Dr. Norman broke the news that my pathology report had come back positive for cancer.

Happy birthday to me.

I smoothed my blouse for the umpteenth time as I waited for Jerry. Of course he was late. The man was always late for anything that wasn't work related.

You'd think that now that he'd retired his days would be his own, but of course he'd filled his time volunteering and serving on the board of several nonprofits. From what I could tell, he was nearly as busy now as when he'd been an attending at Chicago General Hospital.

His retirement had been the straw that broke the camel's back of our marriage. Turned out we weren't actually used to being around each other that much after half a lifetime of Jerry's job monopolizing the lion's share of his time and attention.

He hadn't adjusted well to the transition at first. He'd been restless, bored, maybe even a little depressed. Unsure how to cope with the loss of what had been the central driving force of his life for the last forty years. It had left a hole I hadn't been able to fill for him. Although I'd tried.

I'd done my best to get him interested in a variety of hobbies: bird-watching, gardening, woodworking. I'd signed us up for couples cooking classes and wine tasting classes. I'd even signed us up for a yoga class, which he'd attended exactly once. The only things he seemed to enjoy were golfing and watching documentaries on the History Channel. Our big retirement vacation—the first real vacation we'd taken just the two of us since our honeymoon—had been a miserable experience. Neither of us had enjoyed the cruise ship or being cooped up together in our tiny cabin, we hadn't wanted to do any of the same activities or excursions, and we'd spent most of the week arguing, sniping, and lapsing into unhappy silences.

The hard truth was that we didn't actually like each other that much anymore. We'd made good partners when he'd had a career to navigate and I'd had children to raise. But with Jerry retired and our youngest son headed off to college, we'd each lost the sense of purpose that had bound us together and allowed us to largely ignore each other for years.

I hadn't wanted to admit it, of course. I'd tried to pretend everything was fine. It had taken Jerry's admission that he'd strayed and wanted to separate for me to finally admit we were irrevocably broken. The thing that really drove it home was how little I cared about his infidelity. He'd slept with another woman—a much younger woman, natch, whom he'd met at his golf club—and I was barely even upset about that aspect of it. I was more embarrassed that other people would find out, and worried about how it would disrupt the comfortable life I'd made for myself.

As it turned out, our separation was the best thing Jerry could have done for me. It knocked me out of my fugue and forced me to confront the fact that I didn't need him anymore—and furthermore, I didn't want him.

The waiter came by to refill my water glass and give me a sympathetic glance. I'd been ten minutes early because I was nervous, and Jerry tended to run ten minutes late, which meant I'd been sitting there for quite a while. But Jerry should be along any minute now. He was as reliable as clockwork, so long as you knew the particular pattern his clock functioned on. Which I did. Intimately.

I'd chosen this restaurant because I knew it was one of Jerry's favorite lunch spots. It was near the hospital, and therefore not too far from my yarn store. But I'd chosen it not for my own convenience, but because Jerry liked it. I'd wanted to put him at ease before I broke my bad news.

Only now did it occur to me how silly that was, and how typical of our marriage. I was the one with cancer, and yet here I was trying to make Jerry more comfortable.

"Sorry I'm late," he muttered, arriving at the table exactly when I predicted. "Hope you weren't waiting long."

"Not at all. You're looking well." In fact, he looked old. He was ten years older than me, and he looked every bit of it. I suspected he was working himself too hard with all his post-retirement projects. He'd retired early at fifty-five, ostensibly to slow down and enjoy his golden years after a lifetime of twelve-hour workdays. But Jerry wasn't really cut out for a leisurely lifestyle. He was happiest when he was busy and working.

"What's this about?" he asked, referring to my lunch invitation. I'd told him only that I needed to talk to him when I asked if we could meet. "Is it something to do with the boys?"

"Let's order first," I suggested. "I'm starving."

When the waiter came back, Jerry ordered his usual: clam chowder and half a club sandwich. God, how I despised clam chowder, and how he loved it. The smell made my stomach turn, and he ordered it every opportunity he had, one of many little things that had grated on me during our marriage.

I ordered a small spinach salad for myself. Despite my assertion about being hungry, I'd had very little appetite since the call from Dr. Norman on Tuesday.

"Well," I said once the waiter had collected our menus and retreated. I folded my hands in my lap and laid it all on the line. "I'm having dinner with the boys tomorrow night, and I've got some news to break to them. I wanted to give you a heads-up because they may have questions they want to bring to you, and I didn't want you be caught off guard."

Jerry's perpetually distracted look shifted to a frown of concentration. "That sounds ominous."

"It's not so bad. It could be far worse." I took a breath to steady myself before saying the bad part out loud. "I've been diagnosed with endometrial cancer. According the biopsy, it's only Stage I, thank goodness. I'm scheduled for a hysterectomy a week from Tuesday, and my doctor is optimistic about a surgical cure."

For a moment Jerry didn't react. His face and body remained frozen in place as my words sank in. Then he seemed to recover and cleared his throat. "You've had your consultation with the surgeon already?"

"Yes, yesterday."

"Who is it?"

"Dr. Farzad."

He gave a brisk nod. "She's very good. I've heard excellent things."

"That's nice to know."

Jerry fiddled with his silverware, lining the fork up with his knife so they were perfectly parallel. "I'll call her office next week to make sure you have a good anesthesiologist."

"That's really not necessary."

"You don't want to mess around with anesthesiologists. People overlook them, but having a good one is critical."

I didn't try to argue. Exerting his professional influence on my behalf was Jerry's way of showing he cared.

"You said you're telling the boys tomorrow?" he asked.

"Yes. We're having dinner at the house." It was supposed to be my birthday dinner, and they'd wanted to take me out, but I'd convinced them I'd rather stay in and cook for them. It was a conversation I preferred to have with them at home rather than at a restaurant.

"They'll be upset."

"That's why I wanted to tell you first. So you'd be prepared to support them if they come to you with questions."

Something that almost looked like hurt flashed across Jerry's expression before he schooled it again. "Very practical. You always had a talent for smoothing everyone's way." He looked down and brushed an imaginary crumb off his tie.

It was a new tie I'd never seen before, and not one I would have thought was to his taste. I wondered if he'd picked it out himself or had help. His latest lady friend, perhaps.

I knew very little about Jerry's dating life other than that he had one. More of one than I'd had since the divorce. The bar was much lower when you were a world-renowned doctor—even a fifty-eight-year-old retired one—rather than a frumpy former housewife. I imagined there were quite a lot of women who wouldn't mind being the second wife of Dr. Gerald Botstein.

He cleared his throat again. "You'll need someone to drive you to the procedure and stay with you afterward."

"I've already asked Angie." I'd finally told her what was going on last night, after my appointment with the surgeon. We'd gone through two bottles of wine between the two of us, but overall I thought she took it quite well. Angie was an optimist, and she'd already convinced herself everything would be fine.

Jerry gave a jerky nod before his eyes found mine again. "You know if you ever need me for anything…all you have to do is ask."

"I know," I told him, although I hadn't even considered asking him for anything. I supposed it was nice to know I could if the need arose.

He reached for his water, his hand shaking slightly. "I always thought it would be me."

"What?"

"Of the two of us, I always thought I'd be the one to get sick first."

I hadn't prepared myself for Jerry to reveal so much emotion. I'd expected our conversation to be much more businesslike, and for Jerry to launch into a lecture on the female reproductive system and the results of various studies on life after hysterectomy. Instead, he actually seemed to be upset—albeit in his typically understated way.

I gave him what I hoped was a cheerful smile. "You'll still have your chance. It's really not a very impressive cancer diagnosis. Hardly even a blip on the radar as cancers go."

I'd been feeling steadier since the surgical consultation. I had a concrete idea of what was coming now, and what it would mean for me. It was easier to plan when you knew exactly what was happening—and when I was making plans, I felt safer. A little more in control of something terrifyingly outside of my control.

A surgical cure would be good news. It would mean no follow-up chemotherapy or radiation. One little procedure and I was done. Provided the oncologist agreed.

There was always the chance they'd get in there and realize the cancer had progressed more than expected, necessitating a more aggressive treatment plan.

It would also be up to the oncologist to determine during the surgery whether I got to keep my ovaries. Unlike a simple hysterectomy, an oophorectomy would deprive my body of estrogen and progesterone, plunging me into sudden, premature menopause with all its attendant horrors. If that happened, I could look forward to an increased risk of depression, anxiety, heart disease, arthritis, and bone loss. This was in addition to the usual side effects of menopause like hot flashes, fatigue, mood swings, and vaginal dryness, which were typically more intense for women who hadn't started menopause naturally.

Fun times.

I thought back to just a few weeks ago, when I'd actually been looking forward to menopause. Now that it threatened to fall on me like a ton of bricks, however, I found the idea considerably less appealing.

But I wouldn't know about that until after I woke up from the surgery—after it had already happened—so I tried not to think about it. Far easier to focus on the things I could control. Throw myself into planning and preparing for what was to come. There was plenty to do to keep me busy for the next week and a half. Shopping for a new robe to wear in the hospital, stocking the house with food and supplies to ease my post-op recovery, packing my hospital bag.

And then there was the store. I'd need Chloe to cover the whole day of my surgery alone while Angie was with me, and after that she and Angie would both need to take on extra hours until I was able to come back to work. There were a lot of things I wanted to do before my prolonged absence, inventory that needed to be shelved, returns made, restocking orders placed. Things that had been piling up while I was distracted over the last few weeks needed to be taken care of before my medical leave. I also wanted to buy gifts for Angie and Chloe to thank them for the extra load they'd be taking on to keep the store running in my absence.

So much to do. So much to think about to distract myself from what was happening.

Jerry reached across the table and laid his hand over mine. "You're going to be fine." His voice was soft and uncharacteristically warm.

As I looked into the eyes of this man I'd loved for over half my life, a man who'd been, until a few years ago, my closest family, I felt an unexpected lump form in my throat.

We were still holding hands when the waiter brought our food.

I managed to keep myself busy until the Sunday before my surgery. I'd been doing fine until then. There was so much to do to prepare, there'd hardly been time to stop and think about what I was preparing for.

But now my surgery was only two days away and everything was done. I'd told everyone who needed to be told, including my sons, who'd taken it reasonably well after I'd assured them it was all very minor and nothing to worry about. I may have glossed over some of the details and put an extra rosy shine on it, but I hadn't seen any point in alarming them.

I'd finished getting the store ready for my absence, and cleaned my house from top to bottom so it'd be a pleasant environment to recuperate in. I'd purchased and wrapped the thank-you gifts for Angie and Chloe. No one could ever say I wasn't prepared.

But as I sat alone in my pristine house with a bottle of pinot noir to keep me company on the eve of the eve of my surgery, the reality of what was about to happen finally started to kick in.

In retrospect, the wine had probably been a mistake. But the bottle was open now. I only had until 10:00 p.m. tomorrow night to finish it.

Sunday nights were often when I felt my loneliness most acutely. Because the store was open on the weekend and closed on Mondays, Sunday nights were my Friday nights. The one night of the week I could stay up late and look forward to sleeping in the next morning. But Sundays were when most other people were home with their families, having meals together, spending time together, enjoying a quiet, cozy night of companionship before the start of the new work week.

And I was alone. Week after week after week. It had begun to feel like I would always be alone.

Usually I didn't mind. I enjoyed my own company and relished my alone time. But occasionally Sunday nights hit me hard. Particularly this Sunday night, when I stood on the precipice of a life-changing medical procedure.

I tried to tell myself it wasn't that big of a deal. The surgery was a simple outpatient procedure. Thanks to the wonders of modern robotic medicine, it would be only minimally invasive. I'd be up and walking around almost immediately, back to moderate activity within two weeks, fully recovered within six.

And yet.

It felt like much more than that. The end of my fertility meant something to me— much more than I'd expected it would. Especially when it wasn't happening on its own, but was being forcibly extracted before my body had decided it was time.

Even the name of the procedure was upsetting. Hysterectomy. The word itself was steeped in centuries of misogyny and medical malpractice and cruel myths about femininity and what it meant to be a woman.

I couldn't help worrying about how it would change me. Would I feel different? Would the hormonal changes make me feel less like a woman? Would my sex drive be affected? My ability to enjoy sex?

I hadn't even had the opportunity to enjoy sex since my marriage ended. It had literally been years since I'd been pleasured by anything that wasn't made of medical grade silicone. I'd tried to tell myself it was just as good, but the truth was, I missed the warm touch of a man. I missed sexual intimacy. I missed feeling desirable.

What if I never had that again?

What if this was my last chance to enjoy sex the way I used to and I'd squandered it away because I'd been too afraid to make myself vulnerable?

My phone buzzed on the coffee table, and I leaned forward to check the screen. It was a new text from Mike. He was certainly persistent. I had to give him that.

He'd continued texting me faithfully every day. Sometimes he'd send a funny picture or meme, and sometimes he'd just ask me about my day, or tell me about his. But the underlying message was always the same: to let me know he was thinking about me.

Even though I'd gently declined all his requests to see me again.

He'd accepted my vague excuses with good grace, and without attempting to put pressure on me. But he kept on texting me to let me know he was still there and still interested, if and when I became available.

It was sweet. *He* was sweet. Imagine that. I'd actually found a single man my own age who was good-looking, kind, *and* interested in me. Mike Pilota was the holy grail of men. The Golden Fleece. Willy Wonka's golden ticket.

Every day I cursed our bad timing. Why did I have to get cancer now? Just when I'd run into Mike again after all these years? It was beyond unfair.

I set my wineglass down and reached for my phone. *Look at this loaf,* he'd texted, along with a link to an Instagram post. It was a video of a fat corgi's backside as it hopped up a flight of stairs, posted by an account called "round boys." I'd mentioned in one of our previous text conversations that I had a fondness for cute videos of fat animals, and Mike had taken it upon himself to text me a new one every day. I could have followed the "round boys" Instagram myself of course, but it was much more fun to get personally curated content from Mike delivered randomly throughout the day.

I responded to him with a row of heart-eyes emojis.

Maybe I shouldn't have kept on texting him, knowing what I now knew. I wouldn't be going on any dates with him anytime soon, and I wasn't inclined to tell him the reason why.

I suppose it was silly of me, but I was too embarrassed. I had a crush on this man; I didn't want to tell him about my aging-lady troubles. The fact that he actually liked me back felt like such a fragile, tenuous, remarkable thing. A miracle, really. How would he ever find me desirable after he'd heard all about my endometrial cancer and hysterectomy and sudden onset of menopause?

It was enough to kill anyone's boner. Permanently.

I felt a stir of longing as I gazed at Mike's name. I could have had him. There'd been a window of opportunity.

Maybe there still was.

Emboldened by the wine, I typed out a text:

Dawn: What are you up to tonight?

A benign enough question. If he was otherwise occupied, that was my decision made for me. Window officially closed.

But I didn't think he was occupied. Would he be texting me videos of corgis if he were busy tonight?

I reached for my wineglass and gulped down a mouthful while I watched the screen, waiting for Mike to respond. After a moment, those three lovely little dots appeared to let me know he was typing. I set my wine back on the coffee table and stood up, pacing around the living room as I waited for his reply to come through.

My heart leapt into my throat when it finally did.

Mike: Nothing, as per usual.

I blew out a long breath. Did I dare? My thumbs hovered over the screen.

Dawn: Do you want to come over?

I hit send before I could change my mind. My knees felt wobbly. I sank down on the couch again and set my phone on the table in front of me.

His reply came almost immediately, causing the phone to buzz against the wood surface.

Mike: I can be there in 30 minutes.

CHAPTER SIXTEEN
MIKE

W hen Dawn opened her front door, it was all I could do not to step forward and kiss her. Just wrap her up with one arm, tilt her head back with the other, and lay one on her like a silver age movie idol. Like how Jimmy Stewart kissed the hell out of Donna Reed at the end of *It's a Wonderful Life*. Joyful and direct and just a little bit brutish, because that was how the sight of her made me feel after two weeks apart.

But I didn't.

I didn't know why she'd invited me over. Maybe she had romantic aims or maybe she didn't. Either way, I figured I'd better take it slow. Let her show me what she wanted.

She wore jeans and a loose, drapey pullover that offered alluring glimpses of the curves underneath. I'd never seen her dressed so casually—not since we were teenagers—and the sight set my heart thumping against my ribs.

I got the feeling she was as nervous as I was—which could support the booty call theory, or could be something else—but her smile was wide and her eyes bright. I loved that smile of hers. It shot straight through my chest and warmed me through and through.

Then she surprised me by stepping forward and kissing me. Not a long, deep, hard kiss like I'd been thinking about giving her, but a soft, sweet, too-brief press of her lips against mine. There and gone again before I could properly appreciate it. She tasted like wine, which probably explained the brightness of her eyes, and for the first time in my life, I actually enjoyed the flavor.

"I'm glad you came," she said, and my chest got even warmer.

"I'm glad you asked."

Her gaze flicked downward, and I saw her cheeks flush. She *was* nervous. I hoped it was a good kind of nervous and not a bad one.

"Come in." She stepped back to admit me into her house, and I toed my shoes off and left them on the rack by the front door.

I tried not to gawk at my surroundings, but it was exactly as classy and stylish inside as I'd imagined. All the expensive-looking furniture matched, and every room we passed through was decorated in a palette of soothing colors that seamlessly complemented each other. It was like walking through a catalog spread.

"Nice place," I said as I followed her past a formal living room and dining room to a bright, roomy kitchen across from a more comfortable-looking living area with a big cushy couch facing a TV.

She glanced around self-consciously. "It's a little more house than I need these days, but it's home. And the boys still have rooms here, if they ever need them."

I marveled at how clean the kitchen was. The whole place was immaculate. Not a spot or a crumb anywhere on any of the shiny granite countertops. The stainless steel range gleamed as bright as the smudge-free refrigerator door. There was no clutter of any kind sitting out—no stacks of mail or dirty dishes, no sign at all that the place was lived in—except a single wineglass and an open bottle of wine on the big central island.

"Would you like some wine?" she offered, following my gaze. "I've also got beer if you'd prefer."

"I'd love a beer, if it's no trouble."

"They're in the fridge. Help yourself."

She topped up her glass while I went to the fridge. It was as neat and clean inside as the rest of the house, and packed full of food. I helped myself to a beer from the door

—there was a selection of local craft brews to choose from—and pulled my keychain out of my back pocket to pry the lid off.

"You come prepared," she observed when I turned around, and dropped the bottle opener she'd been about to offer back into a drawer.

"I try." There were also fresh condoms in my wallet. I didn't mention them, but I hoped I'd get a chance to use them tonight.

She held out her hand for the bottle cap, and I dropped it into her palm. "Shall we go sit down?" she asked as she deposited it into a pull-out trash can.

I nodded and followed her to the living room. The couch was one of those huge, cushy ones meant for lounging, with an ottoman at one end. Dawn sat at the end opposite the ottoman, so I chose the middle and turned toward her, resting my arm on the back of the couch.

She swiveled to face me and pulled her feet up underneath her, drawing my attention to the cherry-red polish on her toes. Her fingernails were always bare and trimmed short, so it gave me a little thrill to glimpse her brightly painted toes, like a prize hidden at the bottom of the cereal box.

"You've got sexy feet," I blurted out before I could think better of it.

"Do I?" She unfolded one of her legs and wriggled her toes.

My mouth watered, and I swallowed. "Yeah." I'd always been turned on by a pretty pair of feet on a woman, and hers were perfect. Small and shapely with dainty little toes.

Her forehead creased as she studied her own foot. "I never thought of feet as particularly sexy."

"They're one of my top five parts of a woman's body."

"Really?" She looked up at me, her expression surprised and curious.

"Really." I set my beer on the coffee table and laid my hand over her foot. The skin-on-skin contact seared through me, setting off an electric discharge that changed the atmosphere in the room. The air seemed to crackle with possibility all of a sudden.

I let my thumb caress the inside of her arch and watched her expression change, her cheeks pinking as her eyes grew wide.

You had to have the right touch with a foot. They were sensitive, and a lot of people were ticklish. Go too light and they'd twitch right out of your grip; too firm and you could cause discomfort on a tender spot. Apply just the right amount of pressure though, and you could send a woman into paroxysms.

I saw Dawn's throat move as she swallowed and felt a surge of satisfaction. One corner of her mouth curved in a tantalizing half-smile. "What are the other top five?" she asked in an unsteady voice.

It felt like a test, and I considered my answer carefully as I continued to caress the arch of her foot. After I'd made up my mind, I took her wineglass from her and set it on the table next to my beer. "The hands," I said as I cradled her hand in both of mine. "Yours are beautiful. I noticed them when you were teaching me to knit." I ran my thumbs over her knuckles, then bent my head and brought her hand to my lips. "So graceful," I murmured, and heard her breath hitch as I kissed the back of her hand. "So dexterous." I turned her hand over in my mine and placed another kiss in the center of her palm.

"What else?" Her voice sounded slightly strangled now.

I lifted my eyes to hers, then let my gaze fall pointedly on her mouth. Her lips parted as she puffed out a ragged breath, and I took it as the invitation I'd been hoping for.

Reaching up, I let my fingers stroke lightly over her cheek before sliding them into her soft hair. I cupped my hand around her head, pulling her toward me as I leaned in. Our noses brushed, our lips almost-but-not-quite touching. I felt her shiver as I let the moment stretch out, growing more intimate by the second. We were achingly close. So close I heard her sharp inhale, and the soft, hungry sigh that followed.

I touched my lips to hers in a barely-there butterfly kiss. "Your mouth," I whispered. "I fucking love your mouth."

Then I waited. Held my breath, closed my eyes, and *hoped*.

She let out a quiet whimper and surged toward me, sliding her hands around my torso as we came together in an open-mouthed, desperate kiss. She tasted sweet and savory on my tongue, like dark red wine and courage. There was something almost reckless about the way she threw herself at me, as if something besides just attraction was driving her.

I felt a moment's doubt in the back of my mind. She'd been so cagey with me until now, encouraging me one moment and seeming to pull back the next. Putting me off and then suddenly inviting me over out of the blue. I didn't understand it. There was so much I didn't understand about her, but I wanted to. I wanted to know everything there was to know about her.

Would she change her mind about me after this? Would she regret letting me get this close? Or view me as some sort of short-lived experiment, one and done?

I didn't think I'd be able to stand that. But I couldn't let this opportunity go by either. If this was my one and only chance with Dawn, I'd make the most of it and hope I could convince her to come back for more.

My fingers curled in her hair, releasing the fresh, fruity scent of her shampoo. It mingled with her perfume, making me feel intoxicated. Her mouth slanted over mine, her tongue exploring freely, tasting me, and I made a husky, impatient noise in the back of my throat. I wanted to slip my hands under that sweater of hers, stroke the soft skin that lay hidden under there and feel her tremble. I wanted to touch her all over, but I forced myself to relax and take it slow, to not maul her like an oaf.

I was trying to follow her lead, but I was dying to touch her. Dying to feel her touching me.

Her hands fluttered over my jaw and throat, ghosting over my beard like she wanted to sink her fingers into it but couldn't work up the confidence to do it.

"You like the beard?" I asked, rubbing it against her lips.

She made a low noise that sent a fresh burst of arousal shooting up my spine. "Yes," she moaned, giving in to her desire and full-on stroking my face with both hands. "God, yes."

I kissed my way to her neck, and she shivered at the friction as my beard rubbed against the tender skin there. She hummed low in the back of her throat, and I felt it in my tongue as I tasted her. Her body pressed against mine, straining toward me, her soft curves melting against my hard planes, lighting me on fire from head to toe.

One of her hands slid under my shirt as the other tugged roughly at my beard. I nearly exploded when her fingertips made contact with the bare skin of my stomach.

That's it, I thought. *Touch me. Take me. Make me yours.*

CHAPTER SEVENTEEN
DAWN

I hadn't known it was possible to be this turned on. Mike did something to me. Made me into a different person. Or maybe this was who I'd always been, and he brought out the parts of me I'd forgotten ever existed. The parts that had been tamed and domesticated and suppressed for far too long.

As his mouth moved over my skin, I felt an animal sort of desire building in me. Not just attraction, but hunger. *Need.* Base, wanton, and shameless.

My hands explored his chest, my nails scraping over his skin, my fingertips tangling in his chest hair. But it wasn't enough. I needed to see what I was touching.

"I want to see you with your shirt off." The words slipped off my tongue before I had a chance to second-guess them.

Mike lifted his head, his eyes gleaming with pleasure. "As you wish."

My heart melted a little more. A man who quoted *The Princess Bride* in the middle of a make-out session? I had to reach up and touch his face to assure myself he was real.

But he was very real, and very much taking off his shirt. He dragged his red Henley over his head and dropped it onto the couch behind him.

"You've got tattoos!" I exclaimed in surprise. On the left side of his chest was a scorpion surrounded by the words *loyalty, strength, courage*—his zodiac sign, I guessed.

On his opposite arm an intricate pattern of swirls and shapes that resembled wings covered his whole shoulder and wrapped around his biceps, reaching almost to his elbow.

"Yeah." He ducked his head as if he were embarrassed by them, but I was delighted.

How marvelous to think they'd been hidden under his clothes all this time and I'd had no idea. My gaze traced over the delicately shaded black ink designs, devouring them with my eyes. "They're beautiful."

"You think?"

"Yes." I reached out, running my fingers over his shoulder and down his arm, following the curve of the muscle. He was divine. Absolutely perfect. "When did you get them?"

"In my twenties. Long time ago."

"I like them." I laid my hand over the scorpion on his chest, right above his heart, and felt him shudder a little.

"I like when you touch me."

I lifted my eyes to his and saw my own lust reflected back at me. It intensified the ache between my thighs, which was growing more urgent by the second.

"Come here." He pulled me into his lap and kissed me again, licking into my mouth in a way that felt depraved and exciting.

As I straddled him, sitting back on his thick, muscular thighs, I ran my hands over the planes of his chest, enjoying the way his breath hitched when I encountered one of his nipples. I gave it a little tweak, and he bit down on my lip.

I leaned into him, craving more contact, and the hard bulge in his jeans pressed against me, right at the source of my aching need. My hips rocked against him of their own will, and he let out a pained groan, going momentarily boneless beneath me. His head fell back against the couch, exposing the delicate skin beneath the line of his beard, and I pressed my lips to it, sucking at his throat.

"Fuck," he moaned. "You're killing me." His hands found their way under my sweater, gliding up over my hips to my ribs, his calluses dragging over my skin and sending delicious shivers down my spine.

Next thing I knew, he'd unclasped my bra. He cupped a breast in one palm, kneading the soft flesh, his thumb rubbing over my rock-hard nipple. His other arm wrapped around my hips, pulling me hard against him. Grinding me against his erection.

I let out a little gasp of pleasure, wriggling so the pressure hit me in just the right spot. He let out another groan, half-choked this time, and squeezed his eyes shut as his head fell back again.

I ran my fingers through his lovely beard, caressing his jaw as I bent to kiss him again. Our tongues tangled, the sweet, wet glide sending a buzz of electricity down my spine as the friction between us increased.

I moaned into his mouth, and his eyes blinked open, his pupils dark and lustful.

"I want to see you." His voice was hoarse and needy. "I want to taste you."

I wanted that too. So. Much.

His eyes flicked around the room, taking in all the windows with the shades wide open. "Bedroom?"

I nodded, and he hoisted me off his lap, depositing me on the couch beside him. Twisting to kiss me again, he pushed himself off the couch and wrapped his hands around my wrists, tugging me upright.

He held my hand as I led him up the stairs. As soon as we reached my bedroom, time seemed to compress and speed up. Half frantic with need, we stripped off each other's clothes, devouring every inch of newly revealed skin with our eyes and our tongues. Our pants came off in a blur of wriggling and grunting, and then we were both in nothing but our underwear, and he was laying me down on the bed, lowering his body to mine.

I splayed my fingers over his meaty shoulders as his mouth clamped down on one of my breasts. I loved the way his hands felt as they roamed over my bare skin, loved the way his beard rubbed against my sensitive nipple. But then he moved lower, kissing a trail down my belly, and the nerves I'd managed to ignore reared their ugly heads.

Up until that point, I'd been feeling bold. Impetuous. Excited. Everything felt so good. I didn't want to stop, but the doubt started to creep in.

What did men expect from women these days? I had no idea, and suddenly worried I wasn't up to his standards.

I'd never had a Brazilian bikini wax in my life. I'd settled down and gotten married in the age of grunge and Lilith Fair, when women wore their pubes as bushy as their eyebrows. I kept things trim down there, but not as bare as I suspected he might be accustomed to. And with the lights on, he'd be able to see everything. *Everything.* What if he didn't like what he found?

Shame shimmied over the surface of my skin, dampening my courage. I felt embarrassed suddenly. Shy.

I tried to ignore it, hoping he wouldn't notice. But of course he did. He seemed to notice everything about me. It was both wonderful and terrifying.

Mike lifted his head, his eyes locking on mine with a question in them.

I reached for him, pulling his mouth down to mine. Both for the comfort of his kiss and to distract him, to prevent him from looking at me too closely.

"Dawn." His lips ghosted away, moving to my cheek and then my ear, nuzzling gently. "Do you want to slow down?"

"No. I like it." My fingers curled into his skin possessively, afraid he'd take his heavy warmth away. This was my last shot. I couldn't let this window close. Who knew when I'd have another opportunity?

He pushed up onto his forearms, looking down at me with those piercing dark eyes of his. "We can stop."

"I don't want to stop." I felt my eyes prickle and squeezed them shut, mortified.

The mattress dipped as he shifted his weight to one arm. He lifted a hand to my face. His fingertips caressed my cheek with the tenderest of touches. "Tell me what's wrong."

I almost did. I almost confessed everything. In that moment, I felt like I could have, and he would have listened and talked to me and held me, and it would have been lovely.

But it wasn't what I wanted. I'd invited him here for a reason, and there was a clock ticking. If I opened up the whole can of worms, it would throw a wet blanket over the rest of the evening, and I could kiss my last sexual hurrah goodbye.

So I opened my eyes and told him my other secret instead—which was no small thing for me. Even revealing that much of myself felt monumental. But Mike made it easier. He made me feel safe being vulnerable.

"I think I'm scared."

Dismay clouded his expression as he shifted off me onto his side, propping his head up on his hand. "Do you think I'll hurt you?"

I shook my head. "No, but…I haven't done this in a while." I was acutely conscious of every sound we made. Of how bright and unflattering the overhead light was. Of my naked breasts and bare stomach.

He reached for my hand and squeezed it, tangling our fingers together. "That's okay."

"The truth is…" I looked at our intertwined hands because it was easier than looking at his face or my own body. "The truth is I haven't done this with anyone but my ex-husband for a very, *very* long time. And I'm afraid." It cost me to even admit that much.

"Afraid of what, exactly?"

Everything.

My fear was a large, amorphous blob that encompassed everything relating to sex with another man, so it was hard to pinpoint just one specific thing I was afraid of. "That I'll be bad at it, I guess?" That wasn't exactly it, but it was as close as I could come to putting my fears into words.

Mike smiled, but his eyes were serious. "Not possible."

I let out a snort of disbelief.

"Look at me."

My eyes went to his face of their own accord, as if I were powerless to resist his command.

"I just want to be close to you."

"I want that too."

He nodded, his expression soft. "There's no pressure. We're just getting to know each other better. It's an experiment, not a performance."

His words made me feel a little better, but now that I'd let the apprehension push its way in, it wasn't so easy to push it back out again. My mind seized on a thousand things that could go wrong, could be imperfect, could end up hurting me—not physically, but emotionally. What if he didn't like my stretch marks, the way my breasts sagged when I lay on my back like this, my episiotomy scar, the way I touched him?

What if he didn't like *me*?

He disentangled his hand from mine, and I almost whimpered at the loss of connection. But then he touched my face, his index finger stroking along my jaw and pausing on my chin, exerting gentle pressure to turn my face toward him.

"Close your eyes," he whispered, leaning in until he was just out of reach of my lips.

My heart fluttered in my chest as I obeyed, eager to feel his mouth on me again, craving the delicious friction of his beard.

His lips brushed mine in the gentlest of kisses.

It wasn't enough. I wanted more.

"Shh," he murmured when I arched toward him. "Be still. Just wait."

I didn't want to wait, but I did as he asked, trying to relax my body into the mattress. My eyes were still closed, so it surprised me a little when he touched my chest, right below the divot in my collarbone. His finger stroked a line down between my breasts, slow and deliberate, and I shivered a little.

He surprised me again when he pressed another kiss against my mouth, a little less chaste than the last. Then another, and another, each a little warmer, a little wetter than the one before. I started to lose myself again in the heat of his mouth and the roughness of his beard. By then his finger had journeyed all the way down to my stomach, and I arched toward him as it dipped below my belly button, drawing closer and closer to the place I wanted his touch the most.

I felt him smile against my mouth, and his finger danced over to my hip, tracing hypnotic little loops and swirls on the surface of my skin that made me think of the tattoo on his arm. He kissed me harder as his finger moved down to my thigh, teasing me with light, tantalizing touches. Then he pressed his palm flat against my leg, sliding his calloused hand over my inner thigh.

I swallowed a gasp as he stroked up, up, up…then down again just before he reached the good part. My whole body was on fire with an agonizing blend of pleasure and frustration.

"You like this, don't you?" His breath shivered over my lips. "Being teased a little. The buildup."

I couldn't answer. There wasn't enough oxygen getting to my brain. Instead, I made an animal noise in the back of my throat, somewhere between a grunt and a groan.

"You know what I like?" I could hear the smile in his voice, along with the husky edge of desire. His hand stroked up my thigh again, and I quivered in response. "*This*. I like seeing you so hot for me you're trembling with it. I like touching you and feeling your body react."

This time I did whimper. I was a coil of need, wound so tightly I felt like I would crack under the pressure if I didn't get some relief soon.

His hand traveled up again, but this time he cupped me over my underwear. My hips bucked at the delicious pressure, and we let out matching moans.

"Jesus, you're so wet. Just fucking soaked."

"Please," I gasped, unable to resist rocking against his hand as all pretense of demure behavior shattered.

"I know what you need, don't worry." He hooked one finger under the elastic edge of my underwear, and I nearly shouted with relief. His breathing was hard and heavy, and I felt him shudder along with me as he parted my folds and delved inside me. "God, you feel fantastic. So slick and swollen."

His mouth clamped down over mine like he wanted to consume me, his tongue plunging into my mouth as his fingers plunged inside me. I spread my legs for him, and he went deeper, slipping his whole hand inside my sopping underwear. But even that wasn't enough. I needed…I needed…

He pressed against my aching clit and I cried out, writhing uncontrollably. "That's what you want, isn't it?" His hot breath puffed against my ear as he increased the pressure until it was almost too much. Then he eased up, as if he could read my mind —or my body—applying light, gentle strokes in just the right spot.

I was so close. I could feel the orgasm coiling inside me. I'd never come this quickly before. I bit down on my lip, trying to prolong the pleasure of the moment even as I craved release from the beautiful torture. And then it was on me, my limbs tensing as a pulse of pure bliss crested in my center, washing over me in undulating waves that seemed to go on and on, way beyond anything I'd ever experienced.

"That's it. That's what you wanted." Mike stroked me through it, his mouth caressing mine, his body heavy and solid beside me. "God, you're beautiful when you come."

I opened my eyes blearily, feeling like I was caught in some sort of dream state, and found Mike gazing down at me, his skin flushed and his eyes dark with desire. He was the most gorgeous thing I'd ever seen, and I reached for him, curling my fingers into his hair.

"Touch me." His voice sounded half broken.

I reached down between us, trailing my fingers over his hard stomach until I found his underwear and felt the rock-hard heat straining against the fabric.

His whole body shuddered as I cupped him. "Feel how hard I am? That's what you do to me."

I squeezed, emboldened by his encouragement, and his eyes fluttered closed.

"Harder. Do it harder."

I did as instructed and watched as tremors of pleasure vibrated through his limbs. It was a lovely sight. His broad chest and thick, muscular arms and legs all quivering like gelatin because of something I was doing to him. I considered venturing inside his boxer briefs to feel the soft, velvety skin there without a layer of fabric between us.

Before I could work up the courage, he seemed to snap, pushing himself up on the bed. "Don't move," he instructed in a growly voice that made my blood shimmy in my veins, kissing me hard on the lips once before clambering off the bed and stooping for his jeans.

My breathing quickened as Mike retrieved a condom from his wallet, and my fists squeezed the comforter in anticipation. He pushed down his underwear and his penis sprang free. Instinct told me not to stare, but I couldn't help it. Mike was naked in front of me, and he was magnificent.

My mouth watered as my eyes took him in. His rigid, swollen dick rising out of a nest of salt-and-pepper curls, curving up to kiss his taut stomach.

I wanted it inside me.

He climbed back onto the bed and jerked my underwear down. I reached for him again, eager to touch that satiny pink skin without anything between us, to feel the blood pulsing through him. I squeezed the base of his dick the way I thought he'd like and was rewarded with another full-body shudder.

His jaw clenched, and he caught my wrist in a steel grip. "Stop. Unless you want me to come all over you right now."

It was tempting to see if he really would, if I had that kind of sway over him. But that wasn't what I really wanted—what either of us wanted—so I let go and allowed him to push me back on the bed.

Still holding on to my wrist, he pressed it into the mattress above my head as he lowered his mouth to mine, kissing me with hungry intensity. "What do you want? Tell me."

I was still feeling warm and liquid from my orgasm, but at his words a fresh pulse of need shuddered through me. "You," I moaned as his mouth moved down my throat.

"Where?" His voice was rough, commanding. "Say it."

An electric *zing* of excitement shot down my spine. Who even was I right now? I'd never thought I was someone to get turned on by being given orders, but something about the way Mike did it sent a thrill straight down to my core. His commands were different. There was no force behind them, only promise. *Do this for me, and I'll do something even better for you.* I was helpless to resist. Putty in his hands.

It was a relief, really. Being told what to do and what to say. It took so much of the pressure off. I didn't have to anticipate his needs the way I'd made a whole life out of anticipating everyone's needs. I only had to follow his instructions and reap the rewards.

"Inside me," I replied roughly. "I want you inside me."

At my words, he rose up on his knees again, tore open the condom, and rolled it on with gritted teeth. Holding himself in one hand, he settled between my legs and pushed forward, guiding himself slowly, carefully inside me.

He felt so good, so right. I clutched at him as I took his full length in and shuddered with a jolt of pleasure, consumed by sensation. The powerful thrust of his hips, the scent of his skin, our gasps and moans as we found our rhythm.

The next thing I knew, that glorious tension started building inside me again. I chased it greedily, digging my fingers into the curve of Mike's ass, aching for more pressure. He seemed to know instinctively what I needed and arched his back, increasing the intensity, creating more friction in just...the right...place...until I shattered beneath him, crying out my second release, which was even more powerful than the first had been.

"That's it," he murmured against my skin. "Beautiful. So beautiful."

He kissed my breastbone and then rose up on his knees, lifting my hips off the mattress. His fingers dug into my flesh as he pulled me flush against him, thrusting deep and hard, over and over, our bodies slamming together with the most wonderful intensity. He gazed down at me, his eyes dark and rapt, his jaw set in concentration, until finally, with a groan, his whole body tensed. He thrust one last time, shakily, and collapsed on top of me.

After Mike disposed of the condom, we curled up together in my bed, naked under the covers, our bodies intertwined. I felt happy in that moment. I was so sated and sleepy, so relieved to be physically close to another person again.

I liked him so much. It would be easy to fall for him—*really* fall for him, hard. The kind of fall you didn't recover from. I was already having all kinds of dangerous feelings. On the precipice of losing control. Because he made everything seem easy, even when it wasn't.

I closed my eyes and let Mike hold me in his arms, lying to myself that it was the beginning of something wonderful and not the end.

CHAPTER EIGHTEEN
MIKE

I woke shortly after sunrise, alone in Dawn's bed.

My alarm blared at me from the nightstand. It was Monday morning, and I had to be at work in two hours. Thank god I'd had the foresight to set the damn thing last night before falling asleep.

I rolled over to grab my phone and disentangled myself from the soft ivory sheets that still held Dawn's scent. I'd had my hands full last night and hadn't taken much notice of the decor, but now I let my eyes wander over the room. The furniture was heavy, dark, and classic. Perfectly matched. The bed decorated with a fluffy floral comforter and about a million cushions that had been carelessly swept onto the floor last night in our haste to explore each other's bodies.

For a moment I paused, sitting on the edge of Dawn's mattress, and smiled at the memory of her coming on my fingers. Her sweet little gasps as she fell apart in my arms. The smell of her skin when she nuzzled against me afterward.

Then I came back to reality, to this bedroom she had once shared with a husband. The quiet, combined with Dawn's absence, made me uneasy. I plucked my clothes off the floor, pulling them on hastily, feeling like an intruder in someone else's space.

I made my way downstairs, my socked feet silent on the polished wooden floors. About halfway down, I caught the scent of fresh-brewed coffee and followed it into the kitchen.

Dawn sat at the counter, a mug of coffee in front of her. She hadn't noticed my approach, and for a moment I stood in the doorway watching her. Something about the set of her shoulders and the way she stared into space, lost in her own thoughts, cranked my uneasiness up to the next level.

Then, as if she could feel me watching her, she turned. The way she smiled when she caught sight of me standing there banished some of my apprehension. There was still something off about her. A shadow around her eyes that I'd noticed last night and taken for nerves.

"Morning," she said as I came toward her.

I bent to kiss her, my hand tangling in the collar of her pink terry-cloth robe as our lips touched. "What are you doing up so early?"

"Insomnia." She shrugged lightly, trying to make me think it was nothing.

"You okay?" I asked, fairly certain the answer was no.

A little morning-after uncertainty was to be expected—that normal dance two people did when they were still getting to know each other and weren't sure yet how invested they were, or how to act around one another after a night of blush-inducing intimacy.

This seemed like something else though, and it reminded me how hot and cold she'd been with me these last couple weeks.

The shadow in her expression intensified, and I thought maybe she'd actually tell me what was on her mind. But then she brushed it aside, cloaking herself in a cheerful smile she wore like armor. "Fine. I hope I didn't wake you."

"No, my alarm did that for me." I brushed her hair back, trying to take a mental snapshot of her face, of this moment, of the two of us on this morning after we first came together. My mouth pulled into a regretful smile. "Gotta go home and get ready for work."

She nodded her understanding, and I was gratified to see evidence of disappointment. "I was going to offer to make you breakfast."

"Can't. But I appreciate the thought."

I kissed her again, longer and deeper this time. Her hand curled around the back of my neck and I breathed her in, feeling a peculiar tightness around my heart. There was something so easy, so natural, about the two of us together.

It was too soon to know where we were going or if it would work out, but I hadn't felt this hopeful in a long time.

"Last night was incredible," I told her, holding her face in my hands as I pressed my forehead against hers.

"For me too." Her palms rested on my chest, her warmth soaking into me through my shirt like a sunlamp, and for a second I considered offering to call in sick and spend the whole day with her.

But I didn't know what her plans were for the day, or if she'd even want me to do that, and I hadn't been at this new job long enough to start playing hooky. It wouldn't look good, and I already had enough to prove without throwing in a spotty attendance record.

"When can I see you again?" I asked and felt her tense.

"I'm going to be out of pocket the rest of the week, I'm afraid. I'll have to let you know."

There was that odd caginess back again. I wanted to ask her what she meant, what was keeping her busy, but I assumed she hadn't offered a more detailed explanation for a reason. If she'd wanted to let me into her life, she would have.

For all the intimacy we'd shared last night, there was still a gulf between us I wasn't sure how to cross. I knew I wasn't great at opening up or talking about myself, and I got the feeling that was something Dawn and I had in common. We'd need to make a real effort—both of us—if this was going to be something real.

But for all I knew, she didn't want that. Maybe I was just a temporary experiment. A means to an end. A way to pop her post-divorce cherry so she could move on to more serious pursuits.

I didn't want to believe that of her, but I also had a hard time imagining why a woman like her—a woman with beauty, brains, and money—would want to spend time with a loser like me.

"Right. Sure," I mumbled, trying not to sound hurt. "Let me know. I'll be around."

Her hand fisted in my shirt, pulling me toward her. Our lips brushed, but when I started to pull away, she strained toward me, curling a hand around the back of my neck to hold me there. Her mouth devoured mine in a deep, lingering kiss that left my head spinning and my pulse racing before it dissolved into a string of smaller, gentler kisses, like she was reluctant to let me go.

Then she got up and walked me to the door, and I left feeling more confused than ever.

CHAPTER NINETEEN
DAWN

"A re you comfortable?" the nurse asked, smiling down at me.

I nodded, although I didn't see how anyone could be comfortable in one of these humiliating hospital gowns with a blood pressure cuff on one arm and an IV in the other. I was so tangled up in tubes I could barely reach up to scratch my nose without getting caught on something.

"Right. I'll be back to check on you in a bit, and you've got your call button if you need anything. We're running a little behind this morning, but they should be able to get you in before ten." She pulled the curtain closed around my little cubby in the outpatient pre-op area as she departed.

I was cranky about the delay. According to my phone, it was currently eight o'clock in the morning. Considering I'd gotten to the hospital at six and hadn't had anything to eat or drink since last night, ten felt like a lifetime away.

"What do you want to watch?" Angie asked, taking charge of the TV remote.

"I don't know. Something soothing." I tried not to sound irritable with my friend, who'd gotten up at the crack of dawn to drive me to the hospital and sacrificed her whole day in order to wait on me hand and foot.

I felt guilty about asking for help, and self-conscious for needing it. But I was also tense and anxious about the surgery. Trying not to let it show was wearing me out.

"Home and Garden channel?"

"That's fine."

Angie stopped on a *Property Brothers* rerun and took out her knitting. I tried to watch the show. Usually home improvement shows soothed me, but today I couldn't keep my attention on it. My mind kept haring off to dark places, visualizing different worst-case scenarios. If they had to take my ovaries, plunging me into sudden onset menopause. If they found more cancer than expected and I needed chemo or radiation after all. If I had a bad reaction to the anesthesia and never woke up. Thank goodness I'd updated my will after the divorce. At least the boys were old enough that they'd be okay. Jerry would help them. The store would be a huge problem though. They'd probably have to close it down.

"Do you think these guys are sexy?" Angie asked, pulling me out of my gloomy meditation. Her attention was on the television screen, and I forced myself to focus on it again.

"The Property Brothers?"

"Yeah. People think they're sexy."

"I guess. They're not my type, but they're attractive enough in their own way." To be honest, I'd never given them much thought. My taste in HGTV men ran more to the *Kitchen Cousins*, despite the cringeworthy name of their show. I particularly liked Anthony, with the muscles and the tattoos and the salt-and-pepper beard. Who, come to think of it, looked quite a bit like Mike.

At the thought of Mike, I felt my stomach drop. We'd texted back and forth a few times yesterday, but I still hadn't worked up the courage to tell him about my surgery.

It would change everything between us. I just knew it. I liked that he'd found me sexy, and I felt certain that would cease the second he found out about my medical situation. I wanted him to keep looking at me as an object of desire and not an object of pity or a victim of my aging body.

I just wanted things to stay the same.

"I think they're creepy," Angie said, still preoccupied with the Property Brothers.

"Why?" They seemed perfectly fine to me. Although this was an older rerun from when Jonathan had those unfortunate blond tips. "Is it the twin thing?" I knew some people found adult twins creepy, but I'd never understood why.

"Maybe." Angie frowned. "I don't think so. I think it has to do with their eyes. They're too small. It's like their smiles never seem to reach their beady little eyes. Or maybe it's their haircuts. I don't trust those haircuts."

"Why do so many people find twins creepy, do you think?"

"It's probably the doppelgänger thing. It's like you're seeing someone's double from an alternate universe. Or like seeing a clone. It hints at uncomfortable realities about the known universe that your brain doesn't want to accept."

"Everyone loves twins when they're children."

"That's because people treat them like dolls. But they can be creepy too. Look at those ghost twins in *The Shining*. They're creepy as fuck."

"Hello!" a voice called from the other side of the curtain. "Dawn?"

"In here," I answered, making sure my hospital gown wasn't going to accidentally flash anyone my tits.

The curtain twitched aside, and Nico Moretti's wife, Dr. Elizabeth Finney, peeked her head in. "Are you up for a visitor?" Her maternity leave had ended a few weeks ago, and she was back at work in the emergency room.

"Of course," I answered, glad to see a familiar face.

"How about two?" Elizabeth's friend Sandra Fielding, who also worked at Chicago General Hospital—as a pediatric psychiatrist—appeared alongside her. Both women were avid knitters, and both lived in the building above the store. They were not only regular customers, but welcome company to distract me from my looming medical procedure.

"How'd you know I was here?" I asked once we'd finished exchanging greetings.

Elizabeth's eyes got shifty. "Uhh, someone might have called me and asked me to check in on you."

I pressed my lips together. "Jerry," I guessed. I'd given him strict instructions not to come to the hospital today. The last thing I needed was him showing up to throw his weight around with my doctors. But apparently he'd called his protégé to come in his stead.

Elizabeth straightened her shoulders, keeping her expression studiously blank. "I can neither confirm nor deny that I am here at the request of Dr. Botstein."

"Ohh, what are you knitting?" Sandra asked Angie, deftly changing the subject.

"It's an anatomically correct model of a human uterus," Angie replied. "I'm giving it to Dawn as a consolation prize."

My head snapped around to stare at her in horror. *"What?"*

Angie snort-laughed. "Kidding. It's a Peppa Pig for one of my nieces."

Sandra's lip curled in an expression of distaste. "I rue the day that bacon-limbed hellspawn entered the children's television landscape. It's all I hear in the pediatric ward all day long. That precocious, insufferable little pig haunts my dreams."

Elizabeth chuckled, and Sandra turned on her, lifting an index finger in warning. "Just you wait until Rose is old enough to demand Peppa Pig. You'll see."

"I'm sure I will," Elizabeth said, rolling her eyes as she turned back to address me. "Ashley says to give you her best."

"Oh, that's sweet. How's she doing these days?" Ashley Winston was one of Elizabeth and Sandra's good friends who used to work at the hospital as a nurse practitioner. She'd moved back home to Tennessee several years ago, after her mother died.

"She's absolutely wonderful and said you should check your mailbox in a few days because she's sending you some books to read while you recuperate. She also says to make sure you walk around as much as you can manage after the surgery to dissipate the CO_2 bubbles they use to fill up your abdomen."

Sandra looked at Elizabeth in surprise. "They fill up your abdomen with CO_2? Like a big bottle of Coke?"

"Sort of. It's to keep all your organs in place while they work." Elizabeth's gaze softened as she addressed me again. "How are you? Are you okay? Do you need anything?"

"I'm fine," I assured her.

"Are you scared?" Sandra asked.

I shrugged. "Not really."

"Bull pucky," Sandra retorted.

"Sandra!" Elizabeth nudged her friend with her elbow.

"No, I mean it." Sandra crossed her arms and arched an eyebrow at me. "That's a load of steaming bovine dooky."

Angie snorted from her seat next to the bed but didn't look up from her Peppa Pig knitting.

"Well, I suppose I am a little nervous," I admitted. "I've never had surgery before."

Sandra nodded sagely. "Don't be afraid to advocate for yourself. If you need something—or even if you just feel like you want it—tell someone. Tell the nurses, tell your doctor, tell Angie. That's what they're all here for."

"I will."

"I mean it." Sandra's green eyes grew shrewdly assessing. "I can tell you're a caretaker personality, so you're probably not used to accepting or asking for help. Your instinct is to not be a burden or make trouble for anyone."

I pressed my lips together, disconcerted by the accuracy of her appraisal.

Sandra's smile grew wider as she nodded in satisfaction. "I'm right, aren't I?"

"Right on the money," Angie said.

"I say this as one martyr who abhors asking for help to another: people need people. There's no shame in asking for help."

"Okay, that's enough lecturing," Elizabeth told Sandra. "I think we've bothered her enough."

As if on cue, the nurse popped her head in. "We're ready to take you back now, Mrs. Botstein."

One moment I was counting down from ten for the anesthesiologist, and the next I was in recovery.

I was vaguely aware of other people in the room with me, having a conversation about lunch orders. My recovery nurse was a man with a warm, soothing voice. He fussed with my IV, and I drifted in and out for a bit, waking every fifteen minutes when my blood pressure cuff inflated. There wasn't any pain, thanks to whatever was in my IV, although my throat felt a little raw.

After a while, Angie came in and sat with me.

A while after that, when I was a little less dopey, the surgeon came to talk to me. She told me everything had gone well, they'd gotten all the cancer, and they hadn't needed to remove my ovaries.

I sank back into the pillows and closed my eyes in relief.

Angie drove me home later that afternoon and stayed with me for the next twenty-four hours, insisting on spending the night. I felt guilty about keeping her from her husband for so long, but she waved off my attempts to tell her I was fine.

The pain grew worse as the anesthesia wore off, but it was manageable, and Angie made sure I took my pain medicine on time. She set timers for my meds and made sure I got up and walked around every few hours like my nurse (and Ashley) had instructed. She made sure I drank plenty of water and made me smoothies and milkshakes.

In short, she was a perfect caregiver and friend. I was deeply conscious of how lucky I was to have her in my life, even if I didn't have the words to express it.

She'd texted my boys for me to let them know I was out of surgery and everything was fine. I called them myself that evening, when I was feeling a little stronger. I could hear the worry in their voices, but I repeated the surgeon's good news and reassured them I was fine. They wanted to come see me, but I put them off until tomorrow evening, telling them I was tired and about to go to bed.

I slept on and off through the night, waking occasionally with some discomfort when the pain meds wore off. Overall, the pain wasn't too bad, considering I'd had an entire organ removed.

It hurt quite a bit more the next morning, but once I got up and moved around a little, it subsided. Angie made me toast for breakfast and then talked me into watching a cooking show on YouTube. I didn't even know I could watch YouTube on my TV, or that there was anything worth watching on YouTube, but I always enjoyed cooking shows. We ended up watching it most of the day, with me getting up every hour at Angie's exhortation to shuffle around in my bathrobe for ten minutes.

The boys showed up with dinner in the evening, and Angie went home, promising to drop in and check on me in the morning. I slept better the second night. I still didn't feel quite human, but I was able to do a lot more and I wasn't as tired. I even took a shower when I got up, which helped a little with the feeling human part.

Angie showed up again in the morning, bright-eyed and bushy-tailed, on her way to open up the store. "This is for you," she said, thrusting a large gift bag at me.

"Oh, you didn't have to do that." I already felt guilty about all the time she'd devoted to helping me.

"I was afraid it wouldn't get here in time, but it arrived yesterday." She preceded me into the kitchen and poured herself a cup of coffee.

"In time for what?"

"For you to wear during your convalescence."

I peeked inside and pulled out a clear plastic packet stuffed with something large and fluffy and pastel striped. It looked like a cotton candy machine had upchucked after a hard night of booze and women. Flipping it over, I found the label. "*Adult Unicorn Onesie*," I read in disbelief. It was difficult to imagine when—or why—I might wear such a thing.

"It's for lounging around the house," she explained. "You're gonna love it. It's warm and soft as hell. I've got one, and I never want to take it off."

"Thank you. It's very sweet."

Angie nodded at me over her coffee cup. "Try it on. I want to see how it fits."

"Sure. Okay." I loved Angie, so I wasn't going to tell her I thought her gift was ridiculous. I'd try it on and tell her I adored it, then put it in the back of my closet and never wear it again, except maybe for Halloween.

I shuffled into the downstairs bathroom, shrugged out of my robe, and carefully pulled the onesie on over my pajamas. I was still quite sore, and things like bending over involved considerable effort, so it took me some time.

"You okay in there?" Angie called out. "You need help?"

"Nope, I'm good." I straightened carefully and zipped my new onesie up. Turning toward the mirror, I couldn't help smiling. I looked utterly absurd.

"Come on. Let me see!" Angie begged from the other side of the door.

I pulled it open, and her face lit up in delight. "Oh my god, it's amazing. Even better than I imagined. You have to put on the hood." She reached up and pulled the unicorn head up over my hair, grinning. "Beautiful!"

I had the sense I was being punked. "You're enjoying this, aren't you?"

"I am. How's it feel?"

"Cozy." I had to hand it to her, it was amazingly comfortable and warm, even if it made me feel foolish.

She bit down on her lip as she assessed my appearance. "Looks like it fits okay. I wasn't sure whether to get the small or medium."

"I like that it's roomy." There was no belt or waistband to rub against my incision sites, which was a definite bonus in my current situation.

"But not so roomy you're tripping over it. Let me see the tail."

I peered behind me, wincing a little as my incision pulled. "Oh look, it's got a tail." It was rainbow and furry and matched the mane on the hood.

"And the best part? It's got pockets!"

"Oh! That is nice!" I plunged my hands into the pockets, which were deep enough to hold a cell phone.

"You look great." Her eyes turned shrewdly appraising. "How are you feeling today? You look like you're feeling better."

"Much better. Healing continues apace."

"Good." She carried her coffee cup over to the sink and washed it out. "Is there anything I can do for you before I go?"

"No, I'm all set. I can manage on my own from here on out."

"I want you to call me if there's anything you need. Anything at all."

"I will."

She fixed me with a stern glare. "I mean it."

"Go to work." I shooed her toward the door. "Take care of the store for me." It was the one thing I couldn't do for myself yet.

After she'd gone, I considered changing out of my new onesie, but the thought of wrestling it off again was too exhausting. And it was comfortable. I'd just leave it on for a little while.

I got myself another cup of coffee and sank down on the couch. The whole day stretched ahead of me, empty and dull. I wasn't very good at leisure. My brain was itching to do something—anything—but my body had other ideas. At least I could knit. That would keep my hands busy. I retrieved my knitting and the television remote from the coffee table, pressing a hand to my abdomen as I felt a tug of pain.

As I switched on the TV, my phone buzzed in the pocket of my onesie. I pulled it out, and my chest squeezed when I saw it was a new text from Mike. He'd sent me a video of a small, round hedgehog munching on an apple. The sight of its tiny hands clutching at an enormous piece of fruit unexpectedly brought tears to my eyes.

I hadn't responded to Mike's daily texts since Monday. I wanted to, but I felt overwhelmed whenever I thought about him. It would be two months before I was fully healed and able to have sex again. There was no way I'd be able to put him off for that long without an explanation.

I knew I was being silly, and I should just be straight with him. I couldn't keep stringing him along like this without telling him what was going on. I owed him the truth. He deserved the right to make his own decision about whether he wanted to keep seeing me, under the circumstances.

And yet I hadn't been able to bring myself to do it. Whenever I thought about fessing up to him, I froze up completely. I wasn't a person comfortable talking about intimate personal issues with even my closest loved ones. The thought of broaching the subject with a man I barely knew—and was desperately attracted to—turned my stomach to jelly. We'd barely begun our relationship. How could I expect him to wait patiently for two months? To play nursemaid to me? To see me at my weakest and most unattractive and still want me?

I had a feeling I knew what decision he'd make, and I couldn't face it. Not now. I was too exhausted and sore. I didn't have the energy to deal with it.

So I didn't.

I ignored his text like I'd ignored his last several texts, shoved my phone back in my pocket, and started up the next cooking video on YouTube.

CHAPTER TWENTY
MIKE

When one day went by without Dawn replying to my texts, I didn't think much of it. I figured she must be busy with whatever she had going on this week.

At two days, I started to worry a little.

After three days, I was pretty sure something was wrong.

Still, I kept texting her. Checking in, asking how she was, attempting to make her laugh. I tried to stay hopeful and make up excuses for her lack of communication.

When a full week had gone by with no word from Dawn, I had to face the fact that I'd been ghosted.

It hurt. I wasn't used to being rejected by women. That probably made me sound like an asshole, but usually I was the gun-shy one with commitment issues and finicky taste. Now I'd had a taste of my own medicine, and I didn't like it. Maybe it was karma. Payback for all the Jessicas I'd dropped after one or two dates.

I thought about calling Dawn and asking her straight out what was going on. But what was the point? I already knew, didn't I? She didn't want to see me anymore. That much was clear. The reason didn't matter. It wouldn't change anything.

There'd been a couple women back in Columbus who hadn't wanted to give up on me, even after I'd told them it wasn't working out. They'd tried calling, begging to talk it out. One had even showed up at my apartment hoping to change my mind. All they'd succeeded in doing was making me even more eager to be rid of them.

Calling Dawn wouldn't do any good if she'd already made up her mind about me. Apparently, I was good enough for a one-night stand, but not for anything else.

At least I didn't have to wonder anymore why a woman like her would want to spend time with a guy like me. The answer was simple: she didn't.

Anyway, I had bigger problems to worry about. On Wednesday we had a citywide system outage at work. Every branch library in the city had lost network and internet access, and Rich was crawling up my asshole to get it fixed.

It wasn't like I didn't understand the urgency. I was doing my best to get them back online, but first I had to figure out what the problem was.

I'd already confirmed it wasn't a hardware problem. I suspected the issue was in the network settings somewhere. The thing was, network settings didn't just change themselves. Everything had been fine when I'd gone home yesterday, and suddenly today the network was borked? Someone had fucked with something, and I had a hunch it was Rich. This was exactly the sort of shit he pulled all the time.

So when I went to give him my update, I straight-up asked him if he'd changed anything last night. Not in an accusatory way, just matter-of-factly. I was extra careful to keep my manner neutral, because I knew what a sensitive little shit he was. And I needed him to tell me. If I knew what had been changed, it would save me hours of work trying to figure it out on my own, and I could have the network up and all the branches back in business that much faster. Which ought to be what he wanted.

Rich looked me right in the eye and told me no, acting all annoyed and offended I'd even asked him. Which was a dead giveaway. It was the first logical question anyone would ask, and he should have been expecting it. Why get all defensive unless he had something to be defensive about?

He was lying. I just knew it. This problem had his incompetent fingerprints all over it. The guy thought he was an IT expert and was always trying to do things on his own. Dollars to donuts he'd changed something in the settings that had knocked the branches off the network, got scared, and then lied to cover it up.

And I was gonna prove it. It took some computer archeology, but knowing which user's footprint I was looking for narrowed it down. I found it in the logs pretty easily. Rich had logged into the system last night and changed the SSID but had failed to push the change to all the computers at the branch libraries.

He'd lied to cover his ass. This was who I was working for. This was the person who was supposed to be supervising me—and was likely getting paid double my salary to do it. The guy who was going to write my evaluation at the end of the year and probably stick a knife in my back.

Fuck this place.

I needed to get out. The problem was that I'd likely end up in the exact same situation no matter where I went. Without a degree to my name, I'd pretty much topped out. No one was gonna hire me to be anything more than a grunt, no matter how good I was or how much experience I had.

Something needed to change, and that something was me.

I didn't want to spend the rest of my life taking orders from some college kid with half my experience. Which meant I needed to finish my fucking degree.

It was something I'd been thinking about for a long time. I'd even done a whole bunch of research last year and knew which online program suited me best. But I'd never been able to talk myself into it. And then my dad had died and I'd moved here, and I'd used that as an excuse not to do it.

As soon as I got home that night, I sat down in front of my computer and pulled up the website for the online university I'd looked into last year. They had a solid IT program that offered a bachelor's in cybersecurity and information assurance. It even included a bunch of industry certifications as part of the program, which would make me even more marketable to employers, and hopefully increase my opportunities for advancement and earnings potential.

People didn't change their lives by dithering over simple decisions forever. I could do this. I'd already made the decision. I just had to pull the trigger.

As I started to fill out the admissions application, I thought about my dad. What he'd say about me finally finishing college at my age, and doing it through some online-only university, to boot. It'd be nice to think he'd be proud of me, but I knew he'd have found plenty to criticize and disparage. That was his way. Even when he liked something, he always found something negative to say.

Well, he wasn't here anymore to rub it in or make me feel bad about my choices. There was an unexpected freedom in that. It gave me the impetus I needed to make a long overdue change.

I didn't have to be a loser forever. I could take control of my own life. Get a degree, get a better job, maybe even find a woman I liked as much as Dawn who actually wanted me around.

I almost bailed on the reunion committee meetup Thursday night. If Dawn was there, it was bound to be awkward. And if Dawn wasn't there, what was the point of even going? I'd only joined the committee as a way to get closer to her.

In the end, my loneliness won out over my pride. Sad to say, but this committee I hadn't even wanted to join was my only real social outlet. I'd enjoyed seeing Deon again, and Angie and Yolanda, and even Gina. If nothing else, at least I could have a decent beer and hang around with nonwork people for an hour before heading home to my depressing apartment. And hey, if Dawn was there, maybe I'd get a little closure.

Or not. Whatever.

I chatted with Yolanda when I first arrived and learned she was a hairstylist with two kids in middle school and a boyfriend who was a physical therapist. Then Gina arrived and clamped onto me like a lamprey eel. It made me vaguely uncomfortable, how she kept leaning into me and putting her hand on my arm, but I didn't know how to discourage her without hurting her feelings. I tried to ignore her and talk to Deon when he showed up, but she kept asking me questions, forcing my attention back onto her.

Angie was the next to arrive, and she started the meeting right away, from which I gathered Dawn would be a no-show. I couldn't say I was surprised, but I was disappointed.

Gina continued to hang on me as we moved through the agenda, and I noticed Angie throwing little glares in my direction every time Gina invaded my personal space. I couldn't help feeling this was unfair. I was the one who'd been dropped without so much as an *it's not you, it's me* text. If I wanted to flirt with Gina, I didn't see any reason why I shouldn't.

I had no idea what Dawn had told Angie about me, but as I sat there getting the evil eye from her best friend, I started to wonder. Dawn couldn't have any reason to be pissed at me, could she? I racked my brain for anything I could have done to drive her away and came up empty.

When the meeting was over, Gina asked me if I wanted to grab a bite to eat, and I politely declined, saying I needed to talk to Angie about something. Then I hung around, waiting while Angie said goodbye to everyone before I made my approach.

Her expression was frosty when she turned to me, and I wondered again what she thought I'd done wrong.

"Is Dawn okay?" I asked, electing to play the concerned and clueless angle to feel Angie out.

"Why don't you ask her that yourself?" She was definitely pissed at me, judging by her tone.

"Well, I've tried, but she hasn't been answering my texts. I don't know if she told you, but we'd sort of started seeing each other."

"Oh, she told me. She also told me it didn't work out, but I can read between the lines enough to guess what that means."

I had no idea what she thought it meant, and I was starting to get annoyed about being left in the dark. "Well I wish she'd told me because I have no idea what's going on," I shot back.

Angie's eyes narrowed. "Are you saying you didn't ghost her?"

"Hell no. She ghosted me!"

"Shit." Angie cast her eyes to the ceiling, shaking her head. "I assumed you'd run for the hills when she told you about her surgery."

My stomach dropped. "Surgery? What surgery?" I realized my voice had risen in alarm, and I lowered it again. "Is she okay?"

"She's fine." Angie's expression turned quizzical. "She really didn't tell you?"

"She didn't tell me anything. Just stopped answering my texts last week."

"Figures." Angie shook her head again. "I should have known. That girl. Always trying not to be a burden on anyone else."

"What's wrong with her? Is it serious?" I wasn't annoyed anymore. I was scared.

Angie's lips pressed together. "You should talk to her."

"I tried. She shut me out."

"Don't let her. She thinks she doesn't need anyone, but she's wrong. If you're serious about sticking around, you need to show her."

My brain raced as I tried to process everything Angie had just said and figure out what my next step should be. "Yeah. Okay. Thanks." I nodded goodbye and turned to go.

"Hey, Mike." Angie called out, stopping me. "Don't you dare break her heart."

I had no intention of doing any such thing, and I told her so.

Then I went to go see Dawn.

CHAPTER TWENTY ONE
DAWN

W hen my doorbell rang that evening, I thought it was one of my neighbors bringing over another casserole or some well-intentioned groceries I didn't need.

The last person I expected to find on my doorstep was Mike.

My heart stuttered in my chest as I peered through the peephole. He was still clad in what I assumed were his work clothes: a white pinstriped button-down shirt and a pair of olive chinos that clung beautifully to his muscular thighs. He wore the same black bomber jacket he'd worn on our date. The one he'd loaned me. A sense memory of the scent of that jacket overcame me, and I pressed my forehead against the door to steady myself.

I couldn't just leave him out there on the stoop. I'd have to open the door. Talk to him. Explain myself. I owed him at least that much.

Bracing for an unpleasant conversation, I unlocked the door and pulled it open.

Mike's eyes widened at the sight of me, his mouth falling open slightly. "Uhh…hey?"

I looked down and remembered I was wearing the unicorn onesie Angie had given me. *Super*. Just how I wanted him to see me. Looking like warmed-over death and clad in children's animal pajamas. I'd been dozing on the couch, and there was probably dried drool on my face, or crease marks from the pillow. And my hair—I couldn't even fathom what my hair must look like at the moment.

The corner of Mike's mouth quirked. "Nice onesie. You look like Rainbow Brite."

I crossed my arms over my chest in a gesture that was meant to be dignified, but it only made me more conscious of how absurdly I was dressed. "Rainbow Brite was a little blonde girl in a rainbow dress. I think you mean Rainbow Dash, the *My Little Pony* character."

He didn't try to hide his amusement. "Okay."

"What are you doing here?" I asked, eager to move past the subject of my outfit.

His smile fled immediately as his forehead creased. "Angie told me you'd had surgery?"

I felt a flash of annoyance. "She shouldn't have told you that." I'd purposely avoided telling Angie about the latest developments with Mike because I knew she wouldn't be able to resist butting in. Apparently, she'd managed to butt in anyway.

"Don't be mad at her. She was defending you."

I wondered what I'd needed to be defended from. I knew they'd had the reunion meeting tonight. Had Mike been complaining about me? He was certainly entitled to, after my radio silence for the last week. "She shouldn't have done that either."

"Are you okay?" Mike asked, frowning in concern.

It was exactly the look I'd been trying to avoid seeing on his face. *Pity.* He was looking at me not like I was a desirable woman, but like I was something fragile and in need of help.

I sighed. "I suppose you'd better come in." I stepped back and held the door open to admit him. Once he'd slipped off his loafers and hung his jacket on the rack, he followed me back to the den.

I tried to walk briskly, conscious that he was probably studying me for signs of weakness, but only managed a few steps before I was forced to slow to a more cautious pace. The pain was generally much improved, though it still caught me unawares when I wasn't careful. And I was feeling extra fatigued tonight because I'd overdone it today. I'd been growing restless in my convalescence, so I'd tried to do some work in the garden, which had turned out to be a mistake.

By the time we made it to the couch, I had a hand pressed to my diaphragm and was moving with the sprightliness of a ninety-year-old woman. Not only was I embarrassed by this, I was embarrassed by how messy it was in here. I'd made a sort of burrow on the couch with everything I might need arranged within reach. Too late, it occurred to me we should have just sat down in the front living room, which was much closer to the door and also immaculate since it was hardly ever used. Clearly, my fatigue was affecting my brain function.

There was nowhere for Mike to sit on the den couch, thanks to all my blankets, pillows, knitting, laptop, and tray of dirty dishes and tea mugs. I started to clear a space for him, but he quickly intervened. "Here, let me do that," he said in a chiding voice as he took my laptop out of my hands. "Jeez."

I let him take over tidying as I sank onto the couch. "I'm sorry about the mess. I wasn't expecting anyone to come over."

Mike shot a disapproving glare at me as he transferred the tray of dishes to the coffee table. "I hope you wouldn't have cleaned up if you'd known I was coming."

I didn't reply—since I absolutely would have—and I didn't want to disappoint his hopes any further than I already had.

When he'd finished clearing a space for himself, he sat down next to me, his bulk making the whole couch shake as he settled into place.

I could feel his eyes on me, scrutinizing me, but I refused to look at him. "What did Angie tell you exactly?"

"She just said you'd had surgery. She didn't say for what."

I nodded, girding myself for the confession I'd been avoiding for far too long. "I had endometrial cancer." Mike drew in a sharp breath, and I rushed on to reassure him. "I'm fine. It was just a few cancerous cells, and they got them all. As cancers go, I'm quite lucky. I don't even need chemo or radiation. But I had to have a hysterectomy."

I still wouldn't look at him, but in the silence that followed, I could imagine him nodding slowly as he digested this piece of information.

"When?" he asked finally.

"Last Tuesday."

"So the day you stopped replying to my texts."

I dared a glance at him, moved by the hurt in his tone. "I was…preoccupied." It was a cop-out, and I could see from Mike's expression he knew it as well as I did. Clearly, I wasn't incapacitated. I could have texted him on any of the days that had passed since my surgery. I simply hadn't.

"You didn't want to tell me." It was phrased not as a question but as an accusation. A statement of fact.

"I didn't want to be a burden." As the words left my mouth, I recalled what Sandra had told me in the hospital. Her psychiatrist's instincts were uncannily astute because I'd been doing exactly what she'd warned me against. Exactly what I'd always done.

Angie had accused me once of being too eager to fall on my sword. Whenever things got difficult, my first thought was always of what I could give up to make the situation easier for someone else. The way I cared for the people I loved was by taking care of their problems, which meant not being a problem myself.

And yet I'd always liked being needed because it made me feel important and valuable. When Sandra had reminded me that people need people, all I'd heard was *you need people*.

It hadn't occurred to me that there was another element to it: *people need to be needed*.

I'd denied Mike the chance to feel needed, just like I'd denied it to Jerry and to my sons. I'd even tried to deny Angie as much as I possibly could, pushing myself to self-sufficiency after the surgery so she wouldn't need to take care of me any longer than absolutely necessary. I'd tried to take care of everyone by refusing to let them take care of me.

"How long have you known?" Mike asked.

"I had the biopsy the day we went out on our date."

"Jesus." He looked stricken.

"That's why I wasn't feeling well that night. I probably should have canceled, but I'd been looking forward to it so much."

He ran his fingers through his beard, stroking it thoughtfully. I imagined him replaying the night over in his mind, putting the pieces together. Finally making sense of my behavior.

"Why didn't you want to tell me?" he asked.

I rubbed my palms on my fleece-clad thighs as I searched for a way to put my feelings into words and explain myself. "I didn't know at the time how bad it would be—or if it would be bad at all. I was scared and anxious, and I just wanted an escape from all my worries. You were my escape. The one good thing I had going on in my life."

This was an enormous confession for me. I'd just admitted not only my own fears, but how much Mike meant to me. I braced myself as if I expected something terrible to happen—although what, exactly, I wasn't sure.

Amazingly, the world didn't end because I'd shown my vulnerable underbelly. Instead, Mike took my hand, rubbing his calloused thumb over my knuckles.

His touch warmed me all over. I'd missed him this last week—so much. I felt my defensive walls start to crack, the dam holding back my emotions threatening to break and spill out all over the place.

I swallowed and tried to push on. As difficult as talking was, it was easier than silence. "Anyway, then I found out I needed the surgery, and I was relieved the news wasn't worse, but there was still some uncertainty as to what they'd find and how radical the procedure would need to be."

"And you didn't feel like you could tell me any of that?" The hurt in his voice went straight to the pit of my stomach.

"I'm sorry," I said, feeling like a puppy-kicking jerk. He might look like a big, burly, tough guy, but I was starting to understand that underneath Mike's surface beat a soft, squishy, *kind* heart. One I'd completely underestimated.

He frowned, which made me feel even worse. "I don't want you to be sorry. I'm just trying to understand."

I looked down at his hand covering mine. "We were just starting to get to know each other. I didn't think…" I faltered.

He gave my hand a reassuring squeeze. "What?"

"I didn't think you'd want to stick around and take care of me. I didn't think you should even have to make that choice."

"And so you made it for me?"

"I suppose I did. But I was trying to protect myself as much as you. I thought I knew how you'd respond, and I couldn't face the rejection."

He shifted his hand so his fingers were twined with mine. "So you rejected me first."

"Technically, I didn't reject you. I just froze up and stopped answering your texts."

A faint sort of almost-smile curved his mouth. "You ghosted me."

"I did, didn't I?" I'd never ghosted anyone before. There hadn't been a name for it the last time I'd done any dating, back in the Dark Ages before cell phones and social media. Back then, people just "lost" your phone number and stopped calling when they were done with you.

Mike's face settled into his big, grumbly bear frown. "Because you assumed I'd run the other direction as soon as I found out you were sick."

"Yes." It came out as a whisper, I was so reluctant to admit the truth.

He looked down at where our hands were linked, then back up at me. "You don't know me at all, then." His voice was as soft as his eyes.

"Apparently not." In fact, he'd done the exact opposite. Angie had spilled my big secret, the one I'd been protecting and agonizing over, and instead of running away, Mike had run straight to me.

Imagine that.

And now he was holding my hand and looking at me with compassion, which wasn't nearly as bad as pity, because behind it lay affection. He was here, not because he felt sorry for me, but because he cared about me. My gentle giant. My soft mountain of a man. I'd underestimated him so terribly.

I looked down at where our hands were joined, fingers linked and palms pressed together, and it gave me the strength to keep going. "I wanted to tell you, if that means anything. But I was embarrassed—first to tell you the truth, and then because I'd kept it from you for so long."

"You don't need to be embarrassed."

I shook my head because it didn't work that way. Shame couldn't be erased so easily. It was sticky like chewing gum and embedded itself in everything it touched. "Anyway, now you know everything. My secret's out. And you know what a coward I am."

"No, you're not." His voice had turned low and reproachful. "You're brave. You're so incredibly brave that you think you can do everything on your own, take on everyone else's pain on top of your own without ever asking for help. But you don't have to do that. It's okay to let people see you struggle."

"It's really not."

His mouthed twitched into a smile. "It really is. It's okay to let *me* see. I promise I won't hold it against you."

I wanted to believe him. I almost could.

I swallowed, feeling a lump rise in my throat. "Honestly, I didn't think you'd care if I disappeared on you."

"I care."

"That's going to take some getting used to."

"Then I'll keep reminding you."

My heart felt like it was trying to leap out of my chest and attach itself to Mike. "I suppose I owe you an apology—"

"Stop." The way he growled the word raised feverish memories of our night together —the way he'd growled other commands in that very same voice as his searing lips and intoxicating caresses drove me out of my mind.

It felt so far away now, like it had all been a dream. Like something that had happened to someone else's body.

He shook his head, giving me a reproving scowl. "I told you I don't want you to be sorry. What you've been going through, you're allowed to deal with it however you need to. I just don't like to think of you going through it all alone, is all."

"I'm okay," I told him, and it felt good to say the words out loud and mean them for once. "Really."

The cancer was gone, my recovery was progressing without complications, and Mike was here with me. Holding my hand like he wanted to keep it—like he wanted to keep *me*. I was freaking fantastic.

His eyes traced over my face, searching for the truth, and the look of relief that came into his expression made my heart lurch. I'd been wrong about so many things, it seemed.

From the beginning, I'd resisted the idea that Mike could really like me, refusing to let myself believe it because I was so afraid of disappointment. But now I gave in to it. Let down my defenses and accepted that Mike was here because he *wanted* to be.

The relief was dizzying.

His eyes crinkled at the corners in that way I adored. "There is one thing you can do for me though."

"Anything." As long as his eyes kept crinkling at me like that, his wish was my command.

"Let me hang out with you for a while and keep you company."

I smiled in goofy happiness, feeling like a teenager again. "I'd love that."

CHAPTER TWENTY TWO
MIKE

God, I loved Dawn's smile. She hadn't smiled once since she'd opened the door to me, and it had split my heart in two.

Until I'd asked her if I could stay. The way her face broke open in response stitched my heart back together again. It felt like the two of us had been stitched back together again.

She wanted me. She hadn't quite said it straight out like that—I was starting to realize how difficult it was for her to come right out and say what she was feeling—but it was strongly implied. She wanted me around and had only pushed me away because she'd been scared and trying to protect herself. I could understand that. It was something I could work with.

I drank in the sight of her smiling at me in her adorable unicorn getup. The outfit seemed at once out of character for her and yet somehow utterly perfect at the same time. She wore no makeup, which made the traces of pain and fatigue in her face all the more evident. I could tell from her careful movements that she wasn't feeling herself, but also that she wasn't in a tremendous amount of pain, which was a relief.

I hadn't known what to think when Angie said the word *surgery*. It could have been anything on the spectrum from minor and elective to scary and life-threatening, but my brain had immediately gone into panic mode, fearing the worst.

Once Dawn had explained her situation, I'd still been worried for her, but considerably less so. Now that I knew she was going to be okay, I could breathe freely again.

I brought her hand to my lips and enjoyed the way her eyes danced with pleasure. I wanted to kiss more than just her hand, but I figured anything more had better wait. For how long, I had no idea, but I was willing to go as slow as she needed me to.

"Listen," I said, cradling her hand in both of mine. "I need to make something clear so there's no misunderstanding between us."

She looked crestfallen for a split second before she masked her expression, and I realized she thought I was blowing her off. Even now, after everything we'd just said to each other, she was expecting me to disappoint her. It made me wonder how often she'd been disappointed in her life that she'd learned to expect it reflexively.

I reached up to touch her cheek, wanting to reassure her I wasn't going anywhere. "I find you incredibly attractive, and I loved the night we spent together…"

"But?" she prompted when I paused to consider how I wanted to say the next part.

"But that's not all I'm looking for. The truth is, I could use a friend even more than I need a lover. So if you can't have sex while you're recovering—or even if you never want to have sex with me again—I'd still like to be a part of your life. I like being around you. Talking to you. I don't need to have sex to want to be with you."

Relief flooded her face as she gave me another of those heart-stopping smiles. "I think I'll probably want to have sex with you again. Eventually." Her cheeks pinked, and I felt myself matching her smile with one of my own.

"I'm glad to hear it. Because I want to have sex with you too. Eventually."

"I'm supposed to wait eight weeks."

"That's fine," I said, suspecting she needed the extra reassurance. "That's no problem at all. Okay?"

She bit her lip as she nodded. She was so goddamn cute, and I'd missed her so much this last week, I couldn't help but reach for her—carefully, cautious of surgical wounds I couldn't see and not wanting to cause her any pain. One of my hands rested on her shoulder while the other slid into her hair, stirring up the familiar scent of her shampoo.

I leaned in and pressed my lips to her forehead. Taking her soft sigh as encouragement, I moved to her temple, and then her cheek, rubbing my lips back and forth so my beard brushed lightly against her soft skin. I felt her shiver as she strained toward me, wrapping her hands around my neck. She turned her head, her lips searching for mine, and I let out a sigh of my own as our mouths finally met.

I kept the kiss chaste but took my time, my lips lingering tenderly on hers, leaving her with a promise of more good things to come before I pulled away.

That was enough for now. I didn't want to get too carried away, and I was in danger of doing just that if I let myself have more than a closemouthed kiss.

I stood up and started gathering the dirty dishes on the coffee table. "Have you eaten recently? How are you fixed for food?"

"Please don't clean up my mess," she protested, getting to her feet beside me. "I can do it."

I shot her a disapproving glare. "Sit your ass down and let me help you out. Christ, woman. Have you been trying to do everything on your own all this time?"

She sank back down on the couch again. "No, Angie was with me for the first day." Dawn's lips pressed together, but it didn't dim the smile in her eyes. I could tell she was secretly pleased to have me fussing over her, even if she felt like she needed to protest.

"The first day?" I grumbled as I collected all the dirty mugs and water glasses onto the wooden tray I'd moved off the couch. "That's all?" I didn't know much about the surgery she'd just had, but it seemed like the sort of thing that would necessitate help around the house for more than just twenty-four hours.

Her chin tilted stubbornly. "That's all I needed."

"What about your kids? Didn't they help out?"

"They brought me dinner one night."

I shook my head as I carried the tray of dishes into the kitchen. "Let me guess, you told them you were fine and didn't need anything?" I was trying not to resent them for believing her and being only too happy to fuck off back to their own lives when their mother had just had surgery. I probably would have done the exact same thing at their age, but that didn't make it okay.

I could easily picture Dawn all alone in this big house, hiding from everyone and trying to deal with all her problems herself. It had probably killed her to ask Angie to help for even that one day. But the hospital would have required her to have someone drive her home, so she wouldn't have had any choice.

"I *don't* need anything," she insisted, watching me from the couch.

What she needed was someone to spoil her and lavish her with kindness, and I planned to do exactly that. As much as she'd let me anyway.

"You need to let people take care of you when you're supposed to be recuperating," I chided as I transferred the dishes to the sink. "I'll bet your doctor told you to take it easy."

"I have been."

I moved to the refrigerator and pulled it open. "You didn't answer my question about food. Have you eaten?" I surveyed the inside of her fridge, which was well-stocked with staples, as well as an assortment of plastic containers. I pulled one out and peered through the condensation on the clear lid. It looked like some kind of pasta bake or casserole.

"As a matter of fact, I ate before you came over. I'm capable of looking after myself, you know."

I shut the fridge and narrowed my eyes at her. "I'll be the judge of that." There was a dirty container in the sink, so I figured she was probably telling the truth. My eyes landed on the electric kettle sitting on the counter. "Do you like tea?"

"I don't need any tea."

I ignored her and started pulling open cabinets. "I didn't ask if you needed tea. I asked if you like it."

"Yes, I like tea."

"Maybe *I* want some tea."

"Try the cabinet above the mixer."

I pulled it open and found a collection of black and herbal teas. "I'm helping myself to some of this chai. You want anything while I'm at it?"

"Peppermint, please."

While the kettle was heating, I reached for the dish soap and hand-washed all the dishes in the sink. Apparently, Dawn had given up on getting me to quit helping her, because she didn't lodge any further objections. She even directed me where to put everything away while the tea was steeping. By the time it was ready, the kitchen was spotless.

I carried the two steaming mugs to the couch and handed the peppermint one to her. "Careful, it's hot."

"I know how tea works," she grumbled, but the soft smile on her face warmed me through and through.

I sat down beside her carefully, trying not to jostle the couch too much, and blew on the surface of my tea to cool it down.

"Mike?"

Still cradling my mug in both hands, I turned toward her, eyebrows raised.

"Thank you."

I knew she was talking about more than just the tea, and I felt like I'd just won a major victory. Grasping her free hand, I brought it to my lips again, rubbing my whiskers over her knuckles and enjoying the way it made her eyes spark. "Anytime."

"Do you like cooking shows?" she asked, her eyes skittering away bashfully. "There's this one I've been watching on YouTube—Angie got me hooked on it."

"I love cooking shows." I leaned forward to snag the remote off the table and handed it to her. "Show me."

We settled back to watch a charming young woman attempt to replicate Girl Scout cookies. It was both amusing and stressful, and as the show's host veered off task to clean the microwave and tried to reject the assistance of the other kitchen staffers, insisting that she worked better alone when she so clearly needed help, I began to understand why Dawn liked it so much.

When we'd finished our tea, I took Dawn's mug from her and set it on the table. Leaning back again, I draped my arm on the back of the couch and nodded for Dawn to scoot closer, which she did, snuggling up and laying her head on my shoulder. "Comfy?" I asked, and she nodded, letting out a contented sigh.

"Perfect."

Thirty minutes later, when the woman on the TV triumphantly showed off a tray of perfect Thin Mints, Samoas, and Tagalongs, Dawn was fast asleep on my shoulder.

I let the autoplay roll on to the next episode, even though it was getting late and I had work in the morning. The woman was trying to make Bagel Bites in this one, and I wanted to see how it came out. Besides, I was comfy, and I didn't want to wake Dawn.

I'd missed doing stuff like this. Just spending a quiet evening with someone you liked. I couldn't even remember the last time I'd done it. Not since my divorce, I supposed. By the time my marriage ended, most of my close friendships seemed to have fallen away. That was one reason it had been so easy to pick up and leave Columbus. But I hadn't made any new friends since I'd moved back to Chicago—or bothered to look up any old ones. And although I'd dated my fair share since becoming single, it hadn't been the sort of dating that led to cozy nights on the couch watching TV.

This felt like it was exactly what I'd been searching for. *Dawn* felt like what I'd been searching for. I just hoped she let me stick around for a while.

Gently, so as not to disturb her, I laid my hand on her head and breathed in the sweet scent of her hair.

I stayed that way for a long time.

CHAPTER TWENTY THREE
DAWN

"Do you need to sit down? Maybe you should sit down."

Chloe was fussing over me. It was my first day back in the shop, and everyone was fussing. I was trying very hard to let them, but it was honestly torture for me.

"Here, let me get you the stool out of the back."

"Thank you," I said, trying to sound gracious when Chloe returned with the stool a moment later. I settled my butt onto the hard wooden seat to show my appreciation. "I'm fine. Really."

I was so relieved to be out of the house finally, I felt like I could have run a marathon. If I'd thought anyone would let me get away with it, I would have started back to work sooner than the two weeks the doctor recommended. I'd practically been clawing at the walls by the end. Even Mike's regular visits in the evenings and over the weekends hadn't completely mitigated the long, dull days cooped up in the house alone.

He was the reason I was building up a tolerance for being fussed over. Mike had fussed over me more or less constantly for the last week, and I'd found I liked his fussing. Very much.

He'd been coming over after work most nights with dinner for the two of us. Usually Chinese or Indian takeout, but our first weekend together he brought over all the ingredients to make his mother's minestrone.

I wasn't used to having a man cook for me. I'd always done all the cooking in my house, and the kitchen had been more or less my exclusive domain. My impulse to "help" by second-guessing and micromanaging every move Mike made had gotten me banished from my own kitchen with a grumbly order to sit my ass down on the couch and be quiet while he worked.

The minestrone had been divine, and not having to make it myself or clean up afterward had been equally glorious. Not always having to do everything myself had its perks, I was slowly learning.

I'd learned a lot over the last week, mostly to do with Mike. I'd learned he had a sweet tooth to match his sweet personality, and he was a sucker for anything with chocolate and peanut butter. I'd learned he was allergic to shellfish and had a fear of spiders. I'd learned about his job keeping the library system's computers and networks running, how frustrating he found his boss, and that he got frequent tension headaches that could be soothed by running my fingernails over his scalp until he melted like butter in my arms.

Most importantly, I'd learned I liked everything about him. I liked the way his heavy arms wrapped around me, making a perfect space for me to nestle against his broad chest. I liked the way he smelled, and the gruff rumble of his voice. I liked the gentle ways he touched me with his big, rough hands—pressing them into my back as he maneuvered past me in the kitchen, tucking my hair behind my ear, holding my hand in his as we watched TV together.

It was possible I more than liked him, but I firmly refused to let my mind travel too far down that path. It was too soon to be thinking like that.

"No one believes you when you say you're fine," Angie retorted, snapping me out of my thoughts of Mike. "Although I have to admit, you look pretty great, considering."

"That's because I am pretty great." I hopped off the stool and moved to straighten a display of Angie's handmade stitch markers. Angie and Chloe had taken good care of the store in my absence, but I liked things *just so*, and there were a lot of little tasks I was itching to dig my fingers into. "Modern medicine is a marvel. To think they can use a robot and with only a few tiny incisions remove a person's whole uterus with hardly any scarring at all. It's almost like magic."

"Certainly wasn't like that in my day," Linda said from her seat by the window. "Used to be they'd slit you wide open, take your ovaries for good measure, and slap you on hormone therapy as soon as look at you."

I shuddered at the thought of open abdominal surgery as I rearranged some of the books that had gotten out of order. "Thank goodness for progress."

"There may not be visible scars, but there's plenty of scarring on the inside," Angie reminded me with a scolding look. "That's why it's important that you take it easy."

Chloe's forehead wrinkled. "If the incisions are so small, how do they get your uterus out?"

"They cut it up into bits and remove it through the vagina," I explained, and Chloe's face pulled into an expression of horror. "Yes, that's exactly how I feel. It's really best not to think about it too much."

I'd been experiencing some odd feelings of disassociation from my own body during my recovery. On the one hand, my visible wounds were extremely minor, which made it easy sometimes to forget I'd had surgery. But I was also conscious that internally things weren't quite right. There'd been a good deal of bleeding for one thing, especially in the first week. And although I'd been spared the pain of open abdominal surgery, I'd been left feeling vaguely bruised and tender.

It reminded me a little of the way I'd felt after childbirth, but without so much obvious physical trauma. I'd experienced a similarly odd sensation that my body was not my own after each of my boys was born. Instead of being the comfortable home I was used to, my body felt like something damaged, unfamiliar, and disobedient to my wishes.

I knew the sensation would pass with time—it had before. The scars would heal, and I'd get used to my new normal. But I was impatient.

I wanted to feel like my old self again. Now that I had Mike, I wanted to be able to *enjoy* Mike while feeling 100 percent myself again. It was wonderful how good he was at taking care of me, but I didn't want to be taken care of. I wanted to relive the hot, X-rated night we'd spent together.

More than that, I wanted to *feel* like reliving our hot, X-rated night together.

As attracted as I was to Mike, sex held about as much appeal to me as mountain climbing right now. Not only did I have zero interest in it, but it was difficult to even *imagine* having an interest in it. It seemed like something I'd wanted to do in another life.

I tried to tell myself this was just a normal, natural part of the healing process. Someone had just mucked about in my internal sex organs with surgical implements. Of course my sex drive would be negatively affected. Of course that part of me would feel deadened and defective right now.

It was only temporary. At least I hoped so. I couldn't help worrying that the damage to my sex drive was a permanent side effect. What if I never felt like myself again? What if my hysterectomy had turned me into a sexless old crone? I knew such fears were irrational, but knowing that didn't make them disappear.

"Did we ever get that shipment from the new dyer in Texas?" I asked, pushing aside my negative thoughts for the moment.

"Last week," Chloe said. "It's still in the back. I thought you'd want to look it over before we set it out."

"You're right, I do." I started for the storeroom, but Angie held up a hand to halt me. "I'll get it. You're not supposed to be lifting anything heavy, remember?"

"I wouldn't call yarn heavy," I groused, but let her fetch the box for me. See? I was getting better. Letting people do things for me.

Angie brought the box out and we all gathered around to *ooh* and *ahh* over the new yarn. I'd ordered a selection of colorways from a small-batch dyer I'd fallen in love with on Instagram. The colors were rich and vibrant, and I was pleased with the combinations I'd chosen. Each colorway was inspired by a character from classic literature, with names like Mr. Darcy's Passion and Lady Dedlock's Secret.

"I love this one," Chloe said, cuddling a hank of variegated blues and aquas.

"They're even prettier in person." I'd ordered a couple samples to check for quality, but until now, I'd only seen most of the colorways in pictures on the dyer's website. I reached for a hank of navy blue and soft purples called Captain Wentworth's Agony and turned it over in my hand, feeling for hidden knots. "We should wind a hank and knit up a swatch."

I always tried to do quality spot checks whenever I got a shipment from a smaller supplier—especially new suppliers. Sometimes you'd get a batch with a lot of knots or with dye lots that didn't match, and I liked to make sure I wasn't selling my customers a subpar product. After I'd worked with a vendor for a while, I could get a feel for whether they had good quality control or whether I needed to carefully inspect every single shipment.

"Where do you want to put it?" Chloe asked.

I pursed my lips as I surveyed the inventory space in the store, which was packed close to capacity. "I think we can consolidate the Manos and free up a cubby. That should be enough space for now. If we need to, we can hold back some stock."

"I'll get to work on that," Chloe volunteered, moving toward the shelf of Manos del Uruguay.

"And you can knit the swatch," Angie said, shooting me a pointed look. "It'll be a nice, restful, first-day-back-at-work task." She bent to dig through the box of new yarn. "Which color do you want to play with?"

"I think I'll stick with Captain Wentworth here." I carried it over to the yarn winder and pried off the label before picking apart the knots holding the hank together. Once I'd gotten it untied, I fit it over the yarn swift and fed the end into the winder.

I loved my yarn winder. It was made of high-quality maple with Swiss gears. Sturdy, ergonomic, quiet, and fast, it was worth its weight in gold. As a hobbyist knitter, I'd coveted a winder like this for years but hadn't been able to justify the cost until I'd opened my shop.

I was in the middle of winding my hank of Captain Wentworth's Agony, and pondering a new knitting project I could make with it, when the shop bell rang. I heard Angie greet someone warmly and then call out, "Dawn, you've got a gentleman caller!"

I glanced over my shoulder and felt my chest warm at the sight of Mike. He was holding a beautiful purple orchid plant, and as soon as his gaze locked on mine, the skin around his eyes crinkled in a smile. The warmth in my chest spread out through my limbs and seemed to fill up the space between us as he came toward me.

"Hey, you," I said, presenting my cheek for a kiss. "What are you doing here?"

He pressed a hand to the small of my back and obliged me by rubbing his lips lightly against my face, raising goose bumps down the length of my arms. He'd long since figured out that the sensation of his bristly beard on my skin drove me to distraction and used it against me as often as possible. It was yet another thing I liked about him.

"I was out at one of the north side branches this morning, and I thought I'd drop in on my way back to the office to see how your first day back at work was going." He set the orchid on the counter beside the yarn swift. "That's for you."

"It's beautiful, thank you." I cocked my head, indicating he should lean in so I could return his kiss. When he did, I pushed my face into his beard, rubbing back and forth until his shoulders twitched with a shiver. I wasn't the only one who enjoyed being nuzzled. "My first day back is going excellently."

"You're not working yourself too hard?" His lips pulled down in a frown as he studied me for signs of fatigue.

I glanced over his shoulder to where Angie was helping Chloe make space for the new yarn and pretending not to pay attention to us. "Angie wouldn't let me, even if I tried."

Mike gave an approving nod. "Good." His eyes fell on the ball winder and swift. "What's this contraption?"

"It's for winding yarn."

Three deep creases formed on his forehead as he examined the hank of yarn on the swift. "It doesn't automatically come in balls already?"

I resumed winding as I explained. "Some yarn does. But luxury fibers tend to come in a hank like this, and they need to be wound before they can be used in a project. We offer complimentary winding in the store, but a lot of avid fiber crafters end up purchasing their own swift and winder for use at home."

"Why add the extra step? Why don't yarn companies just sell them all in balls for convenience?"

"To prevent wear and tear prior to sale, mostly. Winding puts strain on the yarn— particularly the finer, more delicate fibers like merino wool, alpaca, or cashmere. If it's left to sit around in tight skeins for a long time, it can leave kinks and creases in the yarn or create tension problems that cause inconsistent gauge. It's also easier to ship and store hanks. They take up less space and don't roll away like skeins do."

"Huh." Mike scratched his beard as he bent down for a closer look at the winder. "That's an impressive piece of craftsmanship. The whole setup reminds me of a Rube Goldberg machine."

"I never thought about it, but it is a bit like that, isn't it?" The yarn pulled free of the swift as I finished winding the last of the hank, and I carefully dislodged my newly created yarn cake, tucking in the free end. When I was through, I reached for Mike's wrist to read his watch. "It's almost lunchtime. Do you want to go get something to eat?"

His face fell. "I wish I could, but I need to get back to the office and check in or my boss'll be breathing down my neck, accusing me of goofing off."

I reached up to stroke his cheek, running my fingernails through his beard. "I'm sorry."

He shivered and grabbed my hand, bringing it to his lips. "I'm sorry too. We'll do it another day. I promise."

"Sounds good."

"I better go. What time are you getting home? I can bring dinner over."

"Actually..." I lifted my eyes to his hopefully. "I was thinking I could come to your place after work. I've never seen where you live."

His forehead creases returned. "Why would you want to do that? It's not much to look at."

"I just want to see where you spend your time."

He leaned in closer, lowering his voice so we wouldn't be overheard. "I've been spending most of my time at your place."

"Do you not want me to see it?" I frowned at him, wondering if there was a reason he didn't want me to come over.

He shook his head. "Nah, it's nothing like that. Well...maybe it's a little like that. It's not very nice, and I guess I'm kind of embarrassed for you to see it."

"I don't want you to be embarrassed. I promise I won't judge. I just want to know you better."

His eyes grew soft. "Yeah, okay. If that's what you really want."

"That's what I really want." I smiled up at him. "I can be the one to pick up dinner tonight for a change. Say around seven o'clock?"

"Deal. I'll text you the address." He leaned in for another cheek kiss, this one just a glancing peck. "I'll see you then."

Smiling giddily, I watched him call out a goodbye to Angie on his way out the door.

"Is that your boyfriend?" Chloe asked, wide-eyed, after the door had shut behind him. "He's yummy."

My smile grew wider. "He is yummy, isn't he? And yes, he's my boyfriend." I hadn't said as much out loud before, but it didn't feel like a presumption.

Mike Pilota was my boyfriend.

I felt a fresh wave of giddiness at the thought.

"Look at you," Angie said, grinning. "I haven't seen you this gaga over a man since...well, since you were gaga for that man in high school."

I rolled my eyes as I went to fetch my favorite ChiaoGoo needles to start my Captain Wentworth swatch. "This is totally different."

Her eyebrows waggled suggestively. "I should hope so." She came closer, lowering her voice. "You're not mad then, are you? That I told him you'd had surgery?"

"No, I'm not." I reached for her hand, giving it a squeeze to illustrate how not-mad I was. I'd been annoyed at first, but I certainly couldn't argue with the results of her meddling. "I'm grateful. I probably would have let him get away if you hadn't intervened."

"Yeah, I figured." The corner of her mouth quirked. "Everyone needs a little fairy godmother intervention from time to time."

"Just don't let it go to your head," I warned, and she laughed.

My phone vibrated in my pocket and I pulled it out to check it. Mike had texted me his address. *See you tonight*, he wrote along with it, and I felt my heart go *ping* in my chest.

"Look at you, you're like a teenage girl." Angie shook her head, smiling, as she went to go help Chloe.

If only I felt more like one, everything would be perfect.

CHAPTER TWENTY FOUR
MIKE

I surveyed my apartment nervously. I'd tidied up when I got home, but no amount of cleaning could disguise the overwhelming bleakness of its appearance. I knew Dawn had said she wouldn't judge, but *I* judged myself for living such a sad existence. How could she help but do the same?

Maybe I was overreacting. Letting the feelings of dissatisfaction and depression I'd experienced while living here color my perception. I tried to view it through a more objective lens, the way a stranger would.

Yeah, no. That didn't do anything to improve the place. It was impossible to imagine a stranger walking in here and seeing anything other than the pitiful home of a sad person who lived a depressing life.

But there was no avoiding it. If I wanted Dawn in my life, I'd have to let her see how I lived. I'd have to let her know me. *All* of me.

And I wanted her in my life, dammit.

A knock at the door pulled me out of my reverie, and I went to answer it. My mood lifted immediately at the sight of Dawn standing on my threshold with a paper bag of carryout.

"It smells like bread!" she announced, grinning at me in delight.

It took me a second to realize what she meant. "Oh, yeah, that's the sandwich shop downstairs. The smell drifts up into the whole building." I'd gotten so used to it I couldn't even smell it anymore, and I'd forgotten how noticeable it was at first.

"That's why you always smell faintly like fresh bread!"

"I guess it is, yeah." I hadn't realized the smell clung to me so much that she'd noticed it.

"I love it. It smells amazing, just like you. Hello, by the way." She stepped forward to kiss me, curling her free hand around my neck as she tilted her head up.

I wound both arms around her waist, pulling her close, and let my lips linger on hers, enjoying the sensation. I'd been reluctant to show too much affection when I'd stopped by her shop earlier, so I made up for it now, kissing her until she grew impatient and squirmed out of my grasp.

"Are you going to invite me in or are we just going to make out on your doorstep all night?" Her voice was lightly teasing as she smiled up at me.

"I guess you can come in, seeing as you brought dinner and all." I took the bag from her and stepped back to admit her into my dismal abode. "Don't be too impressed now. It only got honorable mention in *Chicago* magazine's list of the city's ugliest apartments."

"Oh stop. It's perfectly nice." She gave me a playful tap in the stomach, and I flexed automatically. Her hand idled on my abdomen, her fingertips gliding over the muscles there. "Show-off."

I gave her a wolfish grin. "You like it."

"I do."

I started to reach for her again, but she glided out of range, smiling as she surveyed my living room and pitiful excuse for a kitchen.

"My god, it's so clean. Is it always this spotless?"

I shrugged. "More or less." I hadn't had to do that much cleaning when I got home tonight because I tended to keep the place pretty neat. There wasn't all that much to clean, so it was easy.

"Very impressive."

"You want a beer?" I asked as I set the takeout down on the folding card table that doubled as a dinette. "Afraid I don't have any wine." I made a mental note to pick up a couple bottles of the red I'd seen her drinking at home.

"A beer would be divine."

I went to the fridge and got out two beers while Dawn unpacked the takeout, which turned out to be Indian. We sat down to eat—butter chicken for both of us—and catch each other up on our respective days. I was pleased to hear her first day back at work had been uneventful, and it sounded like she'd mostly taken it easy.

After we were done eating, she helped me clean up. The kitchen was too small for two people, so while I finished putting away the leftovers, she entertained herself by poking around the small apartment. Snooping, really, but I didn't mind. That was the whole point of inviting her over, after all. To let her get to know me better.

"Is this where you play video games?" she asked, sitting down at the computer.

"That's right." I shut the fridge and went to stand behind her, resting my hands on her shoulders. "This is where the magic happens."

"It's a nice setup. I like this keyboard."

It was a gaming keyboard with multi-colored backlighting effects. I usually kept it set to a relatively unobtrusive red, but when I leaned forward and tapped a function key, it switched to a rainbow spectrum.

"Ooh! I love that!" Dawn exclaimed. "I wish my keyboard lit up like that."

"It's for gaming with the lights out so you can see the screen better but still read the keyboard. Also, it's cool."

"Do you game with the lights out?"

"Not usually, no." I wasn't quite that much of a cat-asser. Despite the high number of hours I sank into my hobby, my playstyle was more of a casual gamer than a powergamer. I didn't love grinding or obsessing about my stats, and I didn't belong to one of the big, active guilds. I preferred soloing and exploring the map to raids and dungeon runs, and I enjoyed making new characters to try out their abilities more than maxing out my existing ones.

"Can I see your characters?" Dawn asked.

"Why?" I responded, startled by the question.

She tipped her head back to look at me, smiling. "Curiosity."

"All right." I reached for the mouse and clicked on the League of Magecraft shortcut.

"We had an Xbox when the boys were in high school," Dawn said. "But they mostly played first-person shooters. They never got into role-playing games, which I would have preferred, frankly."

"I've never been much of a console guy. My parents refused to buy an Atari when my sister and I were kids, but they were willing to get us a computer. So I grew up playing games on my Commodore 64, and I guess it stuck."

"I used to play Oregon Trail on my Apple II," she admitted.

I grinned and gave her shoulder an affectionate squeeze. "Fancy-pants."

"Is that why you went into IT? Because you liked computers?"

"I guess, yeah. I sort of fell into it accidentally. I was working in sales for a window and siding company and I was the only one in the office who knew anything about computers, so I ended up troubleshooting whenever there was a problem. Eventually, they offered me a job doing all their desktop support."

"I'll bet you were good at sales, with your charm."

"Not really." I'd never liked it much. I hadn't minded helping people when they needed something, but I'd never been comfortable pressuring anyone to buy stuff they didn't need, and my sales numbers had showed it. It had been a huge relief when I was able to move into a support job instead.

The character screen came up, and Dawn leaned forward for a closer look, using the mouse to click through them. "Wow, you have a lot of characters."

"Yeah, I like to try all the powers out. I'm kind of a perma-lowbie by nature."

"What does that mean?"

"It means I like the early part of the game better than the endgame. I'd rather keep rolling up new characters than max out my existing ones."

"You seem to have a preference for melee classes over ranged classes."

I stared down at her in surprise. "How do you know what a melee class is?"

She tossed a smug look over her shoulder. "I may have played a little D&D in college. That's what these kinds of games are based on, isn't it?"

"Aren't you full of surprises?" I bent to kiss the top of her head.

"I don't know why it's surprising. I was a nerd, remember?"

Funny how in high school I used to think Dawn and I were so different because I was a jock and she was one of the smart kids. But we'd both played computer games and RPGs, which wasn't something any of my so-called friends had been into. If I'd been able to look deeper than what cliques we each belonged to, I might have realized back then how much Dawn and I actually had in common.

"Did you want to play?" she asked me. "I wouldn't mind watching if you did."

Much as I appreciated the offer, I had other plans for this evening. "Maybe another time." I took her by the hand and gently tugged her up out of my computer chair. "Come sit on the couch with me. I'm in the mood to watch our favorite chef try to make Twix and have a breakdown."

Dawn came easily into my arms. "You're not sick of watching a cooking show? Really? You can tell me if you are."

"Are you kidding? I love that show. It's soothing. Besides…" I bent my head to nuzzle the spot under her ear where I knew she was extra sensitive. "It's easier to cuddle with you while watching TV than playing video games." If I was lucky, I might even be able to get her to give me one of those scalp massages I liked so much.

She laughed as my beard tickled her neck, but she didn't squirm away. In fact, she squirmed closer. "I've never known a man as cuddly as you. You're like a touch-starved teddy bear."

I pulled my head back to grin at her. "And I've never known a woman who liked my beard as much as you."

Truthfully, I couldn't get enough of touching her. But since I was trying to be mindful of the fact she was still healing, I was pretty limited in how much and where I could touch her. It was driving me to distraction, in the best possible way. Eight weeks was a long time, but I didn't have any problem with waiting. If anything, the anticipation only made it more exciting. I felt like I used to when I was a kid looking forward to my birthday. Just thinking about the cake and presents in my future made me happy, even if they were still weeks away.

It simply required some adjustments to the way I usually approached my relationships with women. And that meant touching Dawn as much as I could without letting things get too hot and heavy. I worried about getting carried away and making her feel pressured or guilty, so I tried to keep my affection safely outside the bathing suit area. But that still left me a whole world of places I could touch her. Her hands, her shoulders, her neck, her gorgeous legs, her cute little feet. Not to mention her beautiful mouth. So long as I didn't let our kisses get so heated that I lost my head, I could kiss her all night long.

We settled onto the couch and I pulled her up against me as I reached for the TV remote.

"What's that?" she asked, nudging a big fat book under my coffee table with her toes. "It looks like a college textbook."

Cursing myself for not hiding it better, I pretended to be preoccupied by the task of navigating the YouTube menu. "Yeah, it is." I could only hope she'd lose interest when I didn't volunteer any more information.

Instead, she leaned forward and pulled it out for a better look. "*Applied Probability and Statistics,*" she read aloud. "This looks brand-new." She turned a questioning look on me.

My first instinct was to lie. Make up a story about my sister or a friend leaving their book here. But I quickly rejected that impulse. For one thing, a lie like that would trip me up later. But for another, I didn't want to lie to Dawn.

I was embarrassed to admit I didn't have a degree, but I was also tired of hiding it from her. If this thing between us was going to go anywhere, she'd find out about my online classes eventually. It occurred to me maybe I'd left the book out on purpose. Maybe it was my subconscious forcing me to fess up.

"Mike?" She was still waiting for me to explain.

"I'm, uh…" I rubbed a hand over the back of my neck. "I'm taking some college courses online."

"I didn't know that."

I avoided looking at her. "I guess I forgot to mention it."

"Probability and statistics…that can't be for fun."

"No, definitely not for fun. I'm finishing up my degree."

"Your master's degree?"

"My bachelor's." My shoulders were as tense as bowstrings, waiting for her to judge me for my academic failings and find me wanting.

"Good for you," was all she said.

"Uh huh." I still wouldn't look at her. I was too afraid I'd see disappointment in her eyes.

She pushed the book back under the table. "It must be hard, working full-time and taking college courses."

"I just started." I hadn't even cracked the book open yet. To be honest, I was dreading it. The sight of that textbook had brought up all sorts of memories from my last foray into college-level courses, and all the reasons I'd quit the first time. I was feeling a lot less confident than I had been when I'd signed up.

"Well, I think it's impressive."

I let myself look at Dawn finally, studying her to see if she was telling the truth or just trying to make me feel better.

She lifted a hand to my face, cupping my cheek. "I think *you're* impressive."

"Because I dropped out of college?" I couldn't keep the incredulous tone out of my voice.

Her mouth pulled into a frown. "Did you think I'd care about that? Because I don't. I'm sure you had your reasons, and it doesn't change how I see about you."

"Really?" I looked into her eyes, expecting to see some evidence of disappointment or displeasure, but it wasn't there.

"Of course not. College doesn't have anything to do with intelligence." She pulled me in for a soft kiss. "I think you're brilliant."

My parents had never let me forget how disappointed they were that I hadn't finished college. Especially my dad, who'd taken every opportunity over the years to remind me how much I'd let him down. Even Christine hadn't been able to hide her surprise when she found out. She'd tried to push me into taking night classes so I could earn more money, and the more she pushed, the more I'd resisted. We'd ended up having a big fight about it, and after that she'd never mentioned it again. But the bad feelings had lingered as an unspoken sore spot between us—one of many that built up over the years.

I was so used to being made to feel like a failure that I'd come to expect it. But maybe it wasn't that big a deal. Maybe I'd built it up in my head into something much worse than it actually was. Maybe I was being stupid, and it didn't matter at all.

"I can't even imagine going back to school at our age," Dawn said, twining her fingers with mine. "I think it's brave."

I shrugged, unused to taking compliments like that. I was accustomed to women complimenting my appearance, or my manners, or even my skills in the bedroom. But no one ever called me brave or thought I was brilliant. "Come here." I hooked my hand around the back of Dawn's neck so I could kiss her properly.

She melted against me as her lips parted, inviting my tongue to slide against hers. The taste of her mouth, the gentle scrape of her fingernails over my scalp, the willing warmth of her body in my arms, all of it acted like a supercharged healing potion, washing away all my tension and troubles. I could feel all my status bars filling up to max.

She was the cure for everything that ailed me.

Our proper kiss grew hotter and heavier, and I started to feel dizzy from wanting her so bad. Before I got carried away and pushed too far, I broke it off.

"Are we going to watch TV or what?" I grumbled, shifting to adjust the raging hard-on in my pants.

Her eyes locked on mine. Her cheeks were flushed and her breathing heavy, and when her pink lips parted, for a second I had the distinct impression she was going to say "or what." Instead she pressed her lips together again, shaking her head slightly as she reached for the remote. "Which one did you say you wanted to watch tonight?" she asked, putting the remote in my hand and shifting away from me slightly.

"The one where they make Twix."

I navigated to the episode and pushed play before leaning forward to set the remote on the table. When I leaned back again, I pulled Dawn toward me, settling her up against me. She fit perfectly, like she was made to be there, her head resting on my shoulder and my fingers curled around her hip.

As we watched the woman on TV attempt to temper chocolate for her homemade Twix bars, I realized this was the happiest I'd ever felt in this apartment. It didn't even seem ugly to me anymore.

Somehow Dawn made the place homier just by being in it.

"Something's different about you," my sister said the next time I met her for lunch at Ernie's.

"I got a haircut last week?" I offered. It was the exact same haircut I'd been getting for the last four months, but I figured maybe that's what she was talking about.

Kelly frowned at me as she reached across the table to steal one of my french fries. "No, it's not that. You're acting different."

I pushed my plate closer to her. "Different how?"

"Happier. You're smiling more. Actually…now that I'm looking at you, you've kinda got a glow. Are you pregnant?"

I rolled my eyes at my sister. "Yeah, that's it. You guessed it."

She helped herself to another fry and pointed it at me. "Seriously, what's going on with you? Why so happy, big brother? Did something happen?"

I lowered my eyes to the patty melt on my plate. "I've been seeing someone." I didn't know why I felt so bashful admitting it. Maybe because I knew my sister would make a big deal out of it.

It *was* a big deal—or at least it felt like it to me—but I didn't want anything jinxing it. This thing with Dawn still felt precarious, like if I made one wrong move she'd realize she'd made a mistake and it would all fall apart.

Kelly leaned forward excitedly. "Really? Do tell."

"It's someone I knew in high school. Remember Dawn, who used to work with me at Pizza My Heart?"

"Not really."

I reached for another napkin before picking up my patty melt. "Well, we ran into each other again. She owns the knitting store where I got that afghan kit for Mom."

"How long's this been going on?"

"Few weeks." I bit into my patty melt, hoping this was the last of her questions.

She watched me, waiting until I'd finished chewing. "Am I gonna get to meet her?"

I set my sandwich down and reached for my iced tea. "You've already met her, a few times, when you came into the pizza place."

"Okay, but am I gonna get to meet her sometime this millennium?"

I eyed my sister over my iced tea. "Do you want to meet her?"

Outside of high school, Kelly had never met any of my previous girlfriends until things were serious enough for me to bring them home to Chicago to meet my family —which had only happened twice, when I was about to get married. But I hadn't lived in the same city as my sister in all that time. Sharing my life with her was uncharted territory for us.

She gave me one of her patented *don't be stupid* looks. "Of course I want to meet her if you like her."

I contemplated this while I bit into my patty melt again. So far, Dawn and I had been keeping ourselves to ourselves. I told myself it was because we were still in the first blush of our relationship, that part when you want to spend all your time together without having to share the other person with anyone else.

Dawn hadn't raised the subject of me meeting her sons, and I sure as hell wasn't going to push for it. I didn't even know if they knew I existed, or that their mother was seeing anyone. From what I'd been able to gather, they were both pretty caught up in their own lives. Dawn didn't seem to hear from them much, and I suspected they didn't have a clue what was going on in her life these days.

That was fine with me—not that Dawn's kids didn't seem to have time for her, that part seemed kind of shitty—but that they didn't know about me yet. I was in no hurry to rush that introduction. I couldn't imagine it being anything other than awkward at best, and downright unpleasant at worst.

And it wasn't like I'd mentioned Dawn to my mom yet. Mostly because it was so hard to talk to my mom about anything. I found it difficult to imagine she'd care in her current state of mind. I supposed I was also dreading the thought of introducing Dawn to my mom. She'd met her before, back when we were in high school, but my mom was a different person these days. I wasn't sure what kind of reception she'd give Dawn.

But Kelly was a different matter. I could see Dawn and Kelly getting on like a house on fire. Maybe a little too well, in fact. My sister would undoubtedly trot out every embarrassing story in her arsenal just to make me squirm. And yeah, I wanted Dawn to know me—all of me, including meeting my sister and hearing all my humiliating family stories—but it seemed a little too soon to put Dawn through that, unless I wanted her to run for the hills. I needed to take it in stages.

"It's still early days," I told my sister. "I'll let you know."

After our lunch, I thought about what Kelly had said, about me looking happier and smiling more. I hadn't realized it was so obvious, but I definitely felt happier than I'd been in months, and it was all due to Dawn.

For the first time since I'd come back to Chicago, I felt like I had a life here. Dawn had even helped me pick out a few things to spruce up my apartment. Nothing major, just an odd item or two to brighten it up and add some variety to the space. To make it feel more like home.

There were fabric panels for the windows now, a new cushion for the couch, and a soft chenille blanket that Dawn liked to snuggle up under when she came over. But my favorite addition was a League of Magecraft poster she'd found on Etsy, illustrated in the style of a 1950s travel ad, which she'd helped me frame.

I never would have thought to do any of it—or bothered to, even I'd thought of it—but I had to admit it made the place more appealing.

The thing that made the most difference though, was having Dawn in it with me.

Now that she knew about the classes I was taking, she made sure I got all the time I needed to study. Fortunately, I'd found I could study just as easily with her around. I'd bring my books over to her place in the evenings after work—or she'd come over to my place—and I'd do my assigned reading on the couch next to her while she knit or read a book of her own. On Saturdays while she was at the store, I'd study and work on class assignments all day until she closed up the shop. Then we'd meet up in the evening and cook together or go out to a restaurant.

I'd introduced her to Taj's Indian restaurant and we'd become regulars as soon as she tasted their butter chicken. Likewise, she introduced me to some of her favorite places: her favorite diner to get breakfast on the weekends, her favorite coffee shop near the store, her favorite cash-and-carry barbecue joint. She knew the city better than I did after my thirty-year absence, and I enjoyed getting to know Chicago again through her eyes. She even surprised me with Cubs tickets she'd gotten from a season ticket holder friend—in the upper rows of the field box with a great view of home plate—and took me on my first visit to Wrigley Field since I was a kid.

Everything between us was perfect. So perfect I got scared sometimes that it couldn't last. Nothing could stay this good, could it? Part of me was always waiting for the dark clouds to roll in and spoil a sunny day.

But I tried my best to push those kinds of worries aside. Things were great between us. If I didn't screw it up, maybe they'd even stay that way.

"Are we really making our own sprinkles?" I asked Dawn as I surveyed the ingredients laid out on her kitchen counter. "Couldn't we just use store-bought?"

We were attempting to make homemade Pop-Tarts. Dawn had found a recipe on the internet that seemed similar to the one we'd seen on that YouTube cooking show, and we were trying them out for ourselves.

Dawn shot me a disapproving look. "Of course we are, otherwise what's the point? Do you want it to be homemade or not?"

I put up my hands in surrender. "Fine."

She bit her lip as she read through the recipe she'd printed out. It was several pages long. "Maybe we'll just make one color of sprinkles though, instead of five. I don't have enough baking sheets for that many colors." Her eyes were bright and excited, and I adored her so much it made my heart feel too big for my chest.

As I stood there in her kitchen, surrounded by Pop-Tart makings, I felt an incredible sense of belonging, as if I were finally where I was meant to be. Not so much here in this house, but with Dawn. By her side. Wherever she was, that was where I wanted to be.

It had taken me thirty years to figure it out—that's how dense I was. But at least I'd gotten here eventually. I knew what I wanted. And what I wanted was Dawn.

"I think that'll be fine," I told her. "Who needs more than one color of sprinkle? It's not like we're serving them to the queen."

Dawn's mouth curled in amusement. "Do you think the queen eats Pop-Tarts?"

"She might if they're homemade."

My phone started vibrating in my pocket and I slipped it out, expecting it to be another spam call, which was all I ever seemed to get.

It wasn't spam; it was my ex-wife.

CHAPTER TWENTY FIVE
DAWN

"Sorry, I need to take this," Mike said, frowning at his phone. He threw me an apologetic look as he stepped outside the back door before answering it.

I couldn't help wondering who it could be. Whoever it was, he didn't seem happy to hear from them. But it was apparently someone he felt obligated to talk to. And whatever conversation they were having, he didn't want me to overhear.

I tried not to let that bother me. Mike was an intensely private person. He'd been gradually letting down some of his walls for me as we got to know each other better, but it was a slow process I was trying not to rush. There were parts of his life he was still reluctant to talk about. Like his parents. And his past relationships. And his life in Columbus. And his work.

I shook my head. I was probably making nothing into something. For all I knew it was a work call, and he simply hadn't wanted to bore me with it.

Glancing out the kitchen window, I saw him pacing across the deck out back, rubbing his head. He seemed upset. Whatever it was, I hoped it wasn't about his mother.

I decided to go ahead and start the dough for the Pop-Tarts. There was a lot of prep work required for this recipe. If something had happened that meant Mike wouldn't be able to make the Pop-Tarts tonight, the dough would keep in the fridge so we could finish another time.

As I worked, I kept glancing out the window. I didn't want to seem like I was spying, but I was worried about him. After a few minutes, he sat down on one of the Adirondack chairs, but instead of leaning back he stayed hunched forward with his elbows on his knees and his head cradled in one hand. He seemed to be doing more listening than talking. Occasionally I could hear the soft rumble of his voice, too indistinct to make out any words.

A full thirty minutes passed before he came inside again. I'd already finished putting together the pastry dough and was wrapping it up to chill.

"Sorry about that," Mike said. "I didn't mean to leave you to do it all on your own."

"There's still plenty left to do." I put the dough in the fridge and turned to face him. "Is everything all right?"

He gave me a smile that didn't quite reach his eyes. "Yeah, it's nothing."

I recognized that tone. It was his *I don't want to talk about it* tone. I considered letting it go, but if something was wrong, I wanted to know about it so I could try to help.

I closed the distance between us, slipping my hands around his waist. He welcomed me into his arms willingly, which I took as a good sign.

"It didn't seem like nothing," I said quietly. I felt him stiffen, but I only held him tighter. "It wasn't about your mom, was it?"

"No, nothing like that." He kissed my temple and blew out a long breath. "It was my ex-wife. Christine."

I nodded but didn't say anything. I just kept holding him, waiting to see if he'd volunteer anything else. He didn't talk about his marriages much, and I'd never felt comfortable pushing the subject.

"Her mom's going into hospice," he said finally. "She needed a shoulder to cry on."

I tilted my head up to look into his eyes, which were dark and troubled. "I'm sorry. That's so hard."

He shrugged. "She's been fighting breast cancer for a couple years."

"That's what took my mother."

His arms tightened around me and he kissed my temple again. "I'm sorry. I didn't mean to bring the mood down when we're supposed to be having fun tonight."

"I don't care about that. Is Christine okay?"

"Not really. She just made the decision today. I think she's known for a while it was coming though. It's a shame. Her mom's a nice lady."

I rested my head against his chest, giving him an extra squeeze. "She was your family."

"Yeah. She was." He dropped his head, resting it on mine for a moment. "Anyways, there's nothing I can do about it, and we've got Pop-Tarts to make."

"We really don't have to do that tonight. It can wait."

He unclasped my hands from behind his back and slipped out of my arms, moving to the counter. "No way. I've been looking forward to this all week."

"Are you sure?" I asked, biting my lip.

His eyes met mine, clear and earnest. "Positive. I could use the distraction."

I nodded and went to get the strawberries out of the fridge. "All right then. Let's get started on the filling."

"Thanks for being so understanding tonight."

It was hours later, and Mike and I were curled up on my couch in a strawberry Pop-Tart coma. I snuggled closer, pressing my face into his throat. "You mean because you're so bad at rolling out pastry dough? You'll get the hang of it eventually."

I felt his chest rumble with a quiet laugh. "You know I was talking about Christine."

I had known that, but I didn't feel like I'd done anything that required his gratitude. "Did you think I'd be jealous? That your ex called you to talk about her dying mother?"

"I guess jealousy doesn't really seem like your style."

"It's not."

195

"Still, most people wouldn't be thrilled to have their boyfriend's ex-wife calling and ruining their Saturday night plans."

It was the first time I'd heard him use the word *boyfriend* in reference to himself. I felt something squeeze around my heart. "Nothing got ruined," I told him. "And even if it had, I'm not just here for the good times." I lifted my head to look him in the eye. "I want to know what's going on with you—good and bad. As much as you're willing to share. I can take it."

His eyes skated away—my big bashful, grumbly bear—but his arms tightened around me, pulling me on top of him. As my incisions had healed, Mike had gradually gotten less cautious about touching me. At first he'd seemed afraid even to embrace me too tightly, treating me like a piece of handblown glass that might break apart in his hands. But over time he'd grown bolder as he saw me returning to normal activities.

"It's funny, isn't it, how things work out?" His breath warmed the top of my head as he spoke. "You and me running into each other all these years later and reconnecting."

"Mmm." I sighed as his hand stroked up my back. "Who would have thought mousy, nerdy Dawn Czworniak would ever end up with Mike Pilota, the coolest, most popular guy at Taft High?"

He grunted in protest. "I was a douchebag. You were way too good for me."

I made a small scoffing sound. "Sure."

"I'm serious." His fingers squeezed my hip. "I was a real asshole in high school. All the stuff I thought was important, everything I was obsessed with back then, it was all bullshit. None of it was real. I was so busy trying to be cool and popular, I couldn't see what was right in front of my face." He pressed his lips to my hair. "Do you remember, the summer after we graduated, when you asked me if I wanted to go see a movie with you?"

I groaned in embarrassment. "Oh god. You actually remember that? I was hoping you'd forgotten."

"I remember it. I remember wanting to say yes because I always had a good time when we were together. You made me laugh and made that shitty job way more fun than it should have been."

"Then why did you say no?" It still hurt a little to remember the crushing disappointment and humiliation. Even now, safely tucked into Mike's arms.

"Because I knew my friends would give me shit if they saw us together, and I cared way too much about what they thought." His voice sounded rough and bitter. "You might have thought I was cool, but really I was weak. Too busy trying to be who everyone expected me to be. Too scared to follow my heart and say yes when a cute girl asked me to a movie."

I tightened my arms around him. "We were all scared back then. That's the thing you don't know when you're a teenager, that everyone else is just as self-conscious and lost as you. Everyone's trying so hard not to let it show, no one really sees each other."

He drew in a long breath, and I felt his chest rise and fall as he blew it out again. "I've been thinking about that summer a lot lately. Wondering what would have happened if I'd said yes to that movie. How things might have turned out differently."

It was something I'd thought about a lot as well. What if Mike and I had gotten together back in high school? Would we have stayed together? It was impossible to imagine a version of my life without Jerry and my sons.

"The thing is," Mike said, "I don't think I was the right guy for you back then. I wasn't ready yet, to be the kind of man you deserve. You have to mess up in order to grow up, and I had a lot of messing up to do still." He let out a low laugh. "Sometimes it feels like my life has been one failure after another, but maybe it was all worth it if it brought me back here to you."

I lifted my head, and his eyes met mine. Something unbearably vulnerable glimmered in the inky depths, making my chest feel tight. I pressed my lips to his, my hand curling possessively around his neck. His mouth was soft and sweet under mine, but also firm and steady—everything I liked about him. He lifted a hand to cup the back of my head, his fingers tangling in my hair in a way that told me he wanted more than a chaste kiss, but instead he pulled back, his lips brushing over my forehead before he sank back into the couch.

I nuzzled into his chest, breathing in the clean, slightly spicy smell of him—with just a whisper of fresh-baked bread clinging to his clothes. He'd been so patient with me. So tender and solicitous. I wished I could reward him for his devotion.

I loved being close to him. Feeling his body pressed against mine. I loved when he kissed me, and all his little loving touches. I felt attracted to him—quite literally, as if his body was a magnet I couldn't get close enough to.

But what I hadn't yet felt was any sexual desire or arousal. It was as if that part of me was still numb from the surgery. I hoped it was just temporary—I was barely past the halfway mark in the healing process, I reminded myself. But I couldn't banish the fear that my sex drive would never return.

And that Mike would eventually get tired of waiting.

CHAPTER TWENTY SIX
MIKE

I t had been nine weeks since Dawn's surgery. Not that I was counting. Except I was totally counting.

The recommended waiting period before she could try having sex had come and gone, unremarked by both of us. I wasn't going to be the one to bring it up. No way. I knew Dawn was as aware of it as I was, and she'd say something when she was ready. Until then, I wasn't going to pressure her. I had told her I was willing to wait as long as it took, and I'd meant it.

That didn't stop me from hoping.

Every night I wondered if this would be the night. Every time I kissed her, I hoped it would lead to more. But I didn't push it. I let her take the lead. Or not.

The anticipation was starting to get to me though. I had sex on the brain, like some kind of hormonal teenager. I hadn't jerked off this much since junior high. I'd even started having wet dreams again, for the first time in I didn't even know how long.

Even though I was living in a perpetual state of sexual frustration, I kind of enjoyed it in a weird way. Sure, I'd enjoy having sex with Dawn even more. But the waiting gave me something to look forward to.

It didn't do anything to help my focus at work, however. Not that I cared. As far as this job went, my field of fucks was barren. I knew my boss hated me, and I had no hope of advancement, so I was just biding my time while I finished up my degree.

The online university program I was in let me take classes serially at my own pace— as many as I could get through in a semester, as fast as I could get through them. I'd finished my stats class in five weeks and moved on to ethics, which was going much faster. I only had my final left to take and I'd be done with that one. Then I could move on to the classes in my major like IT Foundations, and Network and Security Applications, which I ought to be able to pass in my sleep. It was looking like I might be able to finish the whole program in less than a year.

Then, with the benefit of a bachelor's degree and a stack of certifications under my belt, I could look for a better job. In the meantime, I'd just keep sucking it up at my current one, coasting and not giving a shit what my boss thought of me.

Which left plenty of time for fantasizing about Dawn and all the things I planned to do to her eventually.

I was in the middle of a particularly erotic daydream when my cell phone buzzed. I glanced at the screen and did a double take. It was Tim Goss calling—the executive director of technology at the school district I'd worked for in Columbus.

I stared at it for a second, too surprised to react. I hadn't heard from Tim since I'd tendered my resignation. Our relationship had always been amicable, but since he was my boss's boss, we hadn't exactly been chummy. I had no idea why he'd be calling me out of the blue.

"Hey, Tim," I said, trying to keep my voice even as I answered the phone.

"Hey, Mike. How've you been?" His tone was friendly but brisk.

"Good. Yeah, I've been good." I had a feeling he wasn't just calling for a chat, so I didn't elaborate. "How are things back at City Schools?"

"Oh, you know. The wheels keep turning. That's why I'm calling, actually. Do you have a few minutes to talk?"

I glanced toward Rich's office. He was in there with the door open and liable to get up and start prowling around any second, so I couldn't talk to Tim here. "Can I call you back in five minutes?"

"Yeah, that works," Tim said. "Talk to you in five."

I got up, slipping my phone into my pocket, and headed toward the men's room. I walked past it to the stairwell at the end of the hall and jogged down to the ground floor. Then I made my way out of the main library building and walked a half block down Congress to a nearby coffee bar before calling Tim back.

"Mike," he said, picking up almost immediately. "Thanks for calling me back."

"Sure thing," I said. "What's up?"

"Are you still in Chicago?"

"I am, yeah."

"Right. Well, I don't know if you'd be willing to consider coming back, but the director of tech support position is open, and I was wondering if you'd be interested in throwing your hat in the ring."

I didn't know what I'd been expecting, but it wasn't that. "Bob left?"

Robert Breckler had been my boss when I worked for the school district. He was a good guy, if a little humorless and persnickety. Still, he'd been a decent manager, and I hadn't minded working for him. He'd been at the school district forever and was just about the last guy I'd ever expected to leave.

"His wife took a job at Carnegie Mellon, so they're moving to Pittsburgh."

"Wow, good for her."

"Bob suggested I get in touch to see if we could woo you back. You're his pick to replace him."

"Me?" I always knew Bob appreciated me and the work I did for him, but I never expected him to name me as his successor. It had never even occurred to me he'd need a successor—or that I'd be a serious candidate if he did.

"The district requires that we go through the whole interview process, of course, consider every serious candidate who applies. But Bob's recommendation carries a lot of weight around here. That is, if it's something you think you'd be interested in."

"I, uh…I don't know, to be honest. You kind of took me by surprise."

Three months ago, I would have jumped at the chance. In a heartbeat. It was a good job with more responsibility than I'd ever been offered before. I'd have a staff of my own to supervise, not to mention a nice salary bump. And the cost of living in Columbus was better too. I'd be able to afford a lot nicer place.

I'd moved back here to help Kelly out with Mom, but it didn't seem like my presence was helping all that much. Mom didn't seem to care that I was around. And if I got this job, I'd be able to send Kelly money to hire a cleaning service for Mom and whatever else she needed. I didn't have to be here.

This job was perfect for me. It was everything I'd been wanting.

Except one thing.

Leaving Chicago meant leaving Dawn.

We'd only been together for two months, but I already couldn't imagine my life without her. I couldn't leave her now.

Could I?

"Well, the application's on the district website, and it'll be open for two weeks," Tim told me. "Think about it."

"Yeah," I said. "I will."

After we said our goodbyes and hung up, I stared at the phone in my hand.

Was I seriously thinking about it? I had to, didn't I? A job like this didn't come along often—especially for a guy like me. I had to consider it. I'd be a fool not to.

Why couldn't this have happened sooner? Talk about shit timing. Why'd it have to happen now, when I'd finally started to make a life for myself here? When things were going so well with Dawn? The unfairness of it hit me square in the gut.

I could have the job of my dreams or I could have the woman of my dreams, but I couldn't have both.

CHAPTER TWENTY SEVEN
DAWN

Tonight was the night. I'd decided.

I was ready to have sex. I'd been ready for a while, to be honest, but I'd yet to do anything about it.

I'd dithered for over a week, unable to work up the courage to put the moves on Mike. I knew I was being silly. There was no question about whether he'd welcome my advances. I knew he was as eager as I was, although he tried so hard not to let it show. More importantly, I trusted he'd be understanding about any changes in my body and considerate of any discomfort I might feel.

The problem wasn't him. It was me.

I didn't know what to expect from sex since my hysterectomy, and I was a little afraid to find out. Would it feel different? Would I still be able to orgasm? What if I couldn't?

Like, ever again?

My sex drive had finally returned—with a vengeance. It was all I could think about the last few days, how badly I wanted Mike. When we were together, I felt like I was going to explode. Every little touch sent my heart rate spiking and my blood rushing in my ears. And yet I held back. It wasn't that easy to undo a lifetime of conditioning that told me not to ask for what I wanted.

Even when what I wanted was right there. Waiting for me. Eager to be wanted. And Mike had been so patient and waited so long. He deserved to be put out of his misery. We both did.

No more chickening out. This was happening.

I was going over to Mike's place tonight after I closed up at the store, and I was going prepared. I'd shaved from stem to stern. Worn my nicest underwear. There was even a small bottle of lube tucked in my purse in case it was needed.

As I knocked on Mike's door, I was nervous, but also excited. The last time we'd had sex, I'd expected it to be a one-time event. Now we were together—a real couple—and we knew each other much better. We trusted each other. I could only imagine it would make the experience that much more meaningful.

In light of that, my hesitation to initiate intimacy seemed even sillier. When he opened the door, the sight of him bolstered my courage even more. I could do this. I *wanted* to do this. I was ready.

He pulled me into his arms as soon as I stepped inside and held me in a tight embrace. Tight enough that I started to worry a little. "Is everything okay?" I asked, leaning back to look at him.

"Fine. Great. I just missed you." He smiled and bent to kiss me. "I had a weird day at work, is all."

I reached up to cup his face in my hands, skimming my fingernails through his beard. "Do you want to talk about it?"

His eyes fluttered closed as he sighed happily. "I do not. I want to eat dinner with my girlfriend and forget all about it."

I was used to him sidestepping the subject of his job. I knew he was unhappy there and didn't like to talk about it much. He'd opened up enough to vent to me about it a few times, but mostly he seemed to prefer not to think about work once he came home. If that was what he needed, I could give him that. I suspected I'd be able to provide an ample distraction tonight.

"I'll go heat up the food. You want some wine?" He started for the kitchen, but I caught his wrist and tugged him back into my arms.

Winding my arms around his neck, I rose up on my toes and kissed him. His lips parted easily for me, and I felt my blood hum with desire as our tongues slid together. This wasn't going to be so difficult after all.

As I crushed my mouth against his, I dropped my hands to his shoulders, squeezing the solid muscle there and spinning him around to crowd him up against the door.

He grunted as his back hit the wood. "Wow. Okay." A smile curved his mouth as he continued kissing me.

I pressed my body against his, straining toward him as I tilted my head for a deeper, harder kiss. My hands curled into the front of his T-shirt, then wandered underneath, craving the feel of his skin. "Take this off," I ordered, pulling at his shirt.

He tore it off over his head and dropped it to the floor.

My eyes devoured the sight of him, my hands wandering freely over his skin as I explored the hard muscles of his chest and the thick patch of salt-and-pepper hair trailing down to his firm stomach.

His breath hitched, then his hands caught mine and he gave me a surprised, hopeful, questioning look. "Dawn..."

I met his gaze with as much confidence as I could muster. "I'm ready."

"Are you sure?" His brow furrowed. "Because we don't have to."

"I want to. I've been wanting to for a while."

"Yeah?" A smile curved his mouth, and I rose up to kiss it.

"Hang on." Taking me by the hand, he pulled me toward his bedroom and over to the nightstand. I watched as he bent to retrieve something from the bottom drawer.

"What's that?"

With a somewhat sheepish look, he presented me with a tube of Astroglide. "I bought some lube. I thought—well, I was reading up on hysterectomy side effects and it said some women experience a decrease in vaginal lubrication, so I picked some up. You know, just in case."

I stared at him in wonder. "You were reading up on hysterectomy side effects?"

His shoulders twitched. "Yeah."

"You are the sweetest man in the whole entire world. Did you know that?" Warmth rushed through me, starting down at my toes and spreading out into my limbs and heating my cheeks before finally settling in my chest, where it wrapped around my heart. He was so good and pure. I couldn't get over how lucky I was.

He gave me a cockeyed grin. "I don't know if it was sweet so much as I'm just really, *really* looking forward to having sex with you."

I reached for him, intending to show him how I felt by kissing him, but he twisted out of my grasp.

"That's not all."

My eyebrows lifted as he tossed the lube onto the bed and turned back to the night-stand. I wondered what other sex aids he had stashed in there, but instead he held up a piece of paper.

I squinted at it in confusion, unable to decipher the small type without my reading glasses.

"I went to the doctor," he declared proudly. "It's a clean bill of health. No STDs."

I blinked up at him. "I never thought—"

"Better safe than sorry," he declared with adorable earnestness. "Since we don't have to worry about you getting pregnant, I thought it might be more comfortable for you if we could skip the condom."

A smile tugged at my lips as I shook my head. "You're amazing."

His gaze dragged over me, slow and heavy like molasses. "Come here." The paper in his hand fluttered to the floor as he reached for me.

He sank his fingers into my hair as he kissed me: hungry, hopeful, and so, so loving. The smell of baking bread perfumed the air around us, and I knew this was exactly where I belonged. I adored this man.

No, I realized, the knowledge striking me like a lightning bolt. I *loved* him.

I let the feeling envelop me. The intensity of it was a little frightening—I felt almost drunk with it—but it was exhilarating too.

The urge to tell him, to share this exciting epiphany with Mike, the man I loved and trusted with my whole heart, rose up in me, but I held back. As much as I wanted to be completely honest with him, I couldn't help feeling it was still too soon. I needed to sit with the realization a little longer before I was ready to put myself out on that limb.

Besides, I had a much more pressing goal at the moment, and I didn't want to get sidetracked by emotional declarations. There would be plenty of time for those later. Mike wasn't going anywhere. We had all the time in the world.

I leaned into him, kissing him with renewed vigor. Lust bubbled up in my blood, stirring between my legs and in the pit of my stomach, and I surrendered myself to it. I arched against him, my hips rocking as my breathing grew shallow and ragged. Mike pressed against me, his arousal grinding against my stomach, and I ground back, seeking more friction, feeling needy and desperate for him.

His hands grasped at the fabric of my skirt, lifting up the hem, then pushing my dress up and over my head. I felt a moment's uncertainty as Mike's fingertips skimmed over my stomach, past the small, healed incisions there, but he didn't linger. His big hands cupped my breasts, kneading the soft flesh, his thumbs rubbing my nipples through the lace of my bra. I moaned, then shivered as he dropped his mouth to my neck, licking and sucking at the exact spot where I was most sensitive, his whiskers scraping over my skin.

As he unfastened my bra, my hands plucked at the elastic waistband of his sweatpants, then slipped inside, navigating around his boxer briefs to grasp his hard, heavy cock.

"Fuuuuck," he groaned as I stroked him.

"Yes, please," I said, smiling against his lips and enjoying the full-body shudder I'd provoked from him.

Taken by a sudden fervor, he jerked out of my grasp and shoved his pants to the floor, kicking them off as he pushed me toward the bed. He laid me back and lowered his body over mine, the hard planes of heavy muscle pressing me into the mattress. I melted under the warm weight of him, my limbs loose and pliant as my legs parted, inviting him into my body.

He kissed my throat, then my jaw, then my lips, all with such sweetness it made my heart flutter. "Dawn," he whispered against my skin. "You are so beautiful."

His cock was wedged between us, pressing against me so, so deliciously, but I needed more—more pressure, more friction. I needed him inside me, and I told him so, the words tumbling out of me before I knew what I was saying.

"Goddamn." His lips brushed my ear. "That is so fucking hot. Please feel free to talk like that whenever the mood strikes you."

"Happy to, if you'll hurry up and fuck me."

His hips thrust against me, hitting my clit and sending a shock wave of pleasure rippling through me. "Patience, woman. I won't be rushed." The words were low and growly, and I nearly orgasmed right then.

He kissed me softly, then harder and deeper. The more he kissed me, the more I squirmed beneath him, craving sweet relief. Then his mouth moved to my breasts, and while I was distracted by that his hand went to my underwear. I spasmed beneath him at the sudden, wonderful contact, and let out a ragged moan.

"Jesus, you're so wet. I don't think we're gonna need that lube after all."

I gasped, my hips jerking uncontrollably as his fingers slid inside me, as easily as a hot knife through butter. His mouth found mine again, his tongue thrusting deep as he stroked me. My fingernails curled into his back, probably leaving scratches, but I was so carried away by pleasure I couldn't seem to care. My body shook as he drove me closer and closer to the edge, my breaths coming out in ragged, desperate gasps, unable to form any words as I'd promised.

I felt untethered. Loose and wild. Set free at last from the handcuffs of inhibition and fear. I let the shivery coils of bliss carry me away as Mike's fingers thrust inside me, his thumb rubbing my swollen, aching clit with just the right amount of pressure until I was falling apart beneath him, crying out, and coming so hard I saw stars.

He whispered encouragement into my skin as I slowly came back to myself. My eyes opened, focusing on him again. On his beautiful bare torso, his skin golden in the warm light of his bedroom, and his soft, dark eyes brimming with affection but also lust. He flashed me a smile as he bent to brush a kiss across my lips. "That was beautiful. I love watching you do that."

I reached for him, grasping his head with both hands. "Good. Now get inside me and let's do it again."

His grin turned cocky. "Yes, ma'am." Pushing himself upright, he dragged my underwear down, tossing it over his shoulder. I pulled my knees up, arching my hips in anticipation, and his gaze dragged over my body. It was so obvious he liked what he saw—from the glassy look in his eyes, the ragged hitching of his chest, and the peaks of color in his face—I couldn't even feel self-conscious about my less-than-perfect body. He grasped the base of his shaft and squeezed, his tongue shooting out to wet his lips.

I waggled my hips and made grabby hands. "Get over here now."

Still he hesitated. "There's a chance I'm going to last all of five seconds once I get inside you. Just so you know."

"I'll take it as a compliment."

"I promise to make it up to you." His expression was almost comically solemn.

I pressed my lips together, trying and failing to suppress a smile. "I have no doubt you will. Now I'd like to feel you inside me, please."

Lowering himself over me, he guided his cock to my entrance. "As you wish," he murmured, sliding inside me with agonizing slowness. I knew he was being careful in case I experienced any discomfort, but it was killing me. It was killing the both of us. His whole body was taut as a metal spring from the effort of holding himself back.

It was sweet, but I didn't want sweetness right now. I wanted his hardness. His roughness. I wanted him to plow me like an open field. I grasped the firm curve of his ass and jerked him toward me, driving him deep inside me with a suddenness that had us both gasping. My fingernails dug into his flesh as I rolled my hips beneath him. "More like that, please."

He seemed to shake off his restraint. Grasping my hips, he pressed his face into my neck and thrust. Hard, deep, and powerful. "Yessss," I gasped, and he did it again. And again. Building up to a steady rhythm, driving inside me, wringing moans of pleasure from both of us.

He lasted longer than five seconds—no thanks to me. I did everything I could to coax him over the edge, wanting to unravel him the way he'd unraveled me. I could feel him fighting it, trying to make it last, but I ground against him ruthlessly, arching up into him as I squeezed my walls around his cock.

Finally, I reached around his leg and squeezed his balls. He growled, then shuddered, his body contracting as he thrust one last time before going boneless and collapsing on top of me. I held him, skimming my fingernails over his back in light circles, until he roused himself. With a soft, sweet kiss, he pulled out of me and shifted to the side, cuddling up against me.

"I want a rematch," he murmured, nestling against my neck. "Give me ten minutes."

I sank my fingers into his hair as happiness bloomed in my chest. "You can have anything you want."

I spent the night at Mike's place that night, for the first time. Truth be told, I didn't sleep all that well. In part because we had several rematches lasting long into the night, and in part because I never slept well in a strange bed—even one with the man I loved in it. I drifted fitfully in and out, just on the edge of slumber, coming wide awake every time he rolled over or reached for me in his sleep.

But I didn't mind. It was the best night of insomnia I'd ever had.

Mike, on the other hand, slept like the dead. When his phone started buzzing on the nightstand sometime before sunrise, I had to jostle him several times before he finally rolled over and grabbed it.

"Shit," he muttered blearily, sitting up on the edge of the bed.

"What's wrong?" I rolled toward him and laid a hand on his back.

He dragged his fingers through his hair as he stared at the screen. "It's Christine."

I pushed myself upright and swung my legs out of bed. "I'll go make some coffee," I said, and headed for the kitchen, closing the bedroom door behind me to give him some privacy.

Mike came out fifteen minutes later, looking grim. Wordlessly, I poured him a cup of coffee and put a splash of almond milk in it, the way he liked.

"Thanks." He came up behind me and kissed the top of my shoulder as he reached for the coffee mug. "Christine's mom passed away early this morning."

I turned and wrapped my arms around him, laying my head against his chest. "I'm sorry."

He held me tight, letting out a long sigh. "The funeral will probably be next week."

"You should go."

He pulled back to look at me, his brow furrowed. "You think?"

"Do you want to go?"

He shrugged and lifted his coffee to his lips, blowing across the top to cool it off. "It's a funeral. Who ever wants to go to a funeral?"

"Do you feel like you should?"

His expression turned thoughtful as he sipped his coffee. "Christine did come to my dad's funeral last year."

"You should go," I told him. "She'll want you there."

Of course she would. He must have been one of her first calls after she lost her mother. She was grieving, and she needed help from the people who knew her best.

The fact that I didn't want him to go because I'd miss him didn't even factor into it.

"Yeah." He nodded, his expression faraway. "Maybe I will."

CHAPTER TWENTY EIGHT
MIKE

"Which shirt do you think goes better with these pants?" I held up two dress shirts and turned to face Dawn. I was packing for Columbus. The funeral was Friday and I had a late afternoon flight out tomorrow, so I'd be heading to the airport straight from work.

"The striped one. Definitely."

I put the blue shirt back in my closet and carried the striped one over to the bed where my suitcase was laid open.

"Here, let me," Dawn said, reaching for it. "I know a trick so it won't get wrinkled."

I jerked it back. "You're not here to fold my clothes for me."

"Yes, but I'm better at it than you, so you should just let me do it."

I puffed out my chest in a display of mock offense. "How do you know? Maybe I'm a genius at folding clothes."

She gave me the same *don't be stupid* look my sister always gave me, and I relented.

"Fine." I thrust the shirt at her as I shook my head. "But only because you're such a pain in the ass."

"You love it," she retorted as she laid the shirt out on the bed and proceeded to do some kind of witchcraft that ended up with it folded neat and flat as new with only a few flicks of her wrists.

I couldn't help the big, dumb grin that spread over my face. "You're damn right I do."

Her eyes lifted to mine, her expression startled, and I realized what I'd said. Or almost said. Or sort of indirectly implied.

I hadn't meant to blurt it out like that, all inelegant and half joking.

I'd meant to say it properly, when the time was right. I'd been madly in love with her for a while—more or less since the night she'd answered her door in that unicorn onesie—but I wasn't 100 percent sure she was there yet, and I didn't want to scare her off.

I should have just seized the moment and gone ahead and said it properly right then. Told her exactly what was in my heart. But something made me chicken out.

Instead of telling Dawn I loved her, I fled the room.

"Almost forgot my beard trimmer," I said, pretending nothing out of the ordinary had occurred, and headed for the bathroom so I wouldn't have to look at Dawn or bare my soul to her any more than I already had.

As soon as I got in there, I wanted to kick myself for my cowardice. I wasn't sure why I was being such a wimp about it. Usually I had no trouble telling women how I felt. But something had held me back just now. Maybe it was the look on her face, maybe it was the fact that I was about to see my ex-wife again, or maybe it was the job interview I had on Friday morning.

The one I hadn't told Dawn about.

I hadn't intended to apply for the job in Columbus. I didn't want to move back, so there wasn't any point. But then Christine's mom died, and I was going to be there anyway for the funeral, and Tim had called again, which made me think he *really* wanted me for the job.

I wasn't used to being wanted. It felt good.

So I figured *what the hell?* Why not take a meeting while I was there? What could it hurt to hear them out? That didn't mean I had to take it—even if they offered it to me, which wasn't a given. I could blow the interview, or the superintendent could have someone else in mind, or one of the other candidates could outshine me. But I figured it was good practice, if nothing else. Brush up on my interview skills, get used to talking about myself with more confidence. Maintain a good relationship with someone in a position to give me a reference one day.

And maybe—just maybe—part of me was keeping my options open. Just in case things here didn't work out. I knew how I felt about Dawn, but I was a little less secure in her feelings about me. I still didn't quite get what she saw in me. Now that she was all healed from her surgery, maybe she'd decide she didn't need me so much anymore. Maybe she'd lose interest. Maybe she'd realize she could have any man she wanted, and she could do a hell of a lot better than me.

I tried to talk myself out of those feelings. I didn't want to believe it, but the fear was still there, whispering in the back of my head. Part of me was always waiting for the ax to fall, the bubble to pop, and the dream to come to an end.

Anyway, I wasn't taking the job. I was just having a conversation. It was no big deal.

Except for the fact that I hadn't mentioned any of it to Dawn.

I didn't want her thinking it was serious. I had a feeling no matter how hard I tried to convince her I had no intention of taking the job, she'd believe otherwise. I didn't want to make her think I was leaving her.

This whole job situation had forced me to a crossroads. If they ended up offering it to me, I'd have to choose: Dawn or the job. I'd already made up my mind; I was choosing Dawn. No question about it.

But I was afraid to tell her I'd made that choice. It felt too big. The same doubts that kept me from saying *I love you* were holding me back from admitting just how much I'd come to need her in my life. I cared about her more than I cared about some stupid job. More than I cared about pretty much anything. But I couldn't form my lips to tell her any of that.

It was easier not to say anything at all.

So I dawdled in the bathroom for a minute, digging around in the cabinet like I was gathering up necessities, when what I was really doing was hiding from my feelings like a damn coward. When I finally came out of the bathroom, Dawn had a funny look on her face. I pretended not to notice, hoping it would pass and we could move on from this awkward moment. Then she said something that stopped me cold in my tracks.

"Who's Tim Goss?"

Panic spiked through me. "What?"

She pointed at my phone, which was lying face up on the bed. "I'm sorry, I didn't mean to read your notifications, but your phone was right there and when the screen lit up my eyes just went to it involuntarily."

"That's okay." I didn't give a damn if she read all my texts. I didn't have anything to hide from her.

Except the one thing I'd neglected to tell her.

Her brow lowered in confusion as her eyes met mine. "Someone named Tim Goss just texted to confirm your interview on Friday?"

"Oh. Yeah." I tried to sound offhanded, like it was no big deal, but my voice chose that moment to crack like a pubescent teenager, undermining my attempt to play it cool.

"But the funeral's on Friday," Dawn said, looking even more confused. "Are you going on an interview while you're in Columbus?"

I moved to my suitcase and dropped my beard trimmer into it. My skin prickled all over as my senses jangled a warning that something bad was about to happen. "Um…yeah, sort of."

"A job interview?"

I could hear the hurt in her voice, but I couldn't bring myself to look at her. "Yeah, but it's not a big deal."

"It's kind of a big deal if you're considering taking a job in another city."

I swallowed my fears and made myself face her. "I'm not."

Her eyes, her mouth, her whole expression went flat. "But you're going on an interview." She clearly didn't believe me, just as I'd known she wouldn't.

"It's just for the hell of it. Tim—he's the director of technology at my old job—he called last week to let me know about an opening. Since I'm going to be there anyway, I figured I'd see what it was all about."

She lowered her eyes to the floor and gave a tight little nod. "Is it a good job?" Her voice sounded cold—no, not cold. More like distant. Faraway. Like she was already getting used to the idea of me leaving.

"It's okay." I didn't want to talk about the job. I wanted to pull her into my arms and hold her tight and never have to have this conversation. But I could tell from her tense posture that wouldn't fly. Her walls had slammed down like a reinforced steel roll-up door, and I'd been left standing on the outside. "It's with the school district I used to work for. My old boss is leaving and they're looking for a replacement."

"So it'd be a big step up for you."

I dragged my hand through my hair. "I mean…yeah. I guess." I couldn't stop equivocating. Couldn't bring myself to admit that it was a great fucking job. Because if I admitted that to her, I might have to admit to myself just how goddamn badly I wanted it.

Her eyes lifted to mine, and I knew she could see right through me. "You liked it there, didn't you?" Her tone was softer now. More resigned.

"It was all right."

"You liked it better than your job here."

I took a step toward her. "Dawn, I'm not seriously considering it."

"Why not?" She was still sitting on the bed with her hands folded in her lap. Like we were just making inconsequential small talk instead of having a conversation that could make or break us.

I hated how calm she was. The air in the room felt too heavy to breathe. An iron band of panic tightened around my chest. Acid burned in the back of my throat. Something bad was coming, and it was like she couldn't even see it. Or maybe she didn't care.

I heaved a breath and paced across the room, needing to work off some of my nervous energy. "Because I don't want to move back to Columbus. I'm just going to the interview for the hell of it."

Her eyes followed me. "You keep saying that, but I think we both know it's not true. You're going to the interview because you want the job."

I stopped and blinked at her. "It doesn't matter how much I might want it or not, because I can't move right now."

"Why not?"

Her gaze bored right through me. Like she was daring me to say it. Admit that she was the reason I couldn't leave.

I swallowed. "My life is here now. My mom needs me, my sister needs me..." I paused, considering my next words carefully. "I'd like to think maybe you need me too."

Her lips pressed together, and she looked down at her lap. "That's not a good enough reason to pass up an opportunity like this."

"Dawn—"

"I think you should take the job if they offer it."

Her words struck me like a fist. It wasn't just what she was saying—I'd half expected her to say as much—it was the way she'd said it. Aloof. Unfeeling. Matter-of-fact. Like it should be obvious. Like I was crazy for ever thinking otherwise.

The demon lurking in the back of my head whispered, *She doesn't want you.*

I stood there, stricken. A sick feeling formed in the pit of my stomach. The muscles in my jaw clenched tight, grinding my molars together.

"We need to be practical," Dawn said. "An opportunity like this isn't going to come along every day."

She thinks you're a loser, the demon hissed in my ear. *This job is the best you'll ever be able to do.*

I closed my eyes, swallowing a painful lump of pride, and asked her straight out, "Are you saying you don't want me to stay?"

The question hung in the air between us, suspended in a tension as thick as custard. For a second, she looked like a cornered animal. A tendon jumped in the side of her neck. Then she drew her composure around her like a heavy coat, her expression growing flat and distant again. "It's not about what I want."

My voice grew sharper as my frustration flared. "I'm making it about what you want. Do you want me to stay or not?"

All the blood drained from her face. Her eyes shifted down and to the side, avoiding mine. "Please don't ask me that."

"I'm asking."

"I care about you…" The implied *but* took up all the space in the room. It felt like the walls were closing in on me.

I'd been here before. Had this same conversation with Christine.

I care about you, but…

It's not worth it.

You don't make me happy.

I don't want to be with you anymore.

I don't love you.

I was so caught up in the flashback I didn't realize Dawn had started talking again.

"I can't be the reason you turn down an important professional opportunity. This is your career we're talking about. Your livelihood. And we've been together all of two months? You can't make a decision this big all about me—about us. This job sounds like it could be good for your career. You have to take it if they offer it to you. It'd be stupid not to."

A switch flipped inside me when I heard the word *stupid*. All I heard was her telling me I needed to improve myself. Pushing me to do something I didn't want to do. Haranguing me about my limited opportunities and how I was holding myself back.

I was like a land mine that had been stepped on, and I blew up at her as my insecurities and past failures bubbled up in a toxic combustion.

"It's my goddamn life and I'll decide for myself what job I take."

She flinched at the sudden intensity of my tone, and the anger and resentment dripping from every word. Like poison.

Neither of us spoke for a long few seconds, like we were absorbing the shock of my outburst.

She looked down at her lap and brushed away an imaginary piece of lint. "Well," she said, getting to her feet finally. "I think maybe I should go."

"Dawn, no—let me—I didn't mean to shout like that."

"I know." She gave me a tight smile. "It's getting late, and you need to finish packing."

"I'm sorry." I felt shell-shocked. My ears were ringing and the band around my chest seemed to have acquired iron spikes.

"We'll talk more when you get back." She started for the door, her movements stiff.

"Promise?" I asked her back as I followed her into the living room.

She stooped to retrieve her purse from the coffee table. "Yes."

I didn't have a good feeling about that *yes*. It made me think the next time we talked might be the last.

I took a step toward her meaning to stop her—or kiss her maybe—anything not to leave things like this between us, but I froze at the hard expression on her face.

"Have a safe flight." She could have been talking to a perfect stranger, the way she said it. "I'll see you on Saturday."

I racked my brain for something that would make this all better. A way to fix it. But I didn't know how.

Before I could think of anything else to say, she was gone.

CHAPTER TWENTY NINE
DAWN

"Shit!" I drew my hand back, squeezing my index finger as blood started to well from the cardboard paper cut I'd just given myself.

Angie leaned her head into the back room of the store. "Are you okay?"

"Fine," I replied through gritted teeth. "It's just a paper cut."

"I'm not just talking about the paper cut. You know you just swore, right? Out loud. In the store."

I had, hadn't I? *Fudgsicles.* I usually tried to avoid swearing in general, but especially when I was at work. It wasn't the sort of atmosphere I wanted to offer my customers.

"Are there any customers out there?"

"Only Linda."

"Thank god." I went into the bathroom and cleaned my cut, which hurt like the dickens. Cardboard cuts were the worst because they were thick, deep, and jagged.

Angie followed me, watching from the doorway of the bathroom. "What is going on with you?"

"It's a cardboard cut. You know how those are the worst."

"I'm not talking about that, although I agree that cardboard cuts are the worst. I'm referring to the fact that you've been in a pissy mood ever since I got here. And Linda says you were just as bad yesterday." Angie tore off a paper towel and held it out to me when I shut off the water. "She says you yelled at Chloe."

I accepted the towel guiltily and dried my hands. "I did not yell. I may have corrected her a little sharply when I found out she'd input the wrong price for some very expensive Madelinetosh Pashmina, which resulted in us selling twelve skeins below cost. But I never raised my voice."

Angie leveled me with a disapproving look. "Linda said you made Chloe cry."

"I already apologized! Profusely." She hadn't exactly cried, but her eyes had welled up a little and her face had gone pink with the effort of holding back tears. I'd felt like an absolute monster, but that was par for the course this week.

I twisted my wrist to check my watch as I squeezed the paper towel against my still bleeding finger. It was 3:15 p.m., which meant that at this very minute Mike was at his former mother-in-law's funeral, surrounded by his ex-wife's family and friends— who used to be *his* family and friends. I tried not to let it bother me. It was a funeral, not a party. A solemn occasion of mourning. The odds of him falling in love with his ex-wife again because they were at a funeral together were probably extremely low.

But that didn't stop me from worrying about it. I hadn't heard a peep from him since our fight two days ago, which was beyond unusual. He almost never went more than twelve hours without texting me.

I could only assume he was still angry with me. I hated how we'd left things and regretted the impulse that had driven me to leave his apartment before we'd finished talking it through. At the time, I'd felt we both needed a cooling-off period. Emotions had been high. Apparently, I'd struck a nerve, and his reaction startled me. It had seemed wise for both of us to calm down before attempting to continue the conversation.

But that meant letting him go to Columbus with bad feelings between us. He would have had his interview this morning, and I had no idea how it had gone. And now he was with Christine. He'd be with her for the whole afternoon and into the evening for the wake afterward. I could too easily imagine him providing a kindly shoulder for her to cry on, and one thing leading to another until, under the influence of a few too many drinks, they fell back into old habits.

I tried to tell myself such a scenario was unlikely. I wanted to believe Mike was too honorable to do something like that. But I'd been cheated on once before by a man I'd believed to be honorable, so you never really knew, did you? People were fallible. Mistakes happened.

After our fight, Mike might have assumed we were as good as broken up. Maybe he was so angry he'd changed his mind about staying in Chicago. Maybe his interview had been such a success he'd decided to take the job after all.

Maybe I'd succeeded in pushing him into it.

The entire situation was a mess. I loved Mike and wanted the best for him. What was I supposed to do when what was best for him was to leave me behind? I couldn't very well ask him to pass up a promotion like this. Not when I knew how unhappy he was in his current job, and how much he longed for more responsibility and recognition at work. I wasn't going to hold him back. I loved him too much to do that to him.

Which left me miserable and conflicted. Panicked at the thought of losing him, desperately hoping they didn't offer him the job, and racked with guilt for selfishly wishing such a thing.

"Has it stopped bleeding yet?" Angie asked as she rifled through the first aid kit for a bandage.

I peeked under the paper towel. "I think so," I said when the wound didn't immediately well with blood.

She unwrapped the bandage and handed it to me. "All I know is, when the landlord stopped in to tell us about the water main repairs, you were so surly I think you actually scared him a little. And I didn't think anything could scare Quinn Sullivan."

This felt like an unfair exaggeration. "I was just annoyed because our water is going to be off half the day on Tuesday. We'll have to go all the way around the corner to the coffee bar to pee!" It was a huge inconvenience. A woman my age needed to pee frequently, which wasn't something I imagined a man like Quinn would understand.

"It's more than that, and you know it. Is it Mike? Did you two have your first fight?"

I couldn't help scowling as I wrapped the bandage around my injured finger. "First and possibly last."

"Oh come on, I don't believe that. You two are perfect together."

"Hardly." Avoiding Angie's sharp gaze, I tossed my trash into the bin. "Mike's thinking of moving back to Columbus."

Her mouth fell open in astonishment. "What? He wouldn't."

I pushed past her out of the bathroom. "There's a job there. A really good job. He had an interview this morning."

She followed me back into the stockroom. "He's not going to take it. That man is head over heels for you. He'd never."

"He might."

Angie's eyes narrowed. She crossed her arms, affecting an accusatory stance. "You told him to take it, didn't you?"

"Of course I did." I threw my hands up in frustration. "What else was I supposed to do?"

"Beg him to stay. *Duh.*"

"I'm not going to do that." I still had my pride.

"Okay, but did you at least tell him you *want* him to stay?"

"He knows how I feel."

Angie's eyes narrowed even more. "Does he? Are you sure about that?"

"Of course."

"Have you actually told him though? Like out loud. With words."

Well...

I hadn't actually said the words *I love you* yet. I'd been waiting for...something. I wasn't really sure what. Maybe for him to say it first.

Dammit. Angie knew me too well.

"You have to tell him," she said, not waiting for me to answer. "He deserves to know so he can choose freely. It's not fair to let him make a decision like this without all the facts. He needs to know you're madly in love with him." She fixed me with an appraising glare. "You are madly in love with him, aren't you?"

I answered without hesitation. "Yes."

"Then quit trying to fall on your sword, you freak. You think you're being selfless, but really you're doing it because you're afraid to ask for what you want. Be bold! Tell Mike how you feel about him and trust him to decide for himself what he wants to do."

"What if he doesn't choose me?" It was the thing that scared me most. What if I told him I loved him and it turned out he didn't love me back? What if I asked him to stay and he didn't? Wouldn't it be easier not to ask?

Angie took me by the shoulders, peering directly into my face to make sure I was listening. "Then you won't be any worse off than if you push him away. But at least you'll know how he feels, one way or the other. What have you got to lose?"

My pride. My dignity. My heart.

But as Angie's words sank in, I knew she was right. It would hurt to lose Mike either way. At least if he rejected me, I'd have some closure.

I made up my mind, right there on the spot.

"Can you open the store tomorrow morning?" I asked Angie.

"Sure, why?"

"Because I have to meet someone at the airport."

CHAPTER THIRTY

MIKE

I'd never been so happy to see the inside of O'Hare. Which was saying something, because O'Hare International Airport tied with the dentist's office on the list of my least favorite places on earth.

My head was pounding this morning, and the recycled airplane air and toddler kicking the back of my seat the whole flight hadn't helped matters. I'd indulged in a little too much whiskey at the wake last night and then boarded a plane at the crack of dawn without drinking enough water. I was also exhausted. Seeing Christine's family and so many of our old friends again had been an emotional and draining experience.

And that was after the interview yesterday morning, which had been grueling, but good. *Really* good. My mood lifted a little just thinking about it.

I'd been nervous going in. Convinced I'd fuck it all up. I hated talking about myself. The prospect of doing it for an hour straight while trying to appear smart and professional made my stomach hurt.

But then something funny had happened. As soon as I got in the room, I clicked into autopilot mode. They started asking me questions, and as I answered them, I began to feel more confident. I actually knew what I was talking about. Why had I been so worried? I could do this job. I was exactly the right person to do this job.

I'd never felt like that before. What a fucking rush.

It might have contributed to my overindulgence last night. Aside from needing to grease the conversational wheels at the wake, I'd wanted to celebrate a little. Raise a glass to not completely fucking up.

But now I was paying the price. I was hungover, and all I wanted was to go home.

I almost didn't see her, I was so distracted and so intent on getting the hell through the airport and out of there. But then something caught my eye. Something familiar —some*one* familiar. I turned my head and stopped in my tracks, so startled I nearly caused a pileup as the people behind me were forced to dodge out of the way.

"Sorry," I muttered in response to their irritated grumbles, pulling myself together enough to thread my way through the stream of people and over to her.

Dawn.

She was here. At the airport.

I hadn't heard from her in three days, not since our fight Wednesday. Not since I yelled at her and drove her away.

Guilt twined its ugly tentacles around my gut at the sight of her. I owed her an apology. I'd overreacted and I needed to make it right. I probably should have texted or called or something, but we needed to have a bigger conversation than I felt comfortable having over the phone. I'd hoped it could wait until I got back.

And now she was here, in the last place I'd expected to see her.

I didn't let myself wonder why. I headed straight for her, determined to apologize before I said anything else.

I didn't get the chance.

She launched herself at me, jumping straight into my arms as soon as I got close enough. I caught her easily, supporting her with one arm as she wrapped her legs around my waist.

Surprise drove the apology from my tongue. "What—"

She closed her mouth over mine, smothering my question with a kiss. It was a hell of a kiss she laid on me. Exuberant, amorous, and utterly heedless of all the people streaming past us. For a moment I lost myself in the petal-soft pressure of her mouth. My whole world narrowed to the taste of her on my tongue, the feel of her body pressed tight against mine, the familiar, intoxicating scent of her skin.

"Wow," I said dizzily when she finally let me come up for air. "I should go out of town more often."

Her fingers threaded through my beard. "I missed you." Her voice was warm, sweet, and so delicious, like candy for my ears.

I couldn't stop grinning. "I can tell."

"I love you."

My mouth fell open. It was the third time she'd surprised me in less than a minute, and this one left me speechless. My heart spasmed like it was trying to jump out of my chest, and I prayed I wasn't having a heart attack.

"I don't want you to move away," Dawn continued before I could recover myself enough to react to her declaration. "I'll understand if you decide to take the job—you shouldn't have to give it up for me—but I just want to make sure you know where I stand and that I love you and want to be with you. We'll figure everything else out somehow."

My face spread in a slow grin as I bent my head to brush my lips over hers. "I'm not taking the job."

"But—"

"I don't want that job."

I'd realized it halfway through the interview. As Tim Goss sat there next to the assistant superintendent, explaining the role to me in excruciating detail, I realized it wasn't what I wanted anymore, even aside from the Dawn of it all.

The degree I was working toward would open new doors for me in cybersecurity, which was a more interesting and challenging field. I didn't want to be stuck managing a help desk for the rest of my career. I wanted more, and for the first time in my life, I felt like I could have it.

The more Tim talked about it, the clearer it became the job wasn't right for me. By the time I graduated next year, I'd be overqualified for it. Hell, I was already overqualified for it—I just didn't have the piece of paper to prove it yet. I could easily do everything Tim described in my sleep, and I didn't want another job I could do in my sleep. I was tired of sleepwalking through my life. I wanted a challenge. I wanted to stretch myself. I was too good for this job, and I intended to prove it.

They were going to offer it to me—I was 99 percent sure—and I was 100 percent sure I was going to turn it down.

It was a huge relief. I would have turned it down anyway, because of Dawn. I'd already made up my mind on that. I wanted her in my life more than I wanted any job. There wasn't really any choice to make.

But realizing I didn't actually want the job made everything easier. It meant I wouldn't have to wonder what could have been or suffer any lingering regrets. It would make it easier to explain my choice to Dawn and prevent her from carrying any guilt about it.

We could be together. She wanted that as much as I did. It still hadn't quite sunk in. I'd made all these plans in my head about how I was going to fight for her and convince her to give me another chance and keep me around. But it wasn't necessary, because...

She loved me.

Was it possible to overdose on happiness?

Dawn's forehead creased. "We should talk about it."

"We will," I promised. "But I'm not just turning it down for you. It's not what I want for me anymore. I'm pretty sure I can do better." I touched her cheek, needing to get my apology off my chest before I said or did anything else. "I'm sorry I lost my temper the other night. You didn't deserve that."

She nodded solemnly. "I'm sorry I made you feel pressured. I didn't mean to."

"I know." I set her down and cradled her face in both hands, gazing into her beautiful green eyes, which were wide and glittering under the bright airport lights. "Dawn..."

O'Hare wasn't where I'd envisioned doing this. There was a urinal cake smell drifting over from the men's room and someone had spilled what I dearly hoped was a Frappuccino on the floor a few feet away.

But this was where we were, and where Dawn had chosen to tell me she loved me. I'd be damned if I wasn't going to say it back. Even if it meant I'd be forced to cherish a romantic memory of O-fucking-Hare for the rest of my life.

"I love you." I watched her expression break open, and my heart broke open right along with it in a burst of multicolored, incandescent joy.

I'd do anything to keep this woman in my life. Absolutely anything. I'd slay a dragon, fend off an army of a thousand armed goblins, walk barefoot to the ends of the earth and back. I'd take any risk, face down any demon, conquer any fear. Just for a chance to love her the way she deserved to be loved.

She lunged at me again, but this time I was ready for her. My body bent to make space for her as we came together. My arms wrapped around her, lifting her off the floor a little as I kissed her over and over again, like Jimmy Stewart kissing Donna Reed at the end of *It's a Wonderful Life*.

With every single one of those kisses, I made her a silent promise.

I'll stay with you.

I'll take care of you.

I'll fight for you.

Dawn pulled back, laughing, her cheeks pink and her eyes shining with love. The sight was so beautiful it almost brought tears to my eyes.

At fucking O'Hare. I couldn't believe I was getting so mushy and sentimental at this hellmouth of an airport. It was going to make it so much harder to hate this place.

"Take me home," she said, and wrapped her hands around my arm, tucking herself against my side.

"Which one?" I asked, reaching for my roller bag. "Your home or my home?"

She rested her head on my shoulder as we started for the exit. "Either. It doesn't matter. Wherever you are is where my home is."

I kissed the top her head, breathing in the sweet, familiar scent of her shampoo. "As you wish."

EPILOGUE
DAWN

"Are you ready?" I asked Mike as I stepped out of the hotel bathroom.

He was standing next to the king-size bed, doing something on his phone. Probably playing Pokémon Go. He looked ready to me. And extraordinarily handsome in his suit. It was a new one I'd helped him pick out for tonight.

He looked up from his phone, and I watched his eyes heat at the sight of me in my new dress. A wolfish grin spread across his face. "Do we really have to go to this thing? We've got this nice bed here. It'd be a shame to let it go to waste."

I rolled my eyes. "I just finished getting dressed."

He strode toward me, shoving his phone into his pocket. "You look beautiful." His hands slipped around my waist, and he bent his head to my neck. "And now I'd very much like to get you undressed."

"Later." I pushed him away before he succeeded in changing my mind. "The bed will still be here after the reunion."

We'd been at the hotel all afternoon, setting things up for the reunion. I'd booked us the room so we'd be able to shower and change without having to go all the way home. But obviously there were other advantages, and I planned to make the most of them after we'd fulfilled our duties at the reunion tonight.

I went to grab my phone off the dresser. There was a new text from my younger son, Zach, telling me to have a good time tonight. I'd finally introduced both my sons to Mike a couple months ago. They hadn't exactly embraced him with open arms at first, but they seemed to be slowly coming around to the idea of their mother having a new man in her life—Zach a little more quickly than Brandon.

Likewise, Mike had introduced me to his sister, Kelly, who I adored instantly, and his mother, who seemed to tolerate me okay. Mike said I shouldn't take his mother's lack of warmth personally and assured me she actually liked me quite a lot. We'd even managed to entice her out of the house a few times, which Mike considered tremendous progress.

"We need to get downstairs," I said as I typed a quick reply to Zach. "I promised Angie we'd be there early."

"Hang on a sec. Before we go, I've got something for you."

When I turned around, Mike was bent over, digging in the duffel bag he'd brought. I enjoyed the view until he straightened, holding out something encased in a clear plastic box.

I blinked at the ridiculous flower arrangement in his hand. "You bought me a corsage?"

He shrugged, looking adorably bashful. My big grumbly bear. My soft mountain of a man. "Isn't that what you do for these things?"

"Not usually, no."

"Well that's what you do for proms, and I didn't get to take you to our prom, so I figured I could make up for it tonight."

I tilted my head, smiling. "You could have taken me to our prom, if you'd bothered to ask. But you were too busy dating Gina Laird..."

He scowled. "Don't remind me. We've already established that I was a dumbass in high school. Now hold out your wrist and let me put this thing on you."

I presented my wrist, and he slipped on the corsage. It was a beautiful arrangement of champagne roses and satin ribbon that looked completely ludicrous on a woman my age, but I loved it. It made me feel like a teenager, which was the last time I'd worn such a thing.

"What do you think?" he asked.

I reached up to cradle his face in my hands. "I think it's lovely, and so are you. Thank you." I brushed a light kiss across his lips, mindful of the lipstick I'd just applied. "Now we really do need to get going."

He took my hand and led me out of the room and down the hall to the elevator. On the way down, he stood behind me with his hands on my hips. It took all my willpower not to lean back and rub up against him, which I suspected he knew very well.

We couldn't ever seem to get enough of each other. I'd expected our sexual appetites to have settled down a little once the newness wore off, but we'd been together five months now and the attraction was as strong as ever. Maybe even stronger. So much for my fears of losing my sex drive.

As the elevator descended, Mike reached up to trail a finger down my neck. I felt his breath on my skin and tried to suppress a shiver of anticipation. His lips skimmed the top of my shoulder just as the elevator doors opened.

I stepped away from him and into the lobby while I still had the power to do so. If we weren't careful, we'd never make it to the reunion, and I knew Angie was counting on us to be there.

Mike's hand reached for mine again as we headed for the ballroom we'd spent most of the day helping to decorate. The theme for the reunion was "Night at the Movies." We'd filled the ballroom with posters from classic eighties movies from our high school days and crafted centerpieces for all the tables out of popcorn tubs and candy boxes. It was all Angie's brainchild, and as we entered the ballroom, I felt a moment of pride for what my best friend had accomplished.

She came to greet us with her husband, Charles, in tow. He was a soft-spoken, balding tax attorney who was madly devoted to her, even after twenty years of marriage. I used to envy them, but now with Mike at my side, I knew I finally had something just as good. Maybe we'd even get married one day, although neither of us were in any rush to jump back into the institution. We were happy just as we were. Blissfully.

Angie stopped in front of me, staring at my wrist. "Is that a corsage?"

I showed it off proudly. "Mike got it for me."

She turned and smacked her husband on the arm. "Mike got Dawn a corsage. Why didn't you get me a corsage?"

"Was I supposed to?" Charles asked, looking amiably befuddled. "No one told me."

"Is there anything you need us to do?" I asked Angie. If I'd been in charge, I'd be a frazzled, snappish mess right about now, but she seemed cool as a cucumber.

"Nope, it's all in hand. You two still okay to take the first shift at the check-in desk?"

I'd volunteered us for the first shift so we could get it over with and then have the rest of the night to enjoy the reunion—or cut out early if we chose. There was that nice bed waiting for us in the room upstairs, after all.

"Yep," I told her. "We'll get to it, shall we?"

Mike and I stationed ourselves at the table outside the ballroom, ready to welcome our old classmates with drink tickets and name tags. As they started trickling in, I was quickly reminded how popular Mike had been in high school. Not only did everyone remember him, they were thrilled to see him for the first time in thirty years. I ended up doing most of the checking in myself while Mike caught up with old friends, but I didn't mind. I was proud of him.

I knew talking about himself wasn't his favorite thing, and he'd confessed some feelings of ambivalence going into the reunion. But he seemed fine now. In fact, he seemed to be enjoying himself. It helped that he finally had a job he liked, although he wasn't allowed to talk about it except in the vaguest terms. He'd left the library and accepted a job with a company called Cipher Systems, which was owned by my landlord, Quinn Sullivan.

I'd been chatting one day with Quinn's wife, Janie, a crocheter and frequent customer at the store, about the way Mike's online degree program worked and how optimally suited it was for working adults who needed to balance continuing education with full-time jobs. As soon as she'd heard he was pursuing a degree in cybersecurity, she insisted I forward his résumé to her so she could give it to Quinn.

I did—with Mike's approval—and two weeks later, he had an interview. Mike and Quinn hit it off immediately. Not only did Quinn offer him a job at Cipher Systems, he told Mike the company would pay his tuition, and continue to support him if he chose to pursue a master's degree once he finished his bachelor's.

I didn't know much about Mike's new job because he'd signed an NDA that prevented him from divulging any potentially sensitive information about their security clients. But I knew Mike was a lot happier now, which was all that mattered. I knew he liked the work, whatever it was, and felt challenged and respected at his new workplace.

I saw the evidence of that now, as he caught up with old acquaintances, chatting comfortably about his occupation and professional field—without divulging company secrets, of course—and even bringing up the fact that he was earning his bachelor's degree with none of the self-consciousness he used to exhibit.

After we'd put in our hour at the check-in desk, we were relieved by Yolanda and Gina. I greeted them both warmly—even Gina. Over the last few months, I'd gotten to know them both better and found I liked them very much. If Gina had been surprised or disappointed when Mike and I got together, she hadn't let it show. She'd begun dating an investment banker recently and seemed quite happy with him.

Mike and I ventured into the ballroom, where the reunion was now in full swing. A group of his old football buddies immediately hailed Mike over. It was clear as he introduced me to them that they had no idea who I was, but they were friendly and welcoming, including me in their little circle without a second thought. Funny to think how much things had changed. I hung around to chat with them for a few minutes but soon grew bored with their jock talk and excused myself to check on Angie.

I found her by the bar, looking relaxed and pleased with herself. "Everything seems to be going well," I observed to her.

"Damn right it is. Take that, Bossy Tess." She thrust a glass of wine into my hand and craned her neck to peer around the room. "Speaking of, I haven't seen her highness yet. I wonder if she was brave enough to show up tonight..."

"She's here. I checked her in." There'd been a line of people waiting to claim their name tags at that point, so we hadn't been able to talk much, but I'd promised Tess I'd find her later so we could catch up properly.

"Oh, I think that's her." Angie frowned in the direction of the dance floor. "Who's she with?"

I shrugged as I sipped my wine. "I don't know. She came alone."

"Oh my god, is that Donal Larkin with her?"

I followed Angie's stare across the room to the dance floor. "Looks like it."

"Are they…slow dancing? Together?"

I smiled at the sight of them clenched in a tight embrace. "They certainly are."

"I can't even. I mean, in a million years, would you ever have pictured those two together?"

"Well…" I happened to know a secret about Tess and Donal. Something Tess had confided in me our senior year. I'd never told a soul, and I wasn't about to tell Angie now, even thirty years later. "I always thought they'd make a cute couple."

"Are you kidding? They hated each other. Like, *hated*. I half expected her to poison him over the valedictorian race."

"Mmm. Well. They seem to have gotten over it, don't they?"

Mike came up behind me, slipping a hand around my waist. "Hey. Sorry about all the dull football talk."

"That's okay." I turned to smile up at him. "You can talk to your friends as much as you want."

"Eh." He shrugged and kissed my temple. "I'd rather talk to you."

"Gross," Angie said. "You two are so cute it's nauseating."

Mike's fingers twined with mine. "Come dance with me. They're playing our song."

With a wink, I handed Angie my wineglass and let him lead me to the dance floor. That OMD song from the end of *Pretty in Pink* was playing, but I couldn't remember it ever coming up when I was with Mike.

"Since when is this our song?" I asked as I linked my hands behind his neck. "I wasn't aware we'd chosen a song. Don't I get a vote?"

Mike's hand squeezed my hips as he pulled me close. "Any song I get to dance with you to is our song."

"Any song? What about 'Baby Got Back'?"

Mike rolled his eyes. "Sure, if that's what you want."

I grinned at him, enjoying myself. "Or how about 'Brass Monkey' by the Beastie Boys? Oh! I know! 'I Can't Drive 55.'"

Huffing out a laugh, Mike leveled a faux glare at me. "If you don't cut it out, I'm never gonna take you to another reunion ever again. This is an incredibly romantic moment, and you're ruining it for me."

"Did you just quote *Pretty in Pink* to me?"

His mouth curled in a smirk. "Maybe."

I laughed and leaned up to kiss him. "That's Duckie's line though. Molly Ringwald picked the hot, popular guy over him, remember?"

"Yeah, but Duckie had all the best lines. I always thought she should have ended up with him."

I snuggled closer, resting my head against Mike's chest. "I don't know. I think the popular guy had a lot of potential." My eyes drifted shut, and as we swayed to the familiar song from our youth, I couldn't help thinking about teenaged Dawn and what she'd say if she could see me now, dancing with Mike Pilota.

It was funny to think I'd been right all those years ago, when I'd set my sights on Mike. We *were* meant to be together.

It had just taken us thirty extra years to figure it out and find our way back to each other. But now that we had, I was never letting go.

ACKNOWLEDGMENTS

I owe a huge debt of gratitude to Penny Reid, first and foremost, for writing books about smart, funny, opinionated women that inspired me to start reading contemporary romance and eventually try writing contemporary romances of my own. Your books helped change the course of my life. Thank you for your generosity, encouragement, and insight. I am so grateful you opened up the Knitting in the City sandbox and invited me to play in it.

Thank you to my fellow Smartypants Romance authors for being awesome and fun and talented, and for creating a wonderful community for laughter, learning, support, and collaboration. I'm so glad I've gotten to know all of you, and hope I'll get to hug you all in person before too much longer.

Thank you to Fiona Fischer and Brooke Nowiski for your patience, organization, attention to detail, and for helping make the rest of us look good. That hug offer goes double for y'all. Get ready.

To my editor, Julia Ganis, thank you for your careful, thoughtful corrections and guidance. There's no one I'd rather entrust my books with.

Thank you to my friend Mikaela, for once again providing crucial background for one of my books. I've lost track of how many books you've made possible at this point. Here's hoping this year we'll finally get to celebrate our fiftieth birthdays on vacation together in some fabulous locale.

Finally, to my husband, thank you for being better than any romance hero I could ever write. <3

ABOUT THE AUTHOR

SUSANNAH NIX is an award-winning romance author who lives in Texas with her husband, two ornery cats, and a flatulent pit bull. When she's not writing, she enjoys reading, cooking, knitting, and watching British murder mysteries. She is also a powerlifter who can deadlift as much as Captain America weighs.

Sign up for Susannah's newsletter to get new release alerts and exclusive reader extras like deleted scenes and bonus epilogues.

---

www.susannahnix.com

Connect with Susannah Online:
Facebook
Instagram
Twitter
Goodreads
BookBub

Find Smartypants Romance online:
Website: www.smartypantsromance.com
Facebook: www.facebook.com/smartypantsromance/
Goodreads: www.goodreads.com/smartypantsromance
Twitter: @smartypantsrom
Instagram: @smartypantsromance
Newsletter: https://smartypantsromance.com/newsletter/

ALSO BY SUSANNAH NIX

Chemistry Lessons

(STEM Heroines)

Remedial Rocket Science

Intermediate Thermodynamics

Advanced Physical Chemistry

Applied Electromagnetism

Experimental Marine Biology

Starstruck

(Movie Star Heroes)

Fallen Star

Rising Star

Standalone

Maybe This Christmas

For the most up-to-date book list, CLICK HERE

ALSO BY SMARTYPANTS ROMANCE

Green Valley Chronicles

The Love at First Sight Series

Baking Me Crazy by Karla Sorensen (#1)

Batter of Wits by Karla Sorensen (#2)

Steal My Magnolia by Karla Sorensen(#3)

Fighting For Love Series

Stud Muffin by Jiffy Kate (#1)

Beef Cake by Jiffy Kate (#2)

Eye Candy by Jiffy Kate (#3)

The Donner Bakery Series

No Whisk, No Reward by Ellie Kay (#1)

The Green Valley Library Series

Love in Due Time by L.B. Dunbar (#1)

Crime and Periodicals by Nora Everly (#2)

Prose Before Bros by Cathy Yardley (#3)

Shelf Awareness by Katie Ashley (#4)

Carpentry and Cocktails by Nora Everly (#5)

Love in Deed by L.B. Dunbar (#6)

Scorned Women's Society Series

My Bare Lady by Piper Sheldon (#1)

The Treble with Men by Piper Sheldon (#2)

The One That I Want by Piper Sheldon (#3)

Park Ranger Series

Happy Trail by Daisy Prescott (#1)

Stranger Ranger by Daisy Prescott (#2)

The Leffersbee Series

Been There Done That by Hope Ellis (#1)

The Higher Learning Series

Upsy Daisy by Chelsie Edwards (#1)

Seduction in the City

Cipher Security Series

Code of Conduct by April White (#1)

Code of Honor by April White (#2)

Cipher Office Series

Weight Expectations by M.E. Carter (#1)

Sticking to the Script by Stella Weaver (#2)

Cutie and the Beast by M.E. Carter (#3)

Weights of Wrath by M.E. Carter (#4)

Common Threads Series

Mad About Ewe by Susannah Nix (#1)

Give Love a Chai by Nanxi Wen (#2)

Educated Romance

Work For It Series

Street Smart by Aly Stiles (#1)

Heart Smart by Emma Lee Jayne (#2)

Lessons Learned Series

Under Pressure by Allie Winters (#1)

CPSIA information can be obtained
at www.ICGtesting.com
Printed in the USA
LVHW030422080321
680838LV00005B/168